"Are you her father, Liam?"

"That's what the birth certificate says..."

"What do you say?" she asked. "You have no idea who Jane Smith is, and you haven't brought up any other names of women you dated—"

"I'm going to text some contacts to the sheriff," he interjected.

"Why not to me?" she asked.

He shrugged. "I don't know. Marsh asked—"

"I asked you earlier," she said.

"You asked me if I knew Jane Smith," he said. "And if I had any idea who Lucy's mother is. I really don't have any idea."

She released a shaky breath. "Because you had a lot of groupies on the rodeo circuit?" She understood those groupies since she was charmed by him herself, and he wasn't even with the rodeo anymore.

He was a rancher.

A cowboy.

A father.

"No! That's not what I meant."

"Then tell me what you meant," she said. "Tell me the truth, Liam..."

Dear Reader,

Welcome back to Willow Creek, Wyoming, and more of my Bachelor Cowboys series! I couldn't say goodbye to my lovable matchmakers, Sadie and Lem, not when we have a whole new branch of the family that needs to find the loves of their lives. Lem's grandson Liam finds something in the barn at the ranch where he works with his brothers, but it's a baby, not the love of his life. Even though he knows the infant isn't his, he finds himself falling for her and maybe a little bit for Child Protective Services investigator Elise Shaw. Elise just wants to do her job, and she has no interest in getting involved with anyone—especially not a Lemmon.

Everybody in the family is blaming Sadie and Lem for throwing the unlikely couple together, but they might not be the matchmakers this time. Little Lucy, the baby, brings them together, but she might also tear them apart.

I went through two boxes of tissues while I was writing this book, so I advise you to have some handy when reading it. Elise's character is very near and dear to my heart because my older daughter is a CPS investigator. And the Haven-Cassidy-Lemmon family feels like my own.

I hope you enjoy reading these stories as much as I enjoy writing them!

Lisa Childs

THE COWBOY'S BABY SURPRISE

LISA CHILDS

HEARTWARMING

Harlequin®
HEARTWARMING™

ISBN-13: 978-1-335-05158-5

The Cowboy's Baby Surprise

Harlequin Enterprises ULC
22 Adelaide St. West, 41st Floor
Toronto, Ontario M5H 4E3, Canada
www.Harlequin.com

Printed in U.S.A.

Recycling programs for this product may not exist in your area.

New York Times and *USA TODAY* bestselling, award-winning author **Lisa Childs** has written more than eighty-five novels. Published in twenty countries, she's also appeared on the *Publishers Weekly*, Barnes & Noble and Nielsen Top 100 bestseller lists. Lisa writes contemporary romance, romantic suspense, and paranormal and women's fiction. She's a wife, mom, bonus mom, avid reader and less avid runner. Readers can reach her through Facebook or her website, lisachilds.com.

Books by Lisa Childs

Harlequin Heartwarming

Bachelor Cowboys

A Rancher's Promise
The Cowboy's Unlikely Match
The Bronc Rider's Twin Surprise
The Cowboy's Ranch Rescue
The Firefighter's Family Secret
The Doc's Instant Family
The Rancher's Reunion
A Match for the Sheriff

Visit the Author Profile page
at Harlequin.com for more titles.

For one of my favorite heroines,
my daughter Ashley, who handles one of the
most difficult jobs as a child protective services
investigator with an inner strength and integrity
that fills me with awe and respect!

PROLOGUE

A year ago...

EIGHT SECONDS. That was how long he had to stay on the beast. Just eight seconds. Liam Lemmon ran the rosin over his rope once more. The rope would secure Liam's saddle in place, so he began to wind it around the beast that was bucking already in the chute, so desperate to get out that he nearly knocked Liam loose from where he straddled the top rungs of the enclosure.

The bronco's hair was glossy black, like its eyes and probably its soul. The horse rolled his neck back, and those eyes met Liam's and seemed to stare into *his* soul. Nerves clutched Liam's stomach, twisting it into knots.

But he refused to be intimidated. He had to place in this event, or he had no chance of continuing to the finals. No chance to make any more money—not that he'd made much during his few years in the rodeo.

Other riders gathered around, offering him encouragement and advice that he could barely hear over the crowd of spectators filling the stands.

The loudspeaker cut through the noise. "Nobody has ridden this bronco, Midnight, to the buzzer, not even our reigning champ, Dusty Chaps," the announcer, Shep Shepard, remarked. "Let's see if relative newcomer Billy the Kid can pull off the impossible."

Shep, once a rodeo rider himself, had dubbed Liam Lemmon Billy the Kid when he'd made his rodeo debut, and the name had stuck. But nobody else in Liam's life had ever called him Billy, not even his older brothers or older sister. He'd always been Liam.

Maybe that was why he didn't feel like himself anymore. Like he'd somehow gotten lost or like he didn't belong despite all the years he'd yearned to join the rodeo. Or maybe he was always destined to feel that way because he'd never quite felt like he belonged in his family either. His brothers had auburn hair and green eyes. His sister's hair was more of a strawberry blond, while Liam's was nearly as black as Midnight's, and his eyes were blue. Despite never quite fitting in with them, he missed his family—especially his brothers, who loved animals as much as he did.

If he didn't make the buzzer, he would be done for the rest of the season and could go help his brothers out on the cattle ranch where they'd been working for a couple of years. The Four Corners

Ranch was about an hour outside Willow Creek, Wyoming.

He was lucky to have a backup plan, but making the buzzer would be better. Beating Dusty Chaps at something, being the first to ride the notoriously unrideable bronco, would make Liam feel like he finally belonged in the rodeo world.

With the rope cinching the saddle tightly around the bronco, Liam grasped the buck rein in his glove and he eased himself down into the chute and jerked his head in a sharp nod. The chute opened, and Midnight exploded into the ring, bucking high and hard.

One.

Liam's body jerked, and he tightened his knees, trying to hold on.

Two.

His wrist ached as he clutched desperately to the buck rein.

Three.

His grasp began to loosen from his knees to his hand.

Four.

Midnight bucked so high that he nearly somersaulted through the air.

Five.

The horse came back down, his body twisted. The rein slipped free of Liam's hand, and he hit the ground hard. Then Midnight struck him.

Harder.

And pain exploded in Liam's body like Midnight had exploded into the ring. He didn't have to worry about not placing in the money now; he had to worry about recovering.

If he could…

CHAPTER ONE

WALKING OUT OF the sunshine into the dim light of the barn blinded and disoriented Liam for a moment. But it wasn't just the darkness that made him dizzy; the past few months had been a whirlwind that had left Liam as stunned as he'd been after Midnight bucking him off and falling on him nearly a year ago. Fortunately the horse hadn't been hurt. While Liam had healed quickly, he had been permanently wounded. Just not where anyone else would know. And nobody else needed to know. It was something he wasn't even sure he was ready to deal with yet and he hadn't had to because he'd been so busy.

When Liam had shown up at the Four Corners Ranch nearly a year ago, the owner, Frank Dempsey, and Liam's brothers had welcomed him, and for the first time in a long time he'd felt like he belonged somewhere and that, despite his invisible injury, he was useful. But now Frank was gone, and Liam and his brothers were dealing with losing him and with so much uncertainty.

After attending their grandfather's wedding to the legendary Sadie March Haven a few months ago, Liam and his older brothers, Brett and Blake, had returned to the ranch to find Frank in a coma in the hospital. Tough as they come, Frank had held on for weeks before succumbing to the injuries he sustained working the ranch while they were gone. He hadn't been working alone; they'd had a couple of extra ranch hands then and Frankie.

Frank's niece and namesake was as tough as her uncle and had earned the respect of Liam, Blake and Brett. She worked as hard as they did and definitely harder than the hired hands, even though she claimed ranching wasn't for her. She was ready to go back to her life on the road as a singer, but she'd stayed for her uncle. Along with Frankie, Liam and Blake and Brett had divided their time between the ranch and the hospital.

And now that Frank was gone...

There was even more work to do to make him proud, to keep his ranch going, at least until the estate was settled. But that could take a while since a lawsuit had been filed contesting Frank's will.

As his eyes finally adjusted to the dim light of the barn, Liam pushed the lawsuit from his head. Blake and Brett had sworn they would deal with it through Frank's lawyer, Maci Bluff, or through the lawyers Sadie and Grandpa Lem had suggested to them. But in the meantime, things needed to get done. Especially since they'd had to let the last of the hired hands go.

If young Levi and Tom, who should have been wiser since he was older, had actually been working instead of goofing off while Liam and his brothers had been gone, maybe Frank wouldn't have gotten hurt. Despite how strong he'd been, he hadn't recovered from his fall off his horse.

Maybe that fall was why Liam kept thinking about Midnight. Or maybe it was because his new stepcousin, Dusty Chaps, aka Dusty Haven, was about to start breeding the horse, which he'd won off its previous owner in a bet. Liam found that very ironic given how Midnight had hurt him.

But what did it matter to Liam anyway if he couldn't have biological children? Physically everything else was fine, and he was only twenty-seven and single. So it wasn't as if he was looking to settle down anytime soon…or maybe ever. While he'd dated over the years, it had always been more like hanging out with a friend than a love affair. And fortunately the women had remained his friends even after they stopped dating. So he'd never really even had a serious relationship.

And kids…

He'd never actually thought of having them until he'd been told he couldn't father them. Then he'd realized that he wouldn't be able to be the great dad he'd had growing up and eventually the grandfather who all the kids adored, like his grandpa Lem. And now that he knew he wouldn't have a kid of his own, he felt like he was being taunted in that he kept hearing a baby's cry everywhere.

At his grandpa and Sadie's wedding. But that cry had actually been a squeal of delight from a toddler named Little Jake. And even at Frank Dempsey's funeral. But that cry had actually slipped out of Frankie's lips as they laid her uncle, and guardian, to rest.

Even here in the barn, Liam imagined he could hear a baby's cry. This cry probably came from one of the barn cats people kept dropping off at the ranch. Or maybe it was one of those cats' babies making the noise. Because usually the errant owners dropped off their cats after they were already pregnant. But that cry kept getting louder, so loud that it couldn't be coming from a kitten or even a full-grown cat.

"What in the world…" Liam muttered as he walked farther into the barn.

He'd come in to clean out the stalls and saddle up the horses for himself and his brothers, who'd just returned from Maci Bluff's office in Willow Creek. Liam hadn't gone with them because he'd had to get feed for the cattle; his pickup was loaded down with it.

Blake and Brett had stopped at the house to

change. Frankie was in the house, too. So the barn should have been empty except for Liam and the animals.

He peered into the shadows cast by the stalls and piles of hay bales. Something pink and fuzzy peeked out from behind one of the bales, and he walked over to it. Sitting in the woodchips on the ground was a plastic baby car seat, with a baby lying in it, loosely covered with a pink fleece blanket that matched the headband bow on her tiny head. Her face was scrunched up as she cried harder, her little fists flailing through the air.

He glanced around again, looking for the adult who'd left her here. "Hello?"

The baby cried harder at the sound of his voice.

"Hey!" Panic was hitting him now. Was this baby alone in the barn? No. Liam was here, too, and he had to do something. So he unclasped the buckles holding her in the car seat. But he hesitated before lifting her out.

Support the neck. Wasn't that what everybody warned about babies? That you had to support their necks? She was small but probably not a newborn, not that he really knew anything about babies. After Midnight injured him, he'd thought he would never have any reason to learn.

Once the buckles were out of the way, he noticed the piece of paper taped to the pink blanket covering her: *I don't want to be a mother. You need to take care of her now.*

You? Who needed to take care of her? Since nobody else was around, it fell on Liam at the moment.

"Shh…" he murmured. "Everything's going to be all right." But he wasn't sure if he was trying to reassure the baby or himself.

He slid his hands under her squirmy warm body and lifted her from the plastic contraption, letting the clasps and buckles hit the woodchips on the floor. And he pulled her close to his chest where his heart was beating fast and hard with apprehension.

"Shh…" he murmured again. "It's okay. We'll find your mama." He had to because he had no idea how to take care of a baby. Why would her mother have left her here of all places?

There were no other vehicles in the driveway but for his, his brothers' and Frankie's. And he doubted the mom had walked all the way out to the Four Corners Ranch carrying the infant in a car seat.

So where was she? And why had she left her child here because she didn't want to care for her anymore? Who was the *you* who was supposed to take over now?

THE CALL CAME to Child Protective Services via police dispatch, which was never a good sign to CPS investigator Elise Shaw. Maybe the caller just hadn't known who to contact and called the emergency line. Or as was more often the case, the police were already involved and needed CPS's help with the children.

Over the course of her five years with CPS, Elise had been called out to drug and human trafficking raids to take care of the children at the scene. But those cases, fortunately, had been rare. Usually domestic violence calls were the ones where she joined the police to make sure the children were safe. But the police clearly considered this call a matter for Child Protective Services to handle, not them, since they'd patched it through directly to her work cell, which was hooked up to Bluetooth on the state vehicle Elise was driving.

Having such a big county to cover, Elise worked more out of a vehicle than her CPS cubicle in the Department of Human Services in Willow Creek.

"Hello?" she called out into the ominous silence, wondering if the dispatcher had accidentally disconnected instead of patching through the call.

A click broke that silence, and a deep voice rumbled out of the car speakers. "Um, hi, I'm not sure what to do…" Then a baby's cry echoed from speaker to speaker, nearly drowning out the man who murmured, "Shh…shh…"

"How can Child Protective Services help you?" Elise asked.

"Someone left her baby in the barn," the man said. "And I'm not sure where she went, or if she's coming back. She just left a note that she doesn't want to be a mother anymore. But I don't know why she left her *here*. The police are going to come out later for a report, but they wanted CPS to see about the baby."

Elise sucked in a breath. "Is the baby hurt?" she asked. "Do you need an ambulance?"

"The dispatch already asked me that," he said. "And I think she's fine. Just hungry maybe. Or wet."

"Does she have any supplies with her?" Elise asked. She carried some in her vehicle but could stop for more if necessary.

"I... I..." A breath shuddered out of the speakers as if he was sighing with relief. "I found a bag. It has diapers and some bottles in it and a canister of something."

"Formula?" she asked.

"Yeah, that's what it says."

"Can you follow the directions on the canister?" she asked him.

He chuckled. "I should be able to, but I have no experience with babies. I'm not sure what to do."

"You're going to need to change her diaper, too," Elise said. "Tabs in the back."

"Okay, but..." He cleared his throat. "What if the mom doesn't come back?"

From her years with CPS, Elise could come up with any number of reasons why the mother had abandoned her baby, but she wasn't going to speculate until she had more information.

"I'm coming out to you," Elise said. This was definitely a priority one case. She needed to make contact with the child as soon as possible to make certain she wasn't in danger. "Where are you?"

"The Four Corners Ranch." He gave her the address.

Elise was able to remember the addresses of all the places she'd had to pay an official CPS visit—because she'd usually had to pay them more than one visit. So she knew she hadn't been out to the Four Corners Ranch before. But just to verify she asked, "Are there any other children on the property?"

"No, just calves and kittens," he said. "As far as I know, there haven't been human kids on this ranch for many years. But I haven't been here that long myself."

"And what is your name, sir?" she asked.

"Liam," he replied. "Liam Lemmon."

Lemmon. Everyone in Willow Creek knew that surname. Lem Lemmon had been the town's longest serving mayor, and even now, in his eighties, worked as the deputy mayor. But Elise knew it for another reason.

Dr. Livvy Lemmon, an emergency room attending physician, had taken great exception to Elise questioning why the doctor hadn't abided by her role as a mandatory reporter when a wounded child had come into her ER. A call to CPS had led Elise to believe that the child was being abused, but Dr. Lemmon had hotly denied that was the reason for the injury.

However, Elise had hesitated to believe the young doctor because the woman was too close to that little boy's family. And also because after five years as a CPS investigator, Elise hesitated to believe anyone. Perhaps she shouldn't have believed the caller—a nurse at the ER who seemed to have an issue with the young doctor—but with a child potentially in danger, she'd had to investigate.

"Are you there?" the man asked, with a trace of panic in his voice as the baby continued to cry.

"Yes, I'm still on the line, and I should arrive shortly at the ranch," she assured him. Fortunately she'd already been close when the call had come through.

"What is your name?" he asked.

"Elise Shaw."

"Please hurry, Ms. Shaw," he said. Clearly he hadn't recognized her name. Or he just wanted help so badly that he didn't care who she was.

She didn't care who he was either. She cared only about this poor baby whose mother had left her in a barn. Why at the Four Corners Ranch?

What did Liam Lemmon have to do with this baby or her mother? For the baby's sake, Elise was going to make sure she got the answers to all her questions.

RANCH HAVEN WAS as bustling as ever, but instead of feeling overwhelmed with all the people and activity, Lem felt energized. Alive.

For years after losing his first wife, he'd felt so damn alone. Because he'd kept working, the nights had been the worst. Too quiet.

Nobody would ever say that about Ranch Haven. It was never too quiet. Especially not here in the kitchen, which was the heart of the enormous two-story home.

He sat next to his wife, Sadie, who was seated at the head of the long table with the hearth of the big brick fireplace behind her. She reached over and patted his hand. "You're quiet," she said.

He grinned. "I was just thinking about how it's never quiet here." Sadie's son and all of her Haven grandsons and their families lived on the ranch.

Sadie's grandson Dusty and his wife Melanie's infant twins were crying. Melanie's mother, Juliet, walked one of them around the long kitchen island, trying to settle him or her down while Sadie's son, Jessup, walked the other. Little Jake, the two-year-old son of Sadie's late grandson Dale, followed Jessup around, murmuring, "Bee bee. Bee bee." He loved having someone smaller than himself around as much as Lem did. At five and seven, his brothers, Ian and Miller, and his five-year-old stepcousin Caleb were all older than Little Jake.

"I'm sorry," Sadie said. "This must all be too

much for you, moving in here after having a house to yourself for years."

He shook his head and turned his hand over to squeeze hers. Her knuckles were swollen with arthritis, her skin calloused from all her years of hard work. Around her ring finger was a tattoo of the infinity symbol; he had one to match. The tattoos were their wedding bands.

"I love it here," he said. "I love that it's not quiet."

Her dark eyes lit up and she grinned at him. "Me, too. Neither of us want a quiet, retiring life. That's why I love you, you old fool," she said.

She'd always called him an old fool, but now she said it with such affection that it was an endearment.

"I love you, Sadie March Haven Lemmon," he said.

She grinned again and squeezed his hand back. "I know. But are you really okay?" she asked with genuine concern. "Or are you quiet because you're worried about your grandsons?"

He sighed. "I am worried about Brett, Blake and Liam, but they're confident their lawyer can sort out that lawsuit mess. I wasn't even thinking about that. I was thinking about how nice it is to have little ones around. And it's good that I'm here to enjoy them. I have a feeling my grandchildren might never give me greats."

Sadie shook her head. "Give Livvy and Colton time. They just got engaged."

"They're busy people," Lem reminded her. Livvy as an ER doc and Colton as a firefighter and paramedic. "They might wait while before starting a family."

Sadie shrugged. "They might. But there are plenty of kids and babies around here for you to enjoy."

"And I do," he assured her. "I just want all of our Lemmon grandchildren to find their mates and start families of their own, too."

"Are you two meddling again?" Jessup asked on his pass around the long table, the crying infant in his arms.

"Not yet," Sadie said. "We're holding off for a bit."

Jessup chuckled at her honesty.

"And you can't complain about my meddling," she pointed out.

Jessup grinned, and as he passed Juliet who carried the other twin, he leaned over and kissed her cheek. They had fallen in love and were engaged now, too.

Sadie, with her notorious penchant for matchmaking, had found mates for all her adult family members. Lem had helped her make some of those matches, and they'd planned to focus on his family next. But then Frank Dempsey died, devastating his grandsons.

Lem hadn't wanted to add to the chaos of their current lives. But maybe love wouldn't add to the chaos; maybe it would calm it or at least make it survivable and enjoyable. Because that was how his life with Sadie was—despite the chaos and some of the tragedies, they also had joy.

CHAPTER TWO

THE CRYING WAS so intense that Liam's head pounded from the volume of it. How could something so small scream so loudly?

"Shh…" he murmured as he walked the length of the ranch house's front porch. He was outside because he wanted to keep an eye out for that CPS investigator and for the baby's mother.

Despite the note she'd left about not wanting to be a mother, he couldn't believe that she would just abandon her child.

"Your mama will come back," he told the baby, but he had no way of knowing for certain. What if she didn't change her mind about being a mother?

"Why would anyone leave her here?" his oldest brother, Brett, asked from where he stood at the bottom of the steps leading up to the porch. It was as if he didn't want to get too close, maybe for fear that Liam would hand the baby off to him.

He'd tried that when he'd walked up to the house from the barn juggling the baby, the car seat and the big diaper bag. But Brett had stepped back and held up his hands, looking as scared as if Liam had pointed a gun at him. "I don't know anything about babies."

"Me neither," Blake had said.

And Frankie had shaken her head, too. "Don't look at me. I never even babysat when I was a teenager. I have no experience with kids."

"I don't either," Liam pointed out. Before his accident, they hadn't even been on his radar. He hadn't really noticed kids until he'd learned he couldn't father any of his own. Because of his lack of knowledge, he'd pulled up some online tutorials while waiting for the CPS investigator. One of the videos had been for how to change a diaper, so he understood what she'd meant about tabs in back. Another video had shown him how to mix up a bottle of formula. Fortunately Frankie had helped with the formula, though she'd refused to touch the diaper situation.

Blake and Frankie stood behind Liam in the open doorway to the living room, as if ready to slam the door shut on him if he tried to bring the crying baby back inside the house. They looked as scared of her as Brett did.

"You did call CPS, right?" Frankie asked. "Somebody's on their way?"

He nodded. "She said she was close." But then why wasn't she here yet?

It felt like hours had passed since he'd found the baby, hours of the baby crying. He'd already changed her diaper, so she was dry now. He'd thought she was hungry, but she'd refused the bottle that Frankie had passed to him like it was a baton in a relay race.

And Liam felt like he'd been running a relay with each pass he made across the porch. But nobody was taking the baton from him. Since the baby was dry and apparently not hungry, she must want something else. Probably the same thing Liam wanted, for her mother to return for her.

At this point, Liam would settle for the CPS investigator or anyone else who would willingly take this crying baby off his hands. Her little body was so stiff in his grasp that he smoothed his palm down her back, trying to comfort her. Suddenly a belch slipped out with her cry, so loud that it must have startled her because she got quiet and stared up at him, her eyes big and round with surprise and so very blue like his.

"Wow, I can hear again," Brett said as he patted one side of his head.

His voice startled the baby into scrunching up her face again. But before she could cry, Liam tucked her up against him and rocked her in his arms. "Shh…you're okay. Uncle Brett is an idiot."

"Uncle Brett?" Brett repeated. "Are you admitting that you're her daddy, Liam? Are you the *you* in the note the mother left?"

A laugh bubbled up at the thought, but he swallowed it down, not wanting to startle the baby himself, and softly said, "Not me."

He narrowed his eyes and studied his brothers' faces. They didn't flush with embarrassment, but both looked pale with exhaustion despite their tans from working outside so much. None of them had time to so much as go on a date. The baby didn't belong to either of them any more than she belonged to him. But to whom did she belong?

He focused on Frankie to tease her, not because he actually thought she'd had a baby. "What about Mommy?"

She shook her head. "When I said I had no experience with babies, I also meant having them. Uh-uh, no way. If she was mine, I think you all would have noticed her the past few months I've been hanging around the ranch."

"How old do you think she is?" Liam asked aloud what he'd been wondering for a bit now.

If there was any chance of her being his biologically, she would have to be three or four months old. But he hadn't been seriously dating anyone before his unfortunate incident with Midnight. Maybe he'd had a drink at a bar with someone or a cup of coffee, but nothing had happened that would have led to his having a daughter. No. There was no way that this baby and he shared anything more than the blue of their eyes.

She wasn't his.

Instead of feeling relieved, a pang of regret

struck him that he would never have a family of his own.

Brett was studying him with narrowed eyes. "So you're thinking she could be yours? That's why you're wondering how old she is."

"No. I'm just curious," he said.

"Yeah, we're all curious, but not about how old she is," Frankie said. "Who could her parents be?"

"Nobody saw anyone around the ranch?" Liam asked.

They all shook their heads.

"You got home before we did," Brett said. "Did you see anyone?"

"Just her." Liam stared down at the baby. Her eyelids drooped now, as if she was falling asleep. But each time her eyes closed, she blinked them open again to stare up at him, as if she was afraid that he might abandon her, too.

And he felt a twinge of guilt because that was exactly what he intended to do once the CPS investigator arrived.

If she ever did...

HAVING A LIMITED cell and GPS signal this far from any town, Elise missed the turnoff for the Four Corners Ranch. After backtracking, she finally found the driveway and drove down it a bit too fast to make up for the delay. Her tires kicked up gravel and dust that billowed in a cloud around the state vehicle even after she braked it next to a couple of pickup trucks parked near the front porch of a ranch house. She waited a moment before opening her door, but the cloud hung yet in the air. When she stepped out, the dust coated her glasses and burned her eyes and tickled her nose so that she sneezed. A cry echoed her sneeze, and she peered through her dirty glasses at the long front porch.

She felt a pang in her heart over that cry. She needed to make sure the baby was safe. That was all that mattered—more than her own discomfort or even, in some instances, her safety.

One man stood at the bottom of those stairs, another man stood on the porch and two people hovered in an open doorway behind him.

The man on the porch wore a cowboy hat, like the others, and jeans and boots. What set him apart was the pink wrapped bundle he cradled in his arms. He rocked that bundle back and forth and murmured, "Shh…"

"I'm Elise Shaw from CPS," she said as she approached the steps to the porch.

The man standing at the bottom of them moved quickly to the side as if he was worried she was contagious. Due to the filthy condition of some of the places she had to visit, that wasn't an uncalled-for concern.

"I'm Brett Lemmon," he introduced himself. "My brother Liam is the one who called you." He gestured toward the porch and the man holding the baby. Then he turned and took another step back as if he intended to walk away.

"I need to talk to all of you," she said, and she glanced toward the open door, wondering if they might slam that on her like people so often did when she visited.

"I'm Frankie Dempsey and this is Blake Lemmon," the woman said as she gestured to herself and the man standing next to her. "We really don't know anything about any of this." She had dark hair, like Elise, but hers was very curly whereas Elise's hair was thick and straight.

She'd pulled it into a tight ponytail at the back of her head to keep it out of her way and because of the condition of some of the places she visited. "So none of you has any idea who this baby belongs to?" she asked skeptically.

That was what Liam Lemmon had claimed when he'd called her. They all nodded. But the other two men, Brett and Blake, glanced at the one holding the baby; maybe they thought it was his.

"I told you and the police that I found her out in the barn," Liam replied. "Her car seat was sitting near some hay bales, and nobody else was around."

"Nobody else?" she repeated. The baby hadn't driven or walked herself out to the ranch. She was small, probably only a couple of months old if that.

"No," Liam said.

"Were you all here the entire morning?" she asked.

"No, we were actually all away from the ranch. Blake, Frankie and I had a meeting in town," the one closest to her, Brett, replied. "We just got back."

"And I was gone getting cattle feed," Liam said. "When I got back, I went out to the barn to clean stalls and saddle up the horses. That was when I found her, and when I went to take her out of her car seat, I found the note taped to her blanket."

"That her mother didn't want her anymore," Elise paraphrased. "She left her here while you were all gone?" Her stomach pitched at the thought of a mother abandoning a helpless infant when no other adults were around, and she found herself venting some of her frustration. "How would she know that anyone would return? This child could have been out in the barn all day and night on her own if you hadn't come back…"

The man holding the child tightened his arms protectively around her small body. "That's horrible…" Liam murmured.

"Yes, it is," she agreed. Not unheard of, unfortunately, but definitely horrible.

"So this woman dropped off her kid like people drop off unwanted cats at the ranch?" the woman, Frankie, asked, and she sounded horrified as well.

"Maybe the mother is just overwhelmed right now, and she didn't mean to leave her here forever. I'm sure the baby is not *unwanted*," Liam said, his voice lowered to nearly a whisper as if he was worried that the baby could understand him as he stared down at her in his arms. "Her mother has to be around the ranch somewhere. She couldn't have just left her without making sure someone would find her."

"Do you know the mother?" Elise asked.

"No," he quickly replied. "I just don't think the baby is unwanted. She looks healthy and clean." But as he said that, he made a face. "Or she was."

"That's a good point," Brett said. "We should search all the barns again and make sure that we've looked everywhere for the mother."

As well as slamming doors in her face, people had hidden from Elise before, but she had a feeling the mother of this child wasn't hiding. According to her note, she didn't want to be a mother anymore, so she was gone. But the baby was here, and she was Elise's responsibility right now.

Her stomach clenched a bit; she wasn't good with infants. She much preferred older kids with whom she could have a conversation even though they sometimes refused to talk to her, just like their parents. So she slowly climbed those few steps to join the man and the baby on the porch.

He swung his arms toward her as if to hand her the child. But she stepped back and nearly stepped off the porch. He freed one hand from the baby to grab her arm and keep her from tumbling to the ground. And she felt a little zing from the touch of his strong hand. "Hey, are you okay?" he asked.

She nodded. "Yes, but I want to see that note the mother left before I take her. You can change her while I look at that."

He grimaced.

"You said on the phone that there was a bag of things left with her," she reminded him. "Formula and diapers."

He nodded. "Those things and the note are in the house."

"I made a bottle for her," Frankie said, as Liam walked past her with the baby. "But he couldn't get her to drink it. She just kept crying."

She wasn't crying now but for that one startled cry when Elise had sneezed. She hesitated a moment before following the man and the baby into the ranch house. The boots Liam wore clomped across the hardwood floors, and the baby stiffened and cried again. The living room was big and open with a vaulted ceiling, and those cries echoed. Maybe that was why they'd been standing on the porch when she'd driven up, because of the way the baby's cries were amplified in the house.

Frankie flinched, and she and the man next to her, Blake, edged around Elise to head out the door. "We should go help Brett search the area," the woman said.

Liam sighed. "I know I said that she might be around here yet, but we looked everywhere for her before I called the police nonemergency number. We couldn't find her then."

And now that she'd had more time to slip away, she was undoubtedly gone, just as Elise had already surmised.

"Who just leaves her kid like this?" Frankie asked. Then she frowned, making Elise wonder what her story was.

But the baby was the reason Elise was here, so she intended to focus on her right now. "Where is the note?" she asked.

"In the kitchen," Frankie said as she and Blake slipped out the front door and onto the porch, leaving Elise and Liam alone with the crying child.

"Sorry about how my family rushed off," Liam said as he led the way through a wide archway into a big country-style eat-in kitchen. Like the living room with its leather furniture and dark wood, it was austere. Dark. Masculine with espresso-stained walnut cabinets and slate countertops. "But they do have to feed and water all the livestock. I didn't have the chance to do it yet."

Because he'd found a baby.

Elise picked up the piece of paper from the table. It might have stuck to the wooden surface if not for the pink fleece covering the tape. *I don't want to be a mother. You need to take care of her now.*

Who was the *you*? Liam Lemmon or one of

his brothers? The mother had left her at the Four Corners Ranch because she expected someone else to take responsibility for her child. Did that mean one of them was the father?

"I am going to have to question your family more thoroughly," Elise said. Because she struggled to believe that none of them had any idea to whom the baby belonged. Then she remembered how the older brothers had looked at Liam and how quickly they'd left the baby in his care.

He cuddled the infant against himself as he reached for the diaper bag with one hand. He pulled out a diaper and a pad from the bag. When he unfolded the pad onto the top of the kitchen table, another slip of paper fell out of it. It wasn't lined paper like the note but an official-looking document.

She stooped to pick it up and said, "I have some questions for you, too."

He shrugged. "Go ahead. Ask me whatever you want."

"Do you think you're the *you* in the note the baby's mother left?" she asked as she unfolded the piece of paper.

"No. Nobody would expect me to take care of a baby. I didn't even know how to change a diaper. But like you said on the phone, tabs in back."

"It's a little more complicated than that," she admitted. But she didn't step in to help him. She wasn't a foster parent, like her mother was, or even a social worker for the foster care system. She was strictly an investigator. She was the first on the scene, to assess whether a child needed to be removed from their home or if they were safe to be left with their parents with a care plan in place. Or sometimes, like when exes were making trouble for each other, the case could just be closed because the child was in no danger.

She liked those cases best. They were the easy ones. After reading the document she'd picked up from the floor, she figured this case was probably going to be easy, too. She now knew who the *you* was.

Liam fumbled with the snaps on the baby's onesie as the little one kicked her legs and stared up at him. Her eyes were as big and blue as his were. "I wish I knew her name," he murmured.

"Lucy," she said.

He tensed. "What? How do you know? It wasn't on that note."

She held up the document. "It's on this. It dropped out of the diaper bag when you pulled out the pad. It's her birth certificate."

"Oh, thank God," he said with a heavy sigh. "Now you'll be able to find her parents."

"I've already found one of them," she said.

"Which one? Who is it?" he asked.

"You," she said as she extended the paper toward him to read. "You are who her mother wants to take care of her now. She is Lucy Lemmon.

She's two months old today. And her father is listed as Liam Lemmon."

He didn't even look at the paper. He just shook his head. "No…"

"She's your daughter," Elise said. And for some reason she felt a pang of disappointment either that he was denying his child or that the child was his. Not that she was personally interested in the man.

She was too busy with her job to have a relationship. As one of the few single investigators, she covered most of the on-call shifts, so even when she'd tried to date, she hadn't lasted through an entire cup of coffee before she'd had to leave. Not that she'd ever met anyone she'd wanted to stay with…

Or maybe, after the constant stream of kids going through her home growing up, she'd gotten used to nobody ever sticking around, so she made certain she no longer got attached to anyone. It hurt too much when they left. And she would definitely never get attached to a parent on a case, especially one who wasn't even willing to admit he was the parent.

STANDING IN THE silence of the barn, Brett felt a twinge of guilt. But he breathed deeply for a moment in appreciation of that silence before remarking to the other two who stood inside the

LISA CHILDS 39

quiet barn with him, "Should we have just left him like that?"

Blake chuckled. "He's not alone now."

"He hasn't been alone since he found the baby," Brett pointed out.

"You know what we've always said..." Blake began.

Brett chuckled now. "Finders keepers."

"Even though I wasn't there," Frankie chimed in, "somehow I think the finders keepers was started because you'd found some money or something—"

"Probably the TV remote," Blake admitted.

"Not a kid," Frankie said.

"No, definitely not a kid." Brett couldn't believe yet that someone had just left her baby in the barn with a note to pass her off to someone else. Who? Liam?

"Well, the CPS investigator will figure this out," Frankie said. "That's her job."

Except that Ms. Elise Shaw didn't look much older than a child herself. She was probably younger than Liam was.

Brett felt that twinge of guilt again that he'd left his youngest brother to deal with the abandoned baby. But with their boss dying and the estate left in turmoil, Brett already had more to handle than he was probably capable of handling.

"Let's take a quick look around for the mother, then get the animals fed," he said. "Hopefully by the time we get back, the CPS investigator will have figured out where the baby belongs."

Because she didn't belong here on the ranch. While he felt like he and his brothers belonged, he wasn't sure they would be able to stay much longer either. He sympathized with the baby even more for being turned out of her home. He might soon know how she felt.

CHAPTER THREE

THE LAUGH BUBBLED up and escaped from Liam's lips before he could stop it. The sound startled the baby, who tensed, but she didn't cry. She just kicked her legs, and her mouth sagged open in something like a smile. She thought it was funny, too.

Ms. Elise Shaw did not. Her lips pursed into a thin line, and her dark eyes, behind the dusty lenses of her black-framed glasses, narrowed with irritation. "You think this is funny?" she asked.

"I wouldn't say funny, exactly," he admitted. It was ludicrous. Impossible. An ironic joke. A cruel twist of fate. All of those things. And because of that, it struck Liam as funny, too.

"You wasted my time coming out here," she said.

He tensed now with concern. "What do you mean?"

"This is your baby," she said. "Unless you're going to keep claiming she isn't yours, there is no need for me to get involved."

"I did not see that birth certificate in the diaper

bag," he said. "I had no idea my name would be listed on it." And no idea why it had been since there was no way that he could have fathered this child, especially since she was only two months old. Even if she was older, she wouldn't be his unless he had a case of amnesia he didn't know about. "Who's listed as the mother?"

Miss Shaw's dark eyes narrowed even more with obvious judgment and annoyance. "You don't know?"

"I don't."

Her lips pursed again with disapproval. She had to be thinking that he was promiscuous, which nearly made him laugh again. Even before the accident, he'd been too busy to go out for much more than a cup of coffee. Back then he'd been focused on making it to the finals, on making any money in the rodeo at all, so that he could succeed as a rodeo rider.

She looked at the birth certificate again. "Her name is Jane Smith."

"I guess she thought Jane Doe would be too obvious for a fake name," he remarked. "But she didn't do much better."

"I would think that the doctor or the hospital would have gotten some verification of the mother and father's identity before putting them on the birth certificate," she said.

"What hospital or doctor? They didn't get my verification," he said.

"I can't read the doctor's signature, if that is a doctor, and no hospital is listed..." she murmured.

"Is there a signature for the father?" Because if there was, it certainly wasn't his.

She turned the certificate back toward him. He narrowed his eyes as he studied the very flowery cursive signatures of both parents.

"I'm not a handwriting expert," he said. "But that looks like the same person signed as both mother and father. And neither one is how I sign my name."

"That doesn't mean you're not the father," she said. "Maybe someone didn't witness the signatures or verify identities, but why would the mother list you as the father if you aren't?"

He shrugged. "I have absolutely no idea."

He'd failed at the rodeo and the only thing he had to his name now was one-fifth ownership in the ranch, but a lawsuit might take even that away from him. So there was no reason for anyone to try to pin paternity on him; it wasn't as if he was rich or famous.

"And she left the note with the baby, too, saying that you need to take care of her now," Elise added.

"I don't think she really means *me*," he said. "I think this is all a misunderstanding. You need to find the mother and have her clear this up." But he didn't hold out much hope of anyone finding Jane Smith or whoever Lucy's mother really was.

He doubted that either of his brothers or Frankie would find any clue in the barns or on the property as to where the baby's mother had gone. Liam would probably be lucky to see any of his family again before the sun went down. Of course that was often how late they all had to work on the ranch even when they didn't get a late start like they had today.

He needed to be out there with them, helping them get food and water out to the pastures, checking for any new calves. Making sure that there were no holes in any of the fencing or any predators around to attack the livestock. But instead of focusing on his ranch duties, he found himself changing the baby's diaper and reheating the bottle he'd put in the fridge when she hadn't touched it earlier.

"You're good with her," Miss Shaw said.

He shrugged but found himself admitting, "Thanks to some quick online tutorials I have some clue what to do."

"More parents should watch those," she remarked.

"I'm not her parent," he insisted. "You need to find her real ones."

She sighed. "If you won't acknowledge that she's yours, I will have to find a foster home that's willing to take an infant."

He tensed now and stared down at the baby he held. "What do you mean?"

"Our county is so big, but we don't have enough foster homes for all the kids who need placements in our area. And infants require more care, so not many foster homes are willing to take them."

"So where will she go?" he asked, his pulse quickening with concern for her.

Ms. Shaw sighed again. "I really don't know. We'll have to see if we can find a foster home in a neighboring county that is willing to take her. Sometimes we have to bring them to other states."

"Other states?" he asked. "But how will her mother find her?" Because he had no doubt that the woman would return for her baby, that she would regret leaving her and want her back.

"Jane Smith will have to reach out to the authorities to find out where we've placed little Lucy."

Little Lucy. Warmth spread through his heart with her name. But that wasn't all of it. She was Lucy Lemmon.

"And then we'll need to determine if Jane is even fit to take her back after abandoning her like she did," Ms. Shaw continued.

"The baby looks healthy," he said in her mother's defense. Lucy was staring back at him with her mouth open as if she was either trying to smile at him or maybe she was looking for the bottle. When he put the bottle close to her mouth, she started sucking on it. "*Lucy* looks healthy. She must have been taken care of…" Even though the mother said she didn't want to do it anymore, she had cared for her the first couple of months of Lucy's life.

"I need to bring the baby to the hospital for a wellness check," Ms. Shaw said, "to make sure she is healthy with no signs of abuse."

He sucked in a breath. Abuse. Thinking of someone hurting an infant or any child made him feel physically sick. He'd been upset when animals had been mistreated in the rodeo and on some other ranches he'd worked. That was why he and his brothers had respected Frank Dempsey so much. He'd run his ranch with integrity and respect for his workers and for his livestock.

But Frank was gone. And while Liam and his brothers wanted to honor their former boss's legacy, he wasn't sure they would be granted permission to continue to do that. But Brett and Blake had taken the lead on that fight.

Who would take on the fight for little Lucy? Ms. Shaw?

"You'll find her a good home?" he asked.

She shrugged. "I'm just an investigator. I'll try to find a placement for her if you don't want her, but I won't be in contact with the home after she's placed there. The ongoing social worker will take over her case and handle things for Lucy after that."

If you don't want her...

He stared down at that little face that stared back at him, her big eyes so blue and so trusting and so fixated on him. Like she didn't want him to disappear like her mother had.

He felt sick all over again at the thought of passing her off to Ms. Shaw, who would pass her off to someone else, maybe in another state. And little Lucy would be looking for him, and he would have let her down just like every other adult in her young life already had.

She wasn't his, and he knew that. But how could he turn his back on her?

"YOU TOLD ME you're not her father," Elise reminded the man who held the baby so gently and stared down at her with such a look on his face that something thawed slightly inside Elise. She'd made such a point of protecting herself, of making sure she didn't get involved or attached or let anything get to her. She couldn't do her job if she didn't remain objective; she knew that.

But something about Liam Lemmon affected her. Maybe it was his beautiful eyes or the tenderness with which he held the baby.

"I'm not..."

"Then I'll need to find a placement for her," she said, and that warmth inside her froze over again. Babies didn't sleep through the night; they disturbed other kids in the house. So there weren't as many foster homes willing to take one for even a short-term placement.

But this placement could wind up being long-term if the mother or another family member didn't show up for her.

"It will be that hard to find a home for her?" he asked.

She nodded. "Yes, unfortunately, infants are hard placements. If she were ready for someone to adopt, it might be different. But we can't terminate the mother's or the father's rights until a waiting period of several months. And, as is often the case, the mother might change her mind and want her back." She studied his face now. "Or maybe the father will change his mind and acknowledge that she's his."

"You think she is mine," he said.

"Legally she is," Elise pointed out. "You're listed as her father on her birth certificate."

"So you would just leave her with me?" he asked. "Without proof of that?"

"With you listed as her father, that is proof enough for some courts," she said. "But if you want a paternity test to verify it, we can do that when we bring her to the hospital to get checked out."

He sucked in a breath and shook his head. "That won't be necessary."

"So you're going to acknowledge your daughter?" Elise asked with surprise. He'd acted like he was so certain he had no connection to her, that she couldn't be his. Had he remembered something or *someone*?

"Will you still look for her mother?" he asked.

She nodded. "Yes, we will need to find out why her mother left her here at the ranch." According to the note it was because she wanted the father to take over caring for the child. She was probably tired and stressed and struggling emotionally. And if she got help, she would be able to retain her parental rights. "Hopefully she will come back for her."

He nodded. "Yes, she will. I'm sure she will."

"So you do know who she is?"

He shook his head. "I... I don't know any Jane Smith."

"Maybe it isn't her real name," she admitted. But she still couldn't fathom how the mother had managed to put either of their names on the birth certificate without anyone verifying identities. And she wondered again why no doctor's name or hospital was legibly listed on the document.

"Doesn't sound real," he agreed.

"What about the women you do know? What are the names of any who might be Lucy's mother?"

His blue eyes widened with surprise. "Are you asking me about my love life?"

"My only interest is finding out who Lucy's mother is," she said.

But if Liam wasn't the father on one of her cases, she might have been interested in getting to know him better. He was good-looking and gentle with the baby. But Lucy was probably his daughter, and he was denying her. To Elise, whose own father had denied her and wanted nothing to do with her, that was unforgivable.

So there was no chance of Elise falling for him even if her crazy, unpredictable hours left her any time to date.

"Yeah, of course, that's your only interest," he hastily agreed. "I didn't mean to imply anything else."

"So?" she prodded him. "Who might be Lucy's mother?"

He closed his eyes for a moment. Maybe he was trying to search his memory for names or faces or…

To help him narrow it down, she asked, "Eleven months to a year ago, where were you?"

"Uh, I was with the rodeo then."

She nearly groaned at the thought of him on the back of a bull or a bronco. She could see him riding, could see fans cheering him on and screaming their admiration. Because of a recent case of hers, where a little boy had been hurt because of a former bronco, she'd started watching rodeo videos. Maybe she'd even watched old footage of Liam. "Who were you seeing? Anybody in particular?"

Or a lot of adoring fans?

Finding Lucy's mother might be even harder than Elise had thought.

"I… I…" He was staring down at the baby in

his arms. Then the baby stiffened and rejected the bottle in her mouth as she began to cry. He moved Lucy to his shoulder and patted her back, and she vomited all over his shoulder, soaking his Western shirt. "Oh, no…"

"I'll grab you a towel," she said, and she reached for the one hanging from the dishwasher's handle. But the small tea towel wasn't going to dry his shirt.

"I think there's something wrong with her stomach," he said. "She keeps tensing up like she's in pain. We should get her to the ER and get her checked out."

"Yes, of course," she hurriedly agreed.

That was most important thing, making sure that the baby was healthy. Elise would put aside her questions about his love life until they had confirmation that little Lucy was okay.

Then he held out the baby toward her. "Will you take her so I can change my shirt?"

"Uh…" She really had no excuse not to hold her except that babies didn't seem to like her any more than older kids or their parents did. But Elise didn't do her job to be liked; she did it to help people. Unfortunately a lot of people didn't want her help. But Liam Lemmon had asked for it.

So she wrapped her arms around the baby and took her from him. Lucy's little body was stiff, like he'd said, and she was crying again. "We definitely need to get her to ER," she agreed.

Liam must have felt the same urgency because he only unsnapped a couple of buttons before dragging his wet shirt over his head. Then he pulled a shirt out of the dryer that was in a corner of the kitchen, and he shoved his arms into the sleeves before hastily snapping it back up.

And Elise did her best not to stare at his muscular chest and then his back when he turned away from her. Then he turned back, and her face flushed with heat as she realized he'd caught her staring despite her efforts not to notice how good-looking he was. Not that it mattered.

Nothing mattered but little Lucy.

DR. LIVVY LEMMON had been working at Willow Creek Memorial Hospital for several months now, but she wasn't yet used to the slower pace from the busy downtown Chicago hospital where she'd done her residency. So she hung out in the reception area a lot, waiting for patients to come in when there were none in the ER beds for her to see.

Not that she wanted people to get hurt or sick, but she would rather be helpful than bored. And being at the intake desk saved some of the patients from having to answer the same questions over and over again.

So Livvy was out front when the lobby doors opened, and a young couple walked in with a crying baby. While she felt concern for the child, she tensed with irritation when she recognized the woman whose black hair was bound in a pony-tail and whose black-framed glasses slipped down her nose as she looked at the baby in the man's arms. Child protective services investigator Elise Shaw was not one of Livvy's favorite people. The young woman had probably only been doing her job, but she'd caused some unnecessary tension and angst for some little boys who'd recently lost both their parents in a tragic car accident.

Then Livvy focused on the man carrying that child, and her irritation turned to confusion. What in the world was her baby brother doing with Elise Shaw?

And more importantly, what was he doing with a baby?

CHAPTER FOUR

LIAM SWALLOWED A GROAN of frustration over his sister being the doctor on duty in the ER right now. While he respected Livvy's intelligence and knew that she was an excellent physician, he didn't want to answer the questions she was going to have. Because he was going to have to lie to her like he'd chosen to lie to Elise Shaw.

Not that it was an outright lie. He was listed as the father on the baby's birth certificate. So as Ms. Shaw had explained, that legally made him the child's father even though there was no actual way that he could biologically be little Lucy's daddy.

"Hey, Liam." Livvy greeted him as she stepped out from behind the front desk. "What are you doing here?" And from the way her gaze shot to Ms. Shaw and then the baby in his arms, she was asking more than that.

"Dr. Lemmon," Elise greeted her.

Obviously the two women had met before.

"Ms. Shaw," Livvy shot back at her, and from

the chilliness of her tone, she was not a fan of the child protective services investigator.

But Liam didn't know why she wouldn't be. Elise Shaw seemed determined to do her job of protecting children who couldn't protect themselves.

Like Lucy.

His intention was to protect the little girl as well. That was why he was claiming her for now, just until her mom came back for her. He believed she would, that she hadn't meant to abandon her forever when she'd left her in the barn. She'd just needed a break.

"Why are you here?" Livvy asked again.

But he wasn't sure if she was addressing him or Elise. And he didn't quite know what to say anyway so he hesitated again before answering.

The CPS investigator must have thought Livvy was talking to her because she replied, "We need to have his daughter checked out to make sure she's healthy and up-to-date with her vaccinations."

"What?" Livvy asked, and she blinked her green eyes as if she couldn't believe what she was seeing or, in this case, hearing.

Maybe that confusion caused Elise Shaw to assume his sister wasn't up to the task because she turned to the person sitting behind the intake desk. "Is there a pediatrician on duty?" she asked.

"I can examine a child," Livvy replied, "which

you very well know, Ms. Shaw. What I'm questioning is the fact that you claim this child is my brother's." His sister focused on him again, her forehead all scrunched up. "Why is she calling this baby yours?"

"Because that's what her birth certificate says," he answered honestly.

"Well, that's..." Livvy furrowed her forehead more and asked, "Why haven't you said anything about her? I just saw you a few months ago at the wedding."

Unfortunately he didn't often see his sister, and because she was always so busy and worked strange hours as a doctor, he didn't call or text her either. He left that up to her, and now he felt a pang of regret that they weren't close.

"Wedding?" Elise asked as she spun back toward Liam. "You're married?"

"Not me," he said and shook his head at the unlikelihood of that ever happening. Getting married was something he'd never thought about until he'd gotten hurt. And then, like having kids, it kept coming to his mind, or maybe that was because of all the recent engagements and marriages in his new stepfamily. But why would a woman want to marry him when he wouldn't be able to give her a child? He cleared his throat. "Our grandfather recently got married."

To Sadie March Haven, who was also Lem Lemmon's former nemesis. Liam couldn't help but smile as he thought of the older couple. Despite their age or maybe because of it, they were madly in love and mad about love, wanting to matchmake everyone else in their lives.

Liam's new stepcousins had warned him and his brothers at the wedding that they would need to watch out for the octogenarians' matchmaking schemes, or they might be the next ones at the altar. It was already too late for his sister. Livvy was engaged, but at least now it was to a good guy, not the obnoxious egomaniac she'd been engaged to during med school and her residency.

"Explain how this baby is yours," Livvy prodded him, "and how *I* don't know about her."

While his sister had never been as close to him or his brothers, that was probably more their fault than hers. Her intelligence had intimidated them and made them feel like they had nothing in common with her. When their parents had moved them from Willow Creek to Chicago years ago, Livvy had been the only one of them who'd thrived, excelling in her classes and in the city.

Liam and his brothers had missed the wide-open spaces and the ranches of their hometown. They couldn't wait to get back to the country and had moved back west as soon as they'd graduated high school, while Livvy had only recently moved back home.

"I...uh... I didn't know about her either," Liam admitted. "I just found her today, out in the barn."

"What?" Livvy asked again, her green eyes wide with horror. "Somebody just left her out in the barn like a cat they don't want anymore?"

He hated the comparison that he'd initially made himself when he'd assumed her cry was from a cat. And then Frankie had made it, too. It just wasn't right that a child should be treated so callously. "I found her out there by herself," he confirmed, his heart hurting for her.

Livvy stepped closer to him then and reached for the child. "Oh, this poor little thing."

Liam held on for a moment more, unwilling to hand the baby off to anyone, even his sister. While Elise had briefly held her back at the ranch, he'd been quick to reclaim her and not just because the CPS investigator had seemed uncomfortable holding her. He hadn't wanted Lucy to look for him and not see him around; he didn't want to be another person who seemed to abandon her like her mother had.

Why had her mom left her there? He didn't know the baby's story, but someone had written a part in it for him when they'd forged his signature on her birth certificate, and he intended to play that part for now. Hopefully his sister would forgive him for not being honest with her, but he didn't want to compromise her Hippocratic oath or whatever it was that doctors took. Maybe she had an obligation to tell the truth if he told it to her.

He had more hope Livvy would forgive him

than that Elise Shaw would. But she was the reason he was going along with the lie on the birth certificate. Once she'd told him how hard it would be to find a home for an infant, he hadn't been able to let Lucy go. Just like now.

"If you want me to examine her, I'm going to need to take her," his sister said.

He released her into Livvy's arms but said, "I should stay with her. She looks around for me." As he spoke, her head moved in his direction. She already seemed to recognize his voice.

Livvy must have noticed, too, because she asked, "Are you sure you just found her today?"

"I was thinking that as well," Elise Shaw remarked, her dark eyes narrowed with suspicion.

"I swear that I did," Liam said. "Ms. Shaw, you heard that from my brothers and from Frankie, too."

"Frankie?" Livvy asked. "I thought Frank Dempsey died."

"He did," Liam said. "Frankie is his niece. She's been staying at the ranch the past few months."

"And she's not the mother?" Livvy asked.

"No," he said, chuckling at the thought of Frankie having a child. She was less maternal than he was.

"The mother's name on the birth certificate is Jane Smith," Elise said. "It would be good to look up her name and Lucy Lemmon's to see if Lucy was born in this hospital."

"Lucy," Livvy remarked as she stared down at the baby who was trying hard to look at Liam instead of the woman holding her. She wasn't crying now, but she was still stiff and squirming like she was in discomfort.

"Can you check her out?" Liam asked with concern. "She has been crying a lot."

"I can understand why after someone left her out in a barn like that," Livvy said.

"And her body gets stiff," Liam continued, "and she spit up all over me."

"More like projectile vomiting," Elise said.

"Hmm…" Livvy murmured. "Let's look her over then, and I'll reach out to the pediatrician on duty today as well."

"And the records?"

Livvy turned toward the intake clerk. "Please look up Lucy Lemmon," she said. "See if she's in our database."

The intake clerk nodded. "I just did. No record of her being born or seen at this hospital."

"There wasn't a name of a hospital listed on the birth certificate," Elise Shaw admitted, "but I was hoping…"

"That you might get some information out of me," Livvy finished for her, her voice sharp again.

"I wasn't able to read the name of the official on the birth certificate either," Elise said. "So it's possible it was a home birth with a midwife, or maybe it was at a small clinic."

That was probably why no one had verified the father's identity before writing his name on the certificate. But Liam wasn't about to point that out now or Ms. Shaw might take Lucy away.

"That makes it even more likely that Lucy might not have any vaccinations, or she could have undiagnosed health issues if she hasn't seen a doctor," Livvy said.

"Oh, no," he said, his concern growing even more for the baby.

"We'll take her back and examine her right away," Livvy assured him.

"I'm going with you," he reminded her. He was not going to be separated from that baby girl. It didn't matter that she wasn't biologically his; she had nobody else.

And her last name was Lemmon.

ELISE DIDN'T FOLLOW the Lemmon siblings into the back of the ER. She had to update her supervisor at CPS first about this curious case. She stepped outside the lobby doors, found a quiet area away from the entrance and placed the call on her work cell phone. "Hey, Margaret, this is Elise checking in…"

"So what is the situation?" Margaret asked. "Did someone really leave a baby out in a barn?"

Elise sighed. "Unfortunately, yes."

Unless Liam Lemmon was lying about how he'd found the child. It wouldn't be the first time a parent had lied to a CPS investigator and unfortunately it would not be the last time.

"So have you reached out to fosters for a placement yet?" Margaret asked.

"I actually think I have a placement for her." But dare she leave an infant with a man who initially denied any relationship to her?

"Which home?"

"Her father's."

"You already found a parent?" Margaret said and then chuckled. "I shouldn't be surprised. You are my best investigator, Elise."

She wasn't sure about the best, but she had been with the department for a long time, almost as long as Margaret had. Because of the stress of the job, investigators usually didn't last more than two or three years. The job was notorious for causing burnout.

Elise probably would have burned out already, too, if she hadn't grown up with foster kids and learned coping mechanisms long ago. Like how to not get too attached.

She had a feeling that Liam Lemmon was already attached to that little girl even though he'd initially claimed she wasn't his. Was she, or wasn't she? Maybe Elise needed to force the issue of a paternity test. But that wasn't something she could do without a court order.

"The baby's birth certificate was in the diaper bag left with her in the barn," Elise said. "So it wasn't hard to find the names of her parents. The man who found her is listed as her father."

"Oh…" Margaret chuckled. "That's why she was left there, for him."

"With a note that basically said it was his turn to take care of her now," Elise paraphrased.

"We still need to talk to the mother," Margaret said. "Will the father tell you where to find her so that you can determine if she wants to sign off her parental rights?"

"The father claims he doesn't even know who she is," Elise replied. "The mother's name on the birth certificate wasn't familiar to him."

Margaret snorted. "Yeah, right…"

"The name on the certificate, Jane Smith, sounds more like an alias than a real name," Elise admitted.

"But wouldn't the hospital—"

"She wasn't born in a hospital," Elise said. "But that is where I am now."

Margaret gasped. "Is everything all right?"

"I hope so," Elise said. "The ER doctor is examining the baby now. We're not sure how much prenatal and medical care she's had, if any." And that thought made her stomach plunge with concern for the child and for the mother.

Jane Smith must have been very distraught to abandon her baby like that. Having grown up without a father, Elise had a bit of a soft spot for single mothers. She wanted to make sure that the mother was physically and emotionally all right.

Elise had to get more answers out of Liam about Jane and also about his sudden willingness to take care of a baby he claimed he hadn't even known about. She sighed.

"Hang in there, Elise," her supervisor encouraged her. "You really are the best. You'll get the answers you need to determine how best to close the case."

Closing the case for CPS didn't always mean closing the case completely; sometimes it meant handing it off to the ongoing social workers who were in closer, prolonged contact with the families. But Elise wasn't ready yet to hand off or close this case.

She needed a lot more answers before she could do either. But she wasn't as certain as her boss was that she would get those answers.

"Dr. Lemmon is the doctor on duty today," Elise said.

Margaret sucked in a breath. "She must understand you were only doing your job when you investigated that report we received about the boy she'd seen in her ER."

Dr. Lemmon had taken Elise's investigation of an injury to one of the recently orphaned Haven children personally. She had a connection to those children through their family, but to this one...

"The man who found the baby in the barn is Dr. Lemmon's brother," Elise said.

"So the baby is her niece?"

"So it would seem."

Yet something about how adamant Liam had initially been that the child wasn't his made Elise wonder when he'd been lying to her and when he'd been telling the truth.

But why would he claim the child as his if little Lucy wasn't really his daughter?

AFTER WIPING DOWN the horses in the barn and cleaning out their stalls, Blake was the first one to head back to the house. He wouldn't have stayed out as long as he had, but after searching for the baby's mom, they'd also had to tend the cattle. When he crossed the yard between the barn and the house, he noticed that the CPS investigator's vehicle was gone.

Hopefully the baby was gone, too. A twinge of guilt struck him for thinking that. The poor kid hadn't chosen to get abandoned in their barn.

While he felt guilty, he was also overwhelmed. He and his brothers had enough drama right now with the lawsuit contesting their inheritance of shares of the ranch. Could the baby have something to do with that? A way of discrediting them somehow?

He walked across the porch and pushed open the door to the house. "Liam?" he called out.

But his voice echoed hollowly off the hardwood floor and vaulted ceiling. He walked through the house to the kitchen where the shirt Liam had been wearing lay across the washing machine, and the dryer door was open. Some of the baby stuff remained, like a pad on the table in the eat-in area of the big kitchen.

Was the baby not gone?

And where was Liam? His twinge of guilt was a hollow ache now. He and the others shouldn't have just left Liam to deal with the baby and the CPS investigator on his own. But the cattle had already gone untended for too long while they'd been in town talking to Maci.

He called out for his brother again, just as Brett and Frankie walked into the house, too. They moved quietly, as if afraid of waking the baby up.

"I don't think they're here," Blake said as he glanced into the rooms off the kitchen. Then he crossed the living room and looked into the bedrooms. "Nope. No sign of them."

"The CPS worker's car is gone," Frankie said. "But where's Liam and the baby? He didn't come out for his truck when we were unloading the hay from it."

"He sent me a text that he and the CPS investigator took the baby to the hospital," Brett said as he stared down at the screen of the cell in his hand.

Blake hadn't checked his but now that he did, he saw he had a text, too.

Frankie also nodded and said, "I hope she's okay."

"Me, too," Blake agreed. "Poor kid."

"The baby or Liam?" Brett asked. "I hope he isn't taking that finders keepers thing to heart."

Liam had always had the biggest heart of all the Lemmon siblings, even Livvy. While Livvy had chosen to become a doctor to help people, she wasn't as outgoing as their youngest sibling. Liam was a lot like their grandfather, who'd never met a stranger. He loved people and animals and was always gentle with both.

"Maybe the kid is his," Frankie said. "He was in the rodeo before coming to the ranch. Over the years, riders have come into the bars where I was singing and hit on every woman in the place."

While Liam was outgoing like Grandpa Lem, he hadn't ever been a womanizer. Again like Grandpa Lem and like their father. Both had married young and stayed married until their wives had died.

Even though Liam had never gotten close to marrying, whoever he'd dated had usually wound up becoming a friend even after they broke up. And a friend wouldn't have left the baby for him without asking him for help first.

Who was the baby's mother? And just as importantly, who was the little girl's father?

CHAPTER FIVE

LIAM'S HEART WAS beating fast, like it used to just before he eased down from the top rungs of the chute onto the bronco's back. But now he was watching his sister examine the baby who lay on the gurney, kicking her legs, clenching her fists and crying. "Is she all right?"

Was something wrong with her? Was that why her mother had abandoned her? Because she couldn't deal with her baby's health issues?

Livvy looked up, then pulled her stethoscope away from her ears to dangle around her neck. "Her heart and lungs sound great. Strong. Healthy."

"But she was throwing up—"

"After you fed her?"

He nodded.

"I have a feeling she might be allergic to the formula."

"But it was left in her bag…"

Livvy shrugged. "Maybe the mom was breast-feeding her and didn't know. I recommend trying soy formula and seeing how she reacts to that. I'm also going to prescribe drops for gas. It seems like she is struggling with that and maybe reflux issues."

"So the drops and the soy formula will help?" he asked.

She nodded. "And finding her mom would, too. Are you her father, Liam?"

His heart clenched for a moment, and he glanced around the ER bay. Only a curtain separated them from the rest of the emergency room, and he had no idea where Elise Shaw had gone or when she was coming back.

Or if she was coming back.

He'd need to find a ride back to the ranch if she'd rushed off and left him and Lucy at the hospital.

"Liam?" Livvy prodded him. "Tell me the truth."

But would she be obliged to tell Elise if he told her? "Her birth certificate says her name is Lucy Lemmon and Liam Lemmon is her father."

"I don't care what the birth certificate says," Livvy replied. "I want to know what you say about being her father. Are you?"

"I didn't think so when I first found her."

"But now you believe she's actually yours?"

"Legally, because of the birth certificate—"

"Liam!" Livvy interrupted, her voice sharp with impatience.

And the baby began to cry loudly.

Liam scooped her up from the gurney and held

her close against his heart. "Shh…ignore Auntie Livvy. She didn't mean to scare you."

Livvy's face flushed, and she flinched, maybe at his reprimand, maybe that she'd made the baby cry. "Auntie Livvy… So she is yours?"

He sighed. "I don't really…"

"Don't what?" Livvy prodded, but her voice was softer now.

He really didn't want to lie to his sister, but he had already kind of lied to Ms. Shaw. And now he didn't know where she was. Until he looked down, unable to meet his sister's gaze, and he noticed a shadow on the other side of the curtain. He pulled it aside to find Elise, and he wondered how long she'd been standing there.

Good thing he hadn't given his sister an honest answer to her question. No. He wasn't the baby's father. She wasn't Lucy's auntie anything, but when he'd picked her up, she'd stopped crying. Now she seemed to snuggle up against him, as if she belonged in his arms. But she wasn't really his. And what in the world was he going to do with a baby?

Maybe he wouldn't have to keep her for long, just until her mom returned for her. Once she'd had some rest she would regret leaving her baby like an unwanted animal. Wouldn't she?

WHEN LIAM PULLED the curtain back, both Lemmon siblings turned to Elise, their eyes wide with surprise over catching her eavesdropping. Not that she'd heard anything useful, anything that would help her find Lucy's mother or even reassure her that Liam was really her father. But he was no longer denying she was his. He seemed to have accepted that he was her father, and Lucy seemed to have accepted him. She was quiet in his arms, but just as she seemed about to close her eyes, she would open them again as if checking to make sure that he was the one who held her.

That *he* still had her and nobody else did.

But Elise wasn't any more certain than his sister seemed to be about this whole situation. She asked her, "Dr. Lemmon, how is the baby?"

"Healthy. I was telling my brother she might have an allergy to the formula that was left with her. Or she has reflux. I'm going to prescribe some drops for gas and recommend a soy-based formula to see if that helps with her discomfort."

Elise nodded. "Do you think she's had her vaccinations?"

The doctor sighed. "I would hope so, but without knowing if she was born in a hospital or not…" She shook her head. "I don't know for certain. There are certain shots I can give her now that she wouldn't have received before two months old, so that she'll have some immunities."

"Do that," Liam said. "Make sure she's protected."

"She could have a reaction to the vaccinations," the doctor cautioned him.

Liam gasped. "Bad reactions?"

His sister shook her head. "Some swelling, maybe a fever and more crying from the discomfort. Are you really keeping her, Liam? This isn't like finding a cat in the barn."

He emitted something like a soft growl that had the baby opening her eyes wide. "I'm getting really sick of that comparison. I know she's not a cat, and everybody else should stop comparing her to one."

"Your sister is asking if you can handle taking care of a baby," Elise pointed out. "I have my concerns, too." She didn't want to leave a helpless infant with someone who wasn't equipped to take care of her. But removing a child from the custody of a legal parent required a court order just like a request for a paternity test would. She felt like growling, too, with frustration.

"Tabs in back," Liam replied with a grin.

Her pulse quickened at how handsome he looked, his blue eyes sparkling with amusement. "There's more to taking care of an infant than changing diapers."

"I know," he said. "I'm going to have to get some of that soy-based formula and some other supplies for her."

"Taking care of an infant is a lot of work," she said. "Are you sure you want the responsibility?"

"Her mom will come back for her," he said as if he had no doubt.

"I thought you didn't know who her mother was," Elise said.

He shook his head. "I don't."

Now Livvy Lemmon emitted a low growl. "What are you going to do about that, Miss Shaw? Isn't it your job to find the mother and to take care of the baby?"

"It's the parent's job to take care of their baby," Elise replied. "Do you think your brother isn't the father? Or that he just isn't up to the task?"

Livvy glanced at her brother, then back to Elise. "Again, isn't it your job to determine that?"

"Livvy, back down," Liam said. "Miss Shaw is doing her job, and it can't be an easy one. You probably know that even better than I do."

The young ER's doctor's face flushed a bright pink, but she pursed her lips as if holding back something. Maybe the apology she'd never given Elise.

But Elise was not going to hold her breath for one or hold out hope that she and the doctor would ever be friends. It was good that Elise wasn't really interested in the young woman's brother because she doubted that Livvy Lemmon would ever accept her in his life.

Yet Elise kept thinking about how Liam had looked earlier in the kitchen…without his shirt. She wished she'd never sneaked a peek. Or at least that she could forget what she'd seen. Maybe she would have to check out the dating scene again, if she ever caught up enough with her caseload to go on a date.

She needed to figure out how to close this case as quickly as possible not just because of her caseload but because she didn't want to have any more contact than necessary with either of the Lemmon siblings.

But until she had more answers to her questions about little Lucy, she couldn't close the case. And she would just have to figure out how to ignore her uncomfortable awareness of Liam Lemmon.

PARAMEDIC COLTON CASSIDY gave his patient a reassuring grin as he pushed her gurney through the doors of Willow Creek Memorial Hospital's emergency room. He'd called ahead so they were expecting the woman he'd brought in from the local assisted living center, and Nurse Sue rushed up to direct him to an open bay in the ER.

"You'll be fine, Mrs. Reynolds," he assured his elderly patient. "The smartest doctor in Willow Creek is on duty today."

"Your twin?" the older woman asked.

He chuckled. "No, my fiancée, Livvy Lemmon. And you can tell my brother I said so."

Mrs. Reynolds smiled back at him despite how weak she was. She'd taken a bad fall earlier at the nursing home, but he hadn't detected any broken bones. He was more concerned about what had made her fall, especially because of how low her blood pressure was. She probably was going to need to see his brother, the cardiologist, as well as Livvy. But the older woman reached out and patted his hand on the gurney railing. "I'm so glad Old Man Lemmon's family has moved back home."

Nurse Sue sucked in a breath but looked, as usual, like she'd sucked a lemon instead. "Mrs. Reynolds, the doctor will be with us shortly, but I'm going to check your vitals and hook up an IV."

Colton started to step back from the gurney, but Mrs. Reynolds held on to his hand. "Thank you, young man, for taking such good care of me."

Colton was midthirties but a young man to her, while his stepgrandfather, who was probably younger than she was, was Old Man Lemmon. He knew his grandmother, Sadie Haven, was the reason everybody in town had started calling the mayor Old Man long before he was old, though. Now Lem was the deputy mayor and also Sadie's second husband.

"I just got you here, Mrs. Reynolds," he said. "The doctor and nurse will take really good care of you now." He hoped she would be fine; she really was a sweet woman. He squeezed her hand, then moved back. Just as he turned, the curtain across from him opened.

His pulse quickened at the sight of his beautiful fiancée. As usual her strawberry blond hair was pulled up, but several curly locks had managed to escape and dangled down her back and along her cheek. When she turned toward him, her green eyes lit up with the same emotion he was feeling for her: love.

He loved her so much that he didn't even care that Grandma Sadie and her grandfather Lem had schemed to get them together. Not that they'd had to do much. While Sadie might have been instrumental in getting Colton transferred from the Moss Valley Fire Department to the Willow Creek one, she hadn't had to do anything else to get him to fall for Livvy.

He'd pretty much fallen for the beautiful doctor the first time he'd seen her. And she wasn't just beautiful—she was brilliant and caring, too.

"Wow, you got it bad," Mrs. Reynolds remarked, then she emitted a weak laugh.

He grinned at the older woman, who had obviously caught him staring at his fiancée. "Yes, I do."

"Sadie strikes again," Mrs. Reynolds said and chuckled. Of course the older woman knew about Sadie's matchmaking. Everyone in Willow Creek, and probably the surrounding areas, knew about Sadie March Haven Lemmon.

"Colton," a deep voice called out.

He turned back to see that Livvy wasn't alone in the bay across from him. Her brother Liam was with her. And…

Elise Shaw.

Then something in Liam's arms moved, and Colton noticed that the youngest Lemmon was holding a baby.

He left Mrs. Reynolds with Nurse Sue and walked over to join his fiancée. "What's up? Is Sadie already scheming again?"

Had his grandmother done something to get Liam and the child protective services investigator together?

Colton, his brothers and his Haven cousins had warned the Lemmon brothers that their new stepgrandmother would do her best to pair them off with someone and probably as soon as possible. But would Sadie have chosen Elise Shaw for Liam? Colton knew for certain Livvy wouldn't have, that she didn't want anything to do with the CPS investigator. That was his fault more than Elise's. If he'd been watching his second cousin, five-year-old Ian, better, the little boy wouldn't have opened Midnight's stall and gotten hurt. So he understood why the young woman had had to investigate to make sure the child was in no danger.

Livvy still had a problem with her, though. And that was obvious from the glare she shot first toward him and then the other woman.

"Sadie…" Liam murmured, and his blue eyes widened. Then he stared down at the baby and back at Colton. "You think Sadie could be behind this?"

"What are you talking about?" Elise Shaw asked. "You think Sadie Haven left this baby in your barn?"

Colton gasped and moved closer to where they stood. He glanced down at the child Liam held. She couldn't be more than a couple of months old. "This baby was abandoned in a barn like an un—"

"Don't say it," Liam interrupted him. "She is not unwanted, and she is not a cat."

Colton's eyes widened as he stared at his soon-to-be brother-in-law. Clearly, the baby was not unwanted because Liam already seemed quite attached to her. "But she was left in a barn?" he asked, to clarify the situation.

Liam nodded. "Yes, I found her in the barn at the Four Corners Ranch."

"Ah, that's why you're involved," Colton concluded.

"There's a little more to his involvement than that," Ms. Shaw said. "Why would you think Sadie Haven was behind the baby's mother leaving her in the barn?"

"She wasn't," Livvy said now, shaking her head. "Sadie had nothing to do with that."

She wouldn't have coerced a mother to abandon her baby, but the coincidence of Liam finding her and then having to get in contact with Elise Shaw raised Colton's suspicions.

"Dr. Lemmon, we're ready for you now," Nurse

Sue called across from where she stood next to Mrs. Reynolds' stretcher.

Livvy looked at her brother, her expression serious. "You're sure you've got this?"

He nodded. "I'll get her the soy formula and fill the prescription you gave me. I'll also pick up some baby pain reliever in case she has a reaction to the vaccinations you gave her."

Shocked, Colton asked, "You're keeping the baby?"

Liam gazed down at the infant and nodded. "Yeah, for now."

Livvy sucked in a breath and nodded. "Okay, let me know if you need help with her. My shift ends soon." Then she headed over to Mrs. Reynolds's bed without even a glance at Elise Shaw.

Elise Shaw wasn't looking at Livvy, though. She was looking at Livvy's brother, and the look on her face...

Well, it made Colton's doubts return. He wasn't as convinced as his fiancée that Sadie wasn't behind this. His grandmother would do anything if she thought the end justified the means. And she definitely believed that love was justification for any and all of her actions.

CHAPTER SIX

SADIE?

Until Colton mentioned the Haven matriarch moments ago, the thought hadn't entered Liam's mind that the baby could have anything to do with his new stepgrandmother. But it didn't make any sense.

How was leaving a baby in his barn going to set Liam up with the love of his life? More likely it would scare her away.

Ms. Shaw was clearly judging him and finding him wanting as a father and as a man. First because he'd denied that Lucy was his, and now because he was claiming her but denying he knew the identity of her mother. The CPS investigator obviously thought he was some kind of sweet-talking, love-'em-and-leave-'em rodeo rider. And that couldn't be further from the truth.

But he didn't know how to reveal the truth right now without making things worse for himself and for Lucy.

"Your sister and the paramedic were shocked

you have a child," Elise Shaw remarked as she and Liam walked out of the hospital.

"*I* am shocked I have a child," Liam said honestly, since it was impossible for him to father one.

"You really didn't have any clue you had a baby?" she persisted with obvious suspicion. "No woman called to tell you she might be pregnant or that she had your child?"

He choked on the laugh that threatened to bubble up his throat again. "No."

"So the mother just ghosted you after you dated?" she asked. "Does that happen often?"

Never. But he couldn't admit that without her realizing he was lying about being Lucy's father. And he wasn't sure how much trouble he could get in for that lie. She was the one who'd told him his name on the birth certificate legally made him the little girl's dad, though.

Instead of lying now, he just shrugged and added, "Dating now isn't like it was for our grandparents."

"I don't have grandparents," she said.

"What?"

"My mom grew up in the foster care system," she said. "And I never met my dad."

He felt a pang of sympathy and a sudden understanding for her. "Oh…"

"Oh, what?" she asked.

"That's why you became a child protective services investigator." And it was probably also why she'd been so upset when he'd denied that Lucy was his—her father must have denied her.

Elise shrugged now, as if none of that was of any importance. But it was important to him; she impressed him so much for being strong enough to do the difficult job she had. Now that he knew about her upbringing, he was even more impressed. And he wanted to know *everything* about her like how long and soft her hair might be when she took it out of the tight ponytail. Like what made her laugh and what made her cry, what dreams she had for herself.

Oh, he thought, maybe Sadie had struck again, as Colton suspected. Somehow she had maneuvered it so that Liam would meet Elise Shaw. But he couldn't imagine even the legendary Sadie Haven involving an innocent baby in her matchmaking scheme. Family mattered too much to her, just like it mattered to him.

He was going to need a ride back to the ranch and to get some baby supplies.

"Do you mind taking me to the pharmacy and somewhere to buy some stuff for Lucy?" he asked Elise. "There were only a few diapers in the bag and that pad and not many clothes. She will need more than that." He didn't need to know much about babies to realize that.

"You are serious about keeping her?" she asked.

"You said that because my name is on her birth certificate I could keep her," he reminded her.

She narrowed her eyes behind the lenses of her black-framed glasses and studied his face as they stood next to her vehicle in the parking lot. "Are you her father?"

"Apparently I am," he said. *Legally*, at least. "And I'm willing to take her, unlike most foster homes you mentioned." He had to keep Lucy because he was sure her mother would come back for her. Maybe she'd already come back.

He hoped she had because his brothers and Frankie probably wouldn't be happy that he was going to bring the baby back to the ranch. But if the mom was already there, she could explain that she'd just needed a short break.

"I will find her a home if necessary," Ms. Shaw said. "It just might be a distance away from Willow Creek."

He shook his head. "No. She needs to go back to the Four Corners Ranch with me."

And if Elise wouldn't drive them, he would have to wait until Livvy was done working. Or call one of his brothers to come get him. Though Blake and Brett might refuse to give him a ride if they knew he wasn't coming back alone. They had so much to deal with already.

Dad had moved back to Willow Creek after Mom died, but Liam hesitated to call him. He felt guilty asking him for anything when he hadn't been there to help Dad with Mom's second fight with cancer. His parents hadn't told any of them about the first because Liam and his siblings had been young then. But when they'd reached out and told them about the second, Liam had already been in the rodeo circuit and Brett and Blake had been working on ranches and Livvy had been in med school. They'd insisted that nobody needed to come back, that Mom would beat it again, but she hadn't.

She'd been gone nearly two years now but losing her still hurt so much. He sucked in a breath at the sharp jab of pain. She would have enjoyed having a grandchild, especially a girl, as she'd always been so close to Livvy. She would have loved Lucy, and just as she and Dad had wanted them to focus on their own lives instead of them, she would have wanted him to focus on this child, on taking care of her.

So he held his breath as he waited to see what the CPS investigator had decided. If she would let him take little Lucy back to the ranch…

ELISE WASN'T SURE she was doing the right thing, but without a better option as a placement for Lucy, she really had no choice, especially if Liam pressed the issue. He could contest CPS trying to remove Lucy from his home, and since his name was on her birth certificate, he would win.

So instead of starting a legal battle, she chose

to make certain that he had everything he needed for the baby, and Elise would keep checking on him to make sure he could handle taking care of Lucy. Hopefully the mother would return soon, which was probably what Liam wanted, too.

Once they picked up the prescription from the pharmacy, they headed to the baby store on Main Street. The shop was cute, with mobiles hanging down from the ceiling and stuffed animals everywhere. They had bassinets, changing tables, bouncy chairs and even essentials like diapers and formula.

And clothes. There were racks upon racks of little dresses and overalls and footie pajamas. Little cowboy hats even topped some of the racks.

Everything was adorable, but the store was so crowded it was daunting. Since it overwhelmed Elise, she couldn't imagine how Liam felt about all of it. If he'd truly had no warning he was a father, he had to be reeling from being thrust into the role.

Elise had decided a while ago not to have children of her own because there were so many children who needed homes. She didn't want to foster like her mom because too often those kids had to return to their biological parents. She'd figured when she was older and not as busy as she was with her job, she would adopt. But she was always so busy.

Too busy to take the time that she was with

Liam Lemmon. But it was her job to make sure little Lucy was safe with him.

She turned toward him, and he was looking around as awed as she was. "You don't need to go overboard now. You already have the right car seat for her age and weight. You can make do with a portable bassinet while she's this small. And then soy formula, diapers and some more clothes." There were other things he needed for the baby, like rash cream and wipes and more bottles, but she would make sure he included those with his purchases.

He released a shaky breath and nodded. "Okay."

She didn't know what his financial situation was, but she'd help him not to overspend, especially when the salesperson swooped down on them.

"Welcome, welcome to our shop!" she said with a big smile and a booming voice. "What a beautiful family you are!"

Lucy let out a little cry of alarm while Elise managed to stifle hers. Maybe the baby was reacting to the woman's loudness while Elise wanted to protest that they were not a family.

Family.

Elise wasn't even certain what that was despite how hard her mother had tried to have one, how much it had meant to her to have a family of her own. Elise had done her best to make her mother happy and never complain because her mother had had it so much worse.

Liam was right that Elise was a CPS investigator because her mom grew up in foster care. But she was shocked and unsettled she'd let personal information slip out. She never talked about herself. She always kept the focus on the case she was investigating.

That was all that Liam Lemmon was: a parent on a case. And she wasn't entirely convinced about the parent part. But he was willing to claim Lucy and care for her, and that was all that mattered—maybe a little too much to Elise.

He was so gentle with the baby and so handsome. But they were not a family no matter how flattering and pulse-quickening the thought of them being together was. Still, she didn't correct the salesperson.

"We just need a few things," she told the woman. "And we don't have much time." Inside her open purse, her work phone kept lighting up with incoming text messages. If any emergency had come up, she would have received a call. But she still had to respond to her texts. She had other cases she was working on.

And other parents to deal with—Liam wasn't the only one who needed her help. But his needing her had a different effect on her than any other case she'd worked. He had a different effect on her. That unsettled her, too. Anxious to get away from him, she rattled off the list of things they required. The older lady's smile never slipped, but she glanced at Liam, as if for confirmation.

He nodded. "She's the boss."

"That's what my husband says, too," the woman replied with a wider smile.

Family. Husband.

The woman's assumptions were spiraling and making Elise very uncomfortable. But when she opened her mouth to correct the woman, Liam touched her arm.

"You're in a hurry," he reminded her.

Since the baby had had a couple of vaccinations, she might start getting fussy, so they did need to hurry. Elise let the woman believe whatever she wanted; she just had to remind herself that it wasn't the truth. She and Liam weren't really together. They weren't a family. And they weren't ever going to be.

Elise would focus on finding the baby's mother, and maybe the woman would reunite with Liam and give little Lucy the family this salesperson imagined they were. The thought depressed her for some reason.

While another clerk gathered the things from the backroom that Elise had listed off to her, the salesperson ran around the store pulling outfits off racks. Little dresses and overalls and bibs that said things like: Daddy's Girl, Mommy's Little Angel, I heart My Daddy.

Now Elise wasn't the only one who was uncomfortable because Liam's face was flushed. He opened his mouth, probably to correct the woman, and Elise touched his arm. "We are in a hurry," she said.

As if to prove her point, her work cell rang. She grimaced. "I have to take this."

He nodded. "Of course. I'll pay for this."

She leaned closer and whispered, "Don't let her make you buy more than you need."

But she had no idea how much he would need. Was he going to keep Lucy? Or would he give her up if her mother returned for her?

He leaned closer to her, so close that his breath brushed across the skin of her cheek when he replied, "Don't worry, boss."

But she wasn't his boss or his wife or any other thing this salesperson had assumed. She was nothing to Liam Lemmon but the CPS investigator handling his daughter's case.

Elise needed to keep it that way. Maybe that was why, when she took the call just outside the store, she agreed to take the new case and leave as soon as possible. That meant Liam would have to find his own way back to the Four Corners Ranch. But she knew the less time she spent with him the better. He seemed to be doing well with the baby, but she would still need to follow up to make sure.

"Is everything all right?" he asked when she stepped back inside the store.

She shook her head. "I've just had a priority one case come in, which means I need to make contact with the child right away. Are you able to get a ride back to the ranch?"

"Yes, of course," he said. "My dad lives in town. Go. Take care of that child." He tightened his arms around Lucy, as if to protect her from the danger the other child was in.

Unfortunately too many children were too often in danger. But she trusted Lucy wasn't one of them, not with the way that Liam was taking care of her. He'd really stepped up in a hurry.

"I'm sorry," she said, because of how she was rushing off. And someone else would have taken the case if she'd said she was still busy with him. But she wanted to get away from him and Lucy. She didn't want to start believing that they were together, as the salesperson had.

"Go," Liam urged her. "We'll be fine." But he glanced down at the baby a little nervously, like he wasn't entirely certain.

"I'll check back with you as soon as I can," she assured him. But still, when she walked away from him and the baby, she felt like she was abandoning them just like Lucy's mother had.

SADIE WASN'T SURE going to the baby store was a good idea, not when Lem was already yearning for his grandkids to give him grandbabies. But he'd insisted he wanted to buy something for the twins, and she couldn't refuse him anything. So she'd held on tightly while he drove his vintage Cadillac from Ranch Haven into downtown Willow Creek. He drove faster than she did, and she probably drove too fast.

But he was also a good driver. It just wasn't easy for Sadie to give someone else the wheel. Even in her first marriage, she'd run things more than Big Jake had. And maybe in order to keep the peace, he'd kept things from her. Like his cigars and his drinking.

She and Lem had no secrets between them. They told each other everything. Or so she'd thought until they walked into the baby store, and she saw his grandson Liam standing at the counter.

"Is that why you wanted to come here?" she asked.

"What? Why?" Lem asked distractedly as he studied a collection of stuffed animals just inside the door. He picked up a pink poodle from the top of the pile and chuckled. "This one is so cute."

She tapped his arm to get his full attention. He was getting a little hard of hearing. "Look who's here," she said and pointed out his youngest grandson.

But Liam wasn't alone. He held a baby against

his chest. And he seemed to be buying baby things. A lot of baby things.

"What is he doing here?" Lem asked her, his blue eyes wide. Clearly he was just as surprised as she was to find his grandson in a baby store. And she felt a pang of guilt for thinking even for a second that he might keep secrets from her. But apparently someone else in his family had been keeping secrets.

"Let's ask him," she said, guiding him toward the counter where Liam stood. "Imagine running into you here…"

Liam's lean body tensed, and he hesitated a long moment before turning around to face them. The baby he held had a pink bow headband on and a pink blanket wrapped around her. A little girl. "Well, hello there, Grandpa Lem, Sadie…"

She felt a twinge of disappointment and wished he would call her Grandma. But she hadn't had much contact with Lem's grandkids, not since they'd moved away to Chicago years ago. She hadn't had any contact with some of her own grandchildren, though, and they had come to call her Grandma.

Maybe Lem's would, too.

She just had to be patient and not force things, which was the approach she and Lem had agreed to take with his grandsons because they had so much going on. Apparently even more than they'd known.

"And you were just saying that you needed a ride now," the saleswoman remarked. "What wonderful timing."

"Yes…" Liam murmured, but he looked pale, a little sick even.

"You need a ride back to the Four Corners Ranch?" Lem asked.

Liam seemed to tense even more before giving him a nod. "Yes."

The baby appeared to be falling asleep in his arms, but she blinked her eyes open and looked up at him. She had the same beautiful blue eyes that Liam had, that Lem had.

"And who is this adorable little girl?" Sadie asked.

"Um…" His throat moved as if he was struggling to swallow. Then he glanced back at the clerk who was studying him with a quizzical expression despite the plastered-on smile she wore.

He stepped farther away from the counter and lowered his voice. "If you can give us a ride back to the ranch, I'll tell you when we get there. It's a little complicated."

"Us?" Lem repeated. He'd heard that, and he was totally fixated on the baby his grandson held.

Was she Liam's? Had Lem's wish for his grandkids to have children already been granted?

Sadie hoped so because he was already staring at the baby with such affection and awe that he would definitely be disappointed if she wasn't his great-grandchild.

CHAPTER SEVEN

LIAM HAD ALREADY started worrying that the situation was getting out of hand and that had just been with Elise Shaw. But now…

Now he was floundering even before he uttered a word.

He'd let the clerk at the store believe that not only was the baby his but that Elise Shaw was, too. He'd used the excuse that it would be more trouble to explain the situation to her than to just let her believe whatever she wanted. He'd also liked the idea of being a family…but just for the baby's sake.

It didn't matter what the salesclerk thought.

But what about his grandfather and Sadie?

And his brothers?

And Frankie?

Dare he tell them the truth? Or would that make them complicit in whatever trouble he would get in for not telling the CPS investigator that there was no way the baby was his?

But why would someone name him as her father? Who would do that?

He was both hopeful and afraid that Elise would find out the truth. But she'd been called away to a case where a child was in more danger than Lucy was in. Although, at the speed his grandfather drove, Liam wasn't sure how safe any of them were. He reached across the backseat and checked the straps securing the car seat into place facing the back. Fortunately his grandfather had had aftermarket seatbelts installed in the vintage Cadillac. Instead of being frightened, like Liam was, the baby slept peacefully for the first time since he'd found her.

Maybe that was because her tiny fingers were wrapped around one of his. She didn't have to keep opening her eyes to see if he was there; she was holding on to him.

His heart wrenched in his chest. And he knew that he had to hold on to her, to keep her, at least until her mother returned for her. But until then, he wasn't sure what to say to anyone. So he'd remained silent on the ride to the ranch, using the excuse of the sleeping baby and not wanting to disturb her. Thankfully, she had slept, so he hadn't been lying then.

But as his grandfather turned into the driveway to the Four Corners Ranch, Liam knew his reprieve was over. He had to figure out what to tell everyone. Did he risk the truth, or did he just continue with the lie Lucy's mother had told that he was the baby's father?

Like Elise's vehicle had earlier today, his grandfather's Cadillac kicked up a cloud of dust that engulfed them as they continued down the drive to the ranch house. Grandpa braked near the porch and the dust began to settle.

"So this is the ranch?" Sadie asked.

"Yes," Liam replied with a surge of pride. While the Four Corners wasn't on the scale of Ranch Haven, it was a big spread with several hundred acres of property, well-kept barns and a lot of healthy livestock. Most of that was because of his brothers. Once they'd started working for Frank Dempsey, he'd been able to expand the beef business, and the ranch had prospered from all their hard work. That was why he'd included them in his will—he wouldn't have had as much to leave his heirs if not for them.

But one of those heirs, the daughter who'd gone no-contact with him years ago, thought she deserved it all. And because she was his closest next of kin, a judge might side with her. If he and his brothers lost the lawsuit, he wasn't sure what they would do or where they would go.

The dust settled, and Liam peered around the place. His pickup was still parked over by the big red barn, but the box was unloaded. He felt a twinge of guilt that his brothers had done that without him. But he wasn't sure how much help he would be for them until Lucy's mother came back. Maybe they would have to rehire one of the hands they'd let go. But both of the guys had been pretty irresponsible; they'd been more interested in hearing about his rodeo days than doing any work on the ranch. No. Liam would have to figure out some way to continue carrying his share of the workload while he had Lucy and while they still had the ranch.

It was probably a good thing that she wasn't really his because his future was so uncertain. He might not have a job or a home much longer. Maybe that was why he felt such a kinship with her; her future was even more uncertain than his.

He looked down at her as he used his free hand to unclasp the car seat and noticed her eyes were open. She was staring at him like she seemed to always do. Then her lips parted, and a little bubble escaped with something that sounded like a giggle.

Or maybe it was just gas.

He smiled at her. She was such a cutie.

"Is she okay?" Sadie asked.

He glanced over his shoulder at the older woman and nodded. While Sadie Haven was in her eighties now, she was still as intimidating as she'd always been. He'd grown up hearing the legend of her—how she'd fought off wolves with her bare hands and rode through blizzards on horseback. She was strong, and for so many years, she'd been his grandfather's adversary. So seeing them together was still strange for him and not just because his grandfather barely came to her shoulder. Sadie was tall; Lem was short. Her hair was now as white as his had been for years.

Would his brothers, with the same auburn hair his grandfather had in old pictures, go white prematurely, too?

Maybe Liam was lucky that he looked more like his mother with her black hair. He was also a little taller and lankier than his brothers. They were standing on the porch now with Frankie, staring at the Cadillac.

Liam opened the back door and stepped out just as the older couple emerged from the vehicle. There was a moment of silence before Brett called out, "Grandpa."

"And Sadie," Blake added.

The older woman flinched like she had in the store when Liam had addressed her by her first name. Did she want them to call her Grandma? Considering how intimidating she was, that wasn't something Liam would be comfortable doing until she offered permission. And while he'd heard stories about her, he didn't know her very well.

"Did you pick up a hitchhiker on the side of the road?" Brett asked.

Liam chuckled at the weak joke. Then he reached into the back of the Caddy and pulled out Lucy's car seat. Fortunately the Cadillac was big, so all her things had fit in the trunk.

Blake gasped. "You brought her back?"

"Who is she?" his grandfather asked. "What's going on here?"

Liam wished he knew. But because everybody was looking at him, he had to come up with some answers. "I found the baby in the barn earlier today."

Grandpa gasped now, and his blue eyes widened. "What did you say?" he asked.

Sadie raised her voice and said, "He found the baby in the barn."

"I heard that," Lem said. "I just can't believe it."

Neither could Liam.

"That whole finders keepers thing doesn't apply to people," Blake said. "Why do you still have her? Where's the CPS worker?"

"She got called out for a more important case."

"More important?" Frankie added in her two cents. "This baby was left in the barn. That's pretty important."

Sadie looked at her. "Frances Dempsey?" she asked.

Frankie tensed a bit, perhaps surprised that the older woman knew her name. "Yes, ma'am."

Sadie smiled at her.

Along with warning them about her matchmaking, his new stepcousins had warned them that the older lady seemed to always know everything...

even before the other people involved knew. Was that the case here?

Was Colton's suspicion right that she was somehow involved? She certainly didn't seem as surprised as his grandfather was. But then she'd been through so much in her life that she probably just took everything in stride. That was what Liam had to do now.

So he drew in a breath, then exhaled it in a ragged sigh. "Let's head into the house, and I'll tell you all what the situation is…"

Except his dad.

He really didn't want to dump anything more on his father, who was still struggling with grief over losing their mother. So this was good. The people who needed to hear his explanation were all here on the ranch, and they gathered around him in the living room as he unfastened the car seat and lifted Lucy out. But before he could cradle her in his arms, his grandfather took her and cuddled her against his chest.

As he stared down at her, he looked as if he'd already fallen for her. But then his grandpa had always loved kids. After they'd moved away, Liam's immediate family had returned to Willow Creek every Christmas to visit Santa in the town square. But all of them had recognized that Santa was their grandfather.

For years, Liam had believed, and his older siblings had let him believe, that their grandfather was the real Santa Claus. Lem certainly looked the part with his white hair and his white beard and his rosy cheeks and sparkling eyes.

Sadie sucked in a little breath, and Liam turned to see her looking at his grandfather with such love. And his eyes stung a bit. He'd wanted that for himself, the kind of love that his parents and his grandparents had had. He just hadn't wanted it until he was older. Then, after the accident, he'd resigned himself to thinking that he might never have it.

And now...

"Okay, talk," Brett said. "Why did you bring her back?"

"And why did the CPS investigator let you?" Frankie asked. "It's not like you found a kitten."

He gritted his teeth to hold back a groan. "No. But in addition to finding Lucy—"

"Lucy?" Grandpa Lem asked.

Liam nodded.

"You named her?" Blake asked, as if appalled.

"She had a name on the birth certificate Ms. Shaw found in the diaper bag," Liam continued, as if everybody didn't keep interrupting him.

Sadie smiled. He had no idea if it was over the baby's name or over the mention of the CPS investigator.

"What's her last name?" Brett asked.

"Lemmon."

Frankie looked at him and then Blake and Brett. Both his brothers shook their heads.

"No," Blake said.

"No," Brett said.

Even though nobody had asked them the question.

"I'm listed as her father," Liam admitted. "On the birth certificate."

"That's why the CPS investigator let you keep her," Frankie concluded. "But…is she really yours?"

He didn't want to lie, so he just shrugged. Then he added, "But because I'm listed as her father on her birth certificate, that makes me her legal guardian."

"But you need a paternity test or something to prove that, right?" Blake asked.

"Is that why you went with Ms. Shaw?" Brett asked.

"We had Livvy check out Lucy to make sure she's healthy," he said, which he'd already told them in a text.

"But what about the paternity test?"

"I'll deal with all that once her mother's found," he said.

"Who is her mother?" Frankie asked.

He shrugged. "I don't know. The name on the birth certificate sounds like an alias. Jane Smith."

"You don't know a Jane Smith?" Sadie asked, and from the confusion on her face, it was clear she didn't know one either. She was definitely not behind the woman leaving the baby in the barn. So why had the woman claimed he was Lucy's father and left her here?

ELISE HADN'T HAD to go far after leaving the baby store, just back to the hospital. Fortunately Dr. Lemmon's shift must have ended, or maybe she'd left early to drive her brother back to the ranch. So another doctor answered Elise's questions.

The little boy in the traffic accident was going to be okay. His father, who'd been drunk when he drove into the back of a school bus, was not going to be okay. The sheriff was waiting to arrest him for driving under the influence and for child endangerment. And maybe not just for endangering his child, who he'd picked up from school, but for endangering the kids on the bus, too.

"Todd wasn't supposed to pick him up," a woman said, tears streaming down her face as she stood, shaking in the emergency room waiting area. "My ex doesn't even have a license. His mother was supposed to pick up Beau and bring him over to Todd's for his visitation."

"We'll see what we can do to make sure that your ex won't be able to pick him up from school again," Elise said. She wasn't thrilled that the school had released the little boy to a man who was too drunk to drive. So she would have to follow up with them, too.

"This is all my fault," the young woman said. "I should have fought harder for full custody. I thought a boy needs his father, but I could have lost Beau." Her tear-filled eyes widened. "I won't, will I? Is CPS going to take him away from me?"

"You thought the grandmother was picking him up," Elise said. "You will be fine, and the doctor said that Beau will be fine, too." The boy had bitten his tongue but that was all. Fortunately he'd been buckled up even though it hadn't been in a required booster seat for his height and weight.

The woman cried harder. "I just feel like I failed him. It's my fault, my bad judgment, that he has such a lousy father."

Elise found herself squeezing the young woman's shoulder. "Beau will be fine. He has one parent he can count on. He has you. That's all he needs. Your love and support." Just like all Elise had needed was her mother, but her mother had never felt like she was enough either. "Now go see your little boy."

The woman rushed through the waiting room doors to go back to her son. And Elise looked up to find the sheriff standing behind her.

"That was kind," he said.

She shrugged. "I'm not the ogre some people think I am."

He chuckled, probably because he knew how Dr. Lemmon felt about her. And thinking of Livvy made her think of Liam. No. She'd never stopped thinking about Liam even as she'd dealt with her new case. "I need your help with something, Sheriff."

"I'm going to arrest Todd," he assured her.

She smiled. "I know. I have another case. A woman left her baby in a barn."

"The dispatcher told me about that call. Four Corners Ranch, right?"

She nodded.

"We intended to follow up and make a report, and then this accident happened as well as some other cases. But I still plan to send a deputy out."

"I don't think there's any rush," she said. "The baby is safe with her father."

"You already found her dad?"

"No. That's who the mom left the baby with. He didn't know about his daughter, but he seems willing to step up." She remembered how gently he'd held the baby and how he'd looked at her. Maybe he was all that Lucy would need.

But then she remembered how the store clerk had assumed that they were together, that they were a family. And instead of being unsettled, as she'd been earlier, she felt a strange yearning. Or maybe that was just the hollowness some people thought she had inside when they'd accused her of having no heart.

"So case closed?" Sheriff Cassidy asked.

Elise had so many cases that she should have jumped at the chance to close this one. But she needed more information about little Lucy to make sure she was in the right place. "We should still find the mom. Leaving her baby in a barn was a pretty desperate move."

He nodded. "Of course. It was also child endangerment. What if the dad hadn't found her when he had? Or one of the animals had hurt her?"

He had probably heard about the little boy who'd been hurt at Ranch Haven. But then wasn't he some relation to the Havens? Elise was usually too busy to listen to gossip, but everybody talked about the Haven family.

And the Lemmons.

Was Lucy really a Lemmon?

But if she wasn't, why would someone have written Liam's name on her birth certificate? He had to be her father, which was another reason Elise had to stop thinking about him like she was—about how he'd looked with no shirt, about how his breath had felt against her cheek when he'd leaned close to her in the store.

She couldn't get involved with a parent on one of her cases because it would be a conflict of interest and could sway her judgment. Plus, what if the mother came back and wanted not just her baby back but Liam as well? She had to stay as detached and uninvolved as she could, so that she didn't get hurt and so that nobody else did either. She had to do what was best for Lucy and for herself.

Sheriff Marsh Cassidy had just dropped into the chair behind his desk when his cell began to play a song, the ringtone he'd assigned to his grandmother. Sadie's song.

"Good afternoon, Grandma," he greeted her.

"How are Sarah and Mikey?" she asked about his fiancée and soon-to-be stepson.

"Wonderful. Perfect." The loves of his life as she was well aware.

"And you?"

He grinned. "I'm good." While there had been some accidents today, there had been no fatalities. So it had actually been a good day. But he unlocked his computer and pulled up his emails because Ms. Shaw had promised to email him a copy of the birth certificate for the baby found at the Four Corners Ranch.

"Glad to hear it," she said.

"And you, Grandma?" he asked. "How are you?"

She'd had a scare a while ago with her heart. Before he'd even known he had a grandmother who was still alive, he'd nearly lost her. Now that she was in his life, he couldn't imagine her not being part of it.

"I'm good." And he could hear the smile in her voice. She was happy. Then she added, "But I need your help, Sheriff Cassidy."

He tensed over her using his title because he didn't think she was just kidding around. "Why? What's wrong?"

"Not for me, for one of your cousins," she said.

"Are they all right?"

All the Havens had been through so much after the accident in which Marsh's cousin Dale and Dale's wife, Jenny, had died earlier this year, leaving behind three orphaned boys.

"Everybody is fine," Sadie said with a slight laugh. "But Liam has had an unexpected surprise."

Four Corners Ranch. The baby. "Ah, I think I might know what this is about…"

"You spoke with Miss Shaw?"

"Yes."

"Here—I am going to hand the phone off to Liam, so he can fill you in," Sadie said, "and I'm going to try to get a chance to cuddle that beautiful little baby girl. But Lem is hogging her right now."

Marsh chuckled.

"Easy for you to laugh," a male voice commented.

Grandma must have handed off the phone.

"Liam?"

"Yes. Sadie insisted I talk to you."

"You didn't think you should when you found a baby in your barn?" Maybe he hadn't been as surprised as he'd claimed when he'd spoken to the nonemergency dispatch operator and to the CPS investigator. Marsh had pulled up his email and the attachment of a birth certificate for one Lucy Lemmon.

"I did," Liam said. "She wasn't hurt, so I called the nonemergency number."

"Yes, and they referred you to CPS."

"Elise Shaw…" Liam uttered her name with a strange gruffness to his voice.

"Did she rub you the wrong way like she did your sister?" Marsh asked. He knew about the issue with his brother Colton, Ian, Livvy Lemmon and Ms. Shaw.

"No, not at all," Liam said quickly. "She was very kind. She has a tough job."

Marsh sighed. "Yes, she does. I saw her just a short time ago at the hospital—"

Liam gasped. "Is she all right? What happened?"

"She's fine. She was there on a case," Marsh said, but now he understood that gruffness, and it wasn't because his new stepcousin didn't like Ms. Shaw.

"Oh."

"So she filled me in on the situation at the Four Corners Ranch. She also scanned and emailed me a copy of the birth certificate."

"As busy as she is, she already got you a copy of that," Liam murmured.

"Unfortunately CPS is always busy," Marsh said. "I know she juggles a lot of cases at once. I, uh…checked her out for Grandma a while back—"

"I thought Colton was wrong but—"

"Colton?"

"He thought Sadie might have something to do with all of this."

Marsh tensed for a moment, considered and then shook his head. "No. That would be extreme even for her." To leave a baby in a barn…

"Why did she have you check out Elise?"

"Because there was an issue with her great-grandson Ian a few months ago. He got hurt in the barn with Colton, and somebody reported it as potential abuse. Your sister was involved—"

"Ah, that's why there's tension between them," Liam said.

Marsh was surprised that he hadn't known, but Livvy had mentioned once that she wasn't close to her brothers the way Marsh and his brothers were close.

"I'm sure Elise had to investigate since it had been reported," Liam said, as if he was defending the CPS investigator.

"Yes," Marsh said. "And when I checked her out, everyone had nothing but praise for her. She's very good at her job and very thorough."

"Which probably upsets some people," Liam said.

"Yes, but no matter how uncomfortable that might make some people, she has to be thorough because the children's safety is at stake—sometimes their lives."

Liam expelled a ragged breath. "She must be under so much stress."

"Yes."

"But she doesn't have to worry about Lucy," Liam said.

"She is yours?"

"That's what the birth certificate says," Liam replied.

"This is your signature?"

"No."

"So anyone could have put that on there," he concluded. "And the mother, this Jane Smith?"

"I don't have any idea who she is," Liam said.

"But she left her kid with you?"

"I don't know if that's the mother's real name," Liam said. "None of us saw anyone around the ranch. I just went out to the barn to saddle up the horses and found Lucy with the note that her mother didn't want to be a mother anymore."

"You really don't know she's yours then," Marsh concluded.

"The birth certificate makes her legally mine."

"But you just admitted your signature was forged on the document. You could have handed her off to Ms. Shaw," Marsh pointed out. "Why didn't you?"

Liam's sigh rattled in Marsh's cell phone. "I don't know. I just feel like she needs *me*."

Marsh understood that feeling all too well, of being needed. He'd once considered it a burden, but now he realized it was a gift. To be able to be there for the people you loved. But Liam had just found this baby.

Had he fallen for her already?

CHAPTER EIGHT

LIAM PROBABLY WOULD have been awake all night even if the baby hadn't been crying. The conversation he'd had with Sheriff Cassidy, who was now also his stepcousin, had unsettled him.

Before concluding the call, Marsh had pointed out that the person who'd signed Liam's name on the birth certificate had to know him, so Liam must know her as well no matter what she was calling herself. While Liam should have been lying awake trying to figure out who Lucy's mother was, Elise Shaw was the only woman he'd been able to think about.

She had such a stressful job, but she'd been patient and kind to him and Lucy. She not only handled all the cases assigned to her, but she cared as well. And her personal background with a single mother who'd come up in foster care made her even more impressive to him. He'd never met anyone that strong and capable who wasn't related to him.

Livvy and Sadie were strong women who handled all kinds of stress and tragedy but were still kind and caring. Like Elise Shaw.

Not only was she strong and capable but also naturally beautiful. She wore no makeup and bound her hair back in that tight ponytail. She probably had no time for anything more than that before she headed out on her next case. She didn't need to take any more time with her appearance to make his pulse quicken with awareness of her.

But even if she had the time and inclination to date him, he'd blown whatever chance he might have had with her because he hadn't been honest. He should have told her the truth.

Even the sheriff had asked why he hadn't just handed Lucy off to her.

He stared down into the bassinet where Lucy now slept peacefully, her little lips pursed perfectly into the shape of a rosebud. A stuffed animal lay beside her—the pink poodle his grandfather had insisted on purchasing at the baby store. It had comforted her as much as Liam had last night. Maybe more.

The vaccinations Livvy had given her had caused a low fever. But with the cold washcloths recommended on parenting forums and the baby acetaminophen, he had managed to bring down her temperature. And finally she was sleeping, just as the first light of dawn streaked through the blinds over his bedroom window.

He glanced longingly at his bed. The sheets and

blanket were hardly disturbed. But he doubted he would be able to sleep now even though Lucy was quiet.

And he wasn't the only one awake now. Even though it was Saturday, there was no sleeping in on a ranch on the weekends. Every day was a working day.

Noises drifted in from the kitchen: the refrigerator door opening and closing, the soft hiss of steam escaping the machine as coffee brewed and the clang of a pot or a pan settling onto one of the stove burners.

He glanced back down at Lucy, but she didn't stir at all. She was definitely sound asleep. So he tiptoed across the hardwood floor to his bedroom door and slowly and quietly opened it. Then he stepped out into the living room and crossed it as quietly as he had his bedroom.

After Elise had left the baby store, the salesclerk had talked him into a few more purchases, like baby monitors. He held one in his hand while the other was next to the bassinet. If Lucy made any noise, he would hear it. Something rattled the speaker, and he tensed.

But then she emitted what sounded like a soft sigh, and he released his own breath of relief. Other sighs echoed his as he stepped through the archway into the kitchen. Three people turned toward him, their hair mussed and dark circles beneath their eyes. He wasn't the only one who hadn't slept much the night before.

"She had vaccinations yesterday," he said. "That's why it was a rough night." Or she'd missed her mother. While she'd had a fever, it hadn't been high and her little leg where Livvy had injected her hadn't swelled like he'd been warned it might.

"Not just for her," Brett grumbled.

"I'm sorry," he said. He should have realized how his decision to keep her would affect everyone else in the household. But not keeping her...

Brett sighed. "I just can't believe she's yours."

"How?" Blake asked.

Frankie snorted. "Didn't you all learn where babies come from when you were kids?"

"That's not what I mean," Blake said. "We've all been so busy with the ranch that I didn't think *any* of us were dating. Not just me."

"What's a date?" Brett asked. "I don't remember the last time I went on one."

"Neither do I," Liam admitted.

"Well, apparently you had one about nine months before Lucy's birthday," Frankie said. "You were probably still with the rodeo then."

"No, he wasn't," Blake said. "He's been living here for almost a year. That's why your uncle included him in his will."

"He didn't need to do that," Liam said. His brothers had worked for Frank Dempsey for a few more years than he had; they'd helped the ranch to prosper. They deserved their inheritance, but Liam wasn't sure he did. Sure, he'd worked hard the past several months, but he'd loved it. He loved the ranch and working with his brothers.

"You three were like sons to my uncle," Frankie said. "He loved you all so much."

Tears stung Liam's eyes. He missed the older man a lot, but not like Frankie and his brothers must. He noticed that all their eyes glistened with moisture, too.

"You were like a son to him, too, Frankie," Brett teased her.

She snorted. "I know. And you're all lucky my band hasn't booked a gig for a while. I can stick around and help out." She turned toward Liam. "On the ranch. Not babysitting. That's all you."

Frankie could pull her weight and then some on the ranch, but his brothers needed Liam's help, too. He had to figure out how to take care of Lucy and carry his workload on the ranch.

"The sheriff and Ms. Shaw are both working on trying to find her mother," he said. "But hopefully she'll come back soon on her own."

"But what if she doesn't?" Blake asked. "Are you going to keep her indefinitely?"

"Even if her mother comes back, that doesn't mean Ms. Shaw will give custody of the baby back to her," Frankie said. "She abandoned her in a barn."

"And if she really is yours, she should be your responsibility, too," Brett said.

He sucked in a breath. He hadn't considered what might happen if the mother couldn't be found or didn't come back or if Ms. Shaw deemed her unfit. He hadn't wanted to let Lucy down when she'd already seemed attached to him. And he'd figured he could take care of her for a little while. But what if the mother never came back? Could he take care of her forever?

"You look sick," Frankie told him.

He felt sick.

"You should go back to bed," Brett said. "We'll handle the ranch today. Get some rest while the baby's sleeping."

He hadn't really been to bed, and he wouldn't be able to sleep now anyway. He had even more to worry about than he'd had the night before. Now he knew how badly he'd screwed up. And he didn't know what to do to fix it.

ELISE SHOULD HAVE been able to sleep in. It was Saturday, and she wasn't on call this weekend. But she hadn't been able to sleep much with worrying about Liam and Lucy. Had the baby had a reaction to the vaccinations? Had she slept all right? Was she settling in? Did Liam have everything he needed for her? And was he really her father? He'd seemed so incredulous that someone had claimed he was that she couldn't help wondering, especially since he seemed to have no idea who the mother was. Where was she?

Sheriff Cassidy was on the case now, and Elise was impressed with the young lawman. He was good at his job and had already made some great changes in Willow Creek, like lowering speed limits in certain residential areas and improving the security of all the school buildings as well. He'd also assured her that he would talk to the school about letting Beau leave with his inebriated father.

That had taken one thing off her to-do list, but she'd added a few more to it before the day had ended. A few more cases. None were priority ones, though. So she could take longer before making contact. Nobody was in immediate danger. There were just a couple of complaints that sounded like disgruntled exes fighting over child support and custody issues.

Relationships were messy, which might have been another reason she'd made no time to date. But thinking of relationships brought an image of Liam Lemmon vividly into her mind—with no shirt on.

He was so good-looking. But it wasn't just his physical appearance that affected Elise. The gentleness and sweetness he'd shown with Lucy had affected her as well.

What if the baby's mother didn't return?

Would he be able to handle Lucy indefinitely on his own?

Elise stretched and fought her way out of sheets that she'd tangled from tossing and turning all night. Usually she was so exhausted by the time she went to bed that she had no problem falling asleep no matter what was going on. She'd had to learn to shut off her mind at night or she wouldn't have lasted as long as she had at her job.

But she hadn't been able to shut it off last night. Maybe she just needed to touch base with Liam and make sure that everything was fine; then she would be able to put him out of her mind while the sheriff tracked down Lucy's mother. The sheriff was probably as busy or busier than she was, though, so she couldn't leave the investigation entirely up to him. Even if he found the mother, Elise would still have to investigate her to determine if she was a fit parent for Lucy.

She really needed to make sure that Liam Lemmon was a fit parent for the baby as well. So she grabbed the work cell phone from her bedside table and headed out to her small kitchen.

Her entire apartment would probably fit in the living room of the Four Corners Ranch. But she didn't spend enough time at home to require any more space. While her coffee brewed, she punched in the contact for Liam Lemmon.

"Hello," he said, and his voice seemed to echo.

A grumpy-sounding cry echoed his.

"Oh, no, did I wake her up?" she asked with alarm.

Liam yawned into the cell.

"Oh, no, I woke you both up," she said. "I'm sorry."

"No, I'm not sleeping," he said. "I'm driving, so I need to be fully awake."

Elise grimaced as she remembered the accident the day before with the child in the vehicle. That dad hadn't just been tired, though; he'd been drinking. "If you didn't sleep well last night, maybe you shouldn't be driving," she suggested.

"I power-slammed down a bunch of coffee before I left the ranch," he said.

"Where are you going?" she asked.

"Ranch Haven."

"You know the Havens?"

"I told you about my grandfather getting married," Liam said. "He married Sadie Haven."

"Of course…" She should have remembered hearing that bit of gossip. People had been talking about it for a while, but she'd had more important things to worry about, like the children on her cases.

Now she knew that not only did his sister hate her, but the rest of his family probably did as well. Not that it mattered. All Liam Lemmon was to her was the father on one of her cases. That was the only reason she was interested in him—to make sure that he would be a good caretaker for the baby.

"If you need to see me, to check up on Lucy, you would be welcome at the ranch."

She chuckled. "Oh, I don't believe that for a moment."

"You're talking about when Ian was hurt," he said.

"Someone filled you in," she said, wondering who and how biased their version was.

"The sheriff," Liam said.

"You've talked to him." That was good. Maybe Marsh Cassidy had gotten more information about Lucy's mother out of him than she had.

"Yes. But you'd already told him more than I could to help him find Lucy's mother."

Frustration gnawed at her. "There was nothing else you thought of to help?"

"No. But I would like to find her mother." His yawn rattled her cell phone again.

"Rough night."

"Yes."

"She reacted to the vaccines."

"Or she missed her mother," he said.

"We need to find her," Elise said. "I need to ask you more questions."

"I already told you and the sheriff I don't know any Jane Smith."

That was probably true; the name was likely an

alias. "But I need to find out who you were dating, who might be Lucy's mother."

"Like I said, you can come out to Ranch Haven if you want to interrogate me."

"Using Sadie Haven for protection?" she asked. The woman was powerful and influential in Willow Creek, but then so was his grandfather.

He chuckled. "I don't think anyone uses Sadie Haven Lemmon for anything she doesn't want to do."

"The paramedic, Colton Cassidy, mentioned that she could be behind this…"

"Yet another reason for you to come out to Ranch Haven."

She'd already interviewed the older woman once, when she'd investigated Ian Haven's case. She wasn't sure her career would survive another interview with the Haven family matriarch.

But if Sadie knew the truth about the situation with Lucy, maybe it was a risk worth taking. "I'm not working this weekend," she said.

"Then why did you call me, Ms. Shaw?" he asked.

Because she'd been thinking about him entirely too much. But she wasn't about to admit that to him. "I just wanted to check on Lucy."

"Then come see *her* for yourself," he told her.

Why was he trying to get her to come out to the ranch? Did he want to see her again as much as she wanted to see him?

If she were foolish enough to go out to Ranch Haven, it might be not just her job she was risking but her heart as well.

SADIE WINCED AT the ring of the doorbell and not just because her long-haired Chihuahua Feisty reacted to the sound with frenzied barking. She followed the little ball of black fluff down the hallway, past the formal rooms at the front of the house, to the front door and jerked it open.

"I told you to walk right in," she greeted Liam.

He gave her a sheepish smile. "I know. I'm sorry." Then he lifted the car seat he held higher as the Chihuahua bounced around his legs, pulling at the denim of his jeans and scrambling over his cowboy boots.

"Feisty is harmless," she assured him as she lifted the dog up into her arms. She held the small pooch out toward him, and when he reached out to pet her, Feisty eagerly licked his hand.

"What about you?" Liam asked. "Are you harmless?"

Sadie chuckled. "There's that Lemmon sass," she said with satisfaction.

"I'm sorry," he said again.

"Don't be. I appreciate that," she said. "I would also appreciate if you and your brothers treated Ranch Haven like it's your home."

Liam released a shaky-sounding sigh. "I'm glad

you said that because I extended an invitation to someone you might not want here…"

She was intrigued. "But who could that be? I invited your brothers and Frankie to come out today. So they are all very welcome here." And his sister, Livvy, was already a regular at the ranch.

He drew in a breath and then asked, "What about Elise Shaw?"

"What about Elise Shaw?" she repeated the question back to him.

His face flushed. "I… It's just that…" he stammered. "You know she has a job to do. That's all."

But was it?

"She needs to check on Lucy, make sure that she's doing well."

The baby was sleeping soundly in her car seat despite Feisty's yipping, so she looked like she was doing well. He probably could have sent the CPS investigator a picture of the baby to reassure her.

But instead of doing that, he'd invited her out to the ranch. So Sadie suspected that maybe there was more to whatever was happening between Liam and Elise than just a CPS case. Sadie hadn't considered Elise Shaw as a potential mate for any of her grandsons, but if the CPS investigator had the guts to show up here again, that would impress Sadie. And she suspected that Elise had already impressed—or made an impression on— Liam.

CHAPTER NINE

"But don't worry," Liam told Sadie as he stood just inside the door at Ranch Haven. Maybe she was angry that he'd invited the CPS investigator to her home without asking her first. "I'm sure she won't show up. She's not even working today."

"Yet you must have talked to her today," Sadie mused softly.

His face got even hotter than it already was, like he was getting a fever of his own even though he hadn't had a vaccination. "I...yeah, she was just checking to make sure Lucy was all right."

"And that's why you invited her out here, to see for herself," Sadie said matter-of-factly, as if it made perfect sense to her.

It didn't to him. He had no idea why he'd done that except that he really wanted to see the CPS investigator again. And he didn't care where it was, just that she showed up. But like he'd assured Sadie, she probably wouldn't. "Ranch Haven is a long way from Willow Creek," he said. It wasn't far from the Four Corners, though. The two ranches were much closer than he'd realized. "So I doubt Ms. Shaw will make the trip all the way out here."

"You know where she lives?" Sadie asked.

"I just assumed she lives in town," he admitted. "But her county is big. She said that yesterday. So maybe she lives somewhere else."

"Yes, she might be closer than you think," Sadie said. "Much closer…"

Her slightly ominous tone had a chill chasing the heat from his body and raising goose bumps on his forearms. How thoroughly had Sadie had the sheriff investigate the CPS investigator?

"If you'd like I can call her back and tell her not to come," he said. He should probably do that for Elise's sake and his.

Sadie smiled. "Why bother? You're sure she won't come. And if she does, she will be welcomed."

"What about Liam? Are you going to welcome *him* inside the house?" Grandpa Lem asked from somewhere behind his wife.

Liam hadn't even known he was there; he hadn't been able to see his grandfather around Sadie. She was so much taller and broader than her short husband. She stepped aside and Lem rushed forward. But instead of embracing Liam, he grabbed the car seat from his hands and rushed down the hall with Lucy.

Liam chuckled. "Good to see you, too, Grandpa,"

he called after him, then asked Sadie, "Should I be concerned where he's taking her?"

"To the kitchen," she said, and she reached out to wind her arm around his. "It's the heart of this home."

Instead of letting her tug him down the hall in the direction his grandfather had gone, he studied her face for a moment and murmured, "Hmm…"

"What?" she asked.

"I think that you are the heart of this home, Sadie," he said.

She blinked quickly and then smiled at him. The smile lit up her lined face, making her look beautiful and so very vibrant. "You have your grandfather's charm, Liam," she said.

He chuckled again. "I think a lot of people would be surprised that you're calling him charming. I know you've called him some other things over the years."

She chuckled now. "Yes, we started out as arch-enemies in elementary school, always competing with each other, always pushing each other to do our best."

"I would say that you've both done very well for yourselves," he said. "Grandpa was the mayor of Willow Creek for years, and your ranch is amazing." It comprised many more acres than the Four Corners, which wasn't a small spread at all. And the house was two-stories with what looked to be additional wings, unlike the long ranch house where he lived with his brothers and Frankie and now Lucy.

He followed Sadie as she continued down that hallway to an enormous, light-filled kitchen. Grandpa wasn't alone with Lucy in the space. A bunch of little boys were gathered around them, and adults stood behind them, cooing and smiling at the baby.

"Our family is what is amazing," Sadie said, and she squeezed his arm. "That's what we're most proud of and what has brought us the greatest joy."

He felt a sharp jab in his chest. Family. He wouldn't be able to have a biological one of his own, to carry on the Lemmon genes. He'd lost that ability when he'd lost his matchup with Midnight. And once Lucy's mother returned for her, he would lose her, too.

"And yes," Sadie said with a sad smile, "sometimes they've brought us the greatest pain, too, over the ones we've lost much too soon. Like your grandmother and your mother." She looked at him, and there were tears in her dark eyes. "I knew your grandmother well. We were friends. I know that I can never replace her, but I would like you and your brothers to know that your grandfather and I consider our families one big family now."

He smiled back at her. "That's good. I don't think we can ever have too much family." But he knew now that he didn't have enough, that not having a child of his own, a family of his own, would affect him.

But he couldn't keep Lucy forever. She wasn't really his no matter that his name was on her birth certificate. If Elise showed up at the ranch, it would only be because she wanted to find the baby's mother. It wouldn't be because she wanted to see him as badly as he wanted to see her. And even if she did, if he had a chance at all with her, when she learned that he'd lied, she would probably never forgive him.

ELISE WASN'T SURE what compelled her to drive out to Ranch Haven. Even though Liam had almost begged or maybe dared her to come, it wasn't his request that had her making the nearly hour-long drive from Willow Creek.

Maybe it was concern about the baby. But she did trust that Lucy would come to no harm in his care. So maybe it was curiosity. About the baby's mother. About Liam's relationship with the Havens.

About him.

She was entirely too curious about Liam Lemmon. While he'd stepped up admirably once he'd seen his name on Lucy's birth certificate, he still couldn't figure out who the baby's mother was. So was he an indiscriminate playboy or a responsible father?

Elise really wanted to know and not just because of the case or for Lucy's sake but for her own sake. If she knew that he was a playboy, she wouldn't waste any more time or lose any more sleep thinking about him.

And she certainly wouldn't make this drive. As she pulled her personal SUV onto the road that led to Ranch Haven, she considered slamming on her brakes. It wasn't too late to stop herself from making what was doubtless a mistake. While Liam had invited her, nobody else would welcome her here, especially not the little boys. Since it was Saturday, they would be home.

But she continued down the road, driving past pastures and barns and other outbuildings, including an old schoolhouse. She parked a good distance from the two-story farmhouse so that she wouldn't get blocked in when she wanted to leave.

Even before she stepped out of her vehicle, she wanted to leave. This was a bad idea. She wasn't working today; she had no real reason to be here. But…

She was here, so she might as well see this through and check on little Lucy. And Liam…

She shut off her SUV and pushed open the door. With each step that brought her closer to the porch, her heart beat a little harder.

But Elise wasn't a coward, or she wouldn't be able to do her job. So she wasn't backing out now. Her knees felt a little wobbly when she climbed up the porch steps, and her finger trembled a bit when she reached out to press the doorbell.

Sharp barking drowned out the sound of the chimes, and then there was scratching at the door. She'd met Feisty before and knew that the dog was harmless. She wasn't worried about her at all.

But she was worried about the people. Hopefully they wouldn't all treat her like Livvy Lemmon did, with open hostility. The doorknob rattled, then turned, and she came face-to-face with Feisty. The little Chihuahua was in the crook of Sadie Haven's arm.

"He was wrong," Sadie remarked almost idly.

Uncertain if the older woman was even talking to her, Elise tentatively asked, "Who was wrong?"

"Liam. He didn't think you would come."

"Is it all right that I have?" Elise asked. "Because if I'm not welcome, I'll leave." It wasn't as if she was on the clock right now; she was here on her personal time. She nearly laughed at the concept of personal time; she'd taken very little of it over the years.

Sadie studied her for a moment, then a smile spread across her face. She stepped back and gestured for Elise to come inside. "You are very welcome at Ranch Haven, Miss Shaw."

Little butterfly-like nerves flitted through Elise's stomach. Sadie's welcome made her feel like she was walking into a trap. But she suspected the only one in this house who might hurt her was Liam, if she got too attached.

If she was smart, she would have turned around and run back to her vehicle. But instead she stepped across the threshold and into the house. As she passed Sadie, the little dog jumped from the older woman's arm. Reflexively Elise caught it, and the furry little body squirmed against her, licking her arm and then climbing high enough up to lick her neck. She grimaced at the swipe of the rough little tongue against her skin.

"You can put her down," Sadie said.

But Elise liked having the furry, warm little body in her arms, so she kept holding the dog. And when she followed Sadie down the hall and into the crowded kitchen, she was glad that she had. She used Feisty like a shield, but the dog couldn't protect her from the glares of some of the people in that room.

"What are you doing here?" Taye Cooper asked. The woman, who Sadie had hired as a cook at the ranch, was going to be the Haven orphans' legal guardian, along with her fiancé, Baker Haven. As soon as they were married, they intended to submit the paperwork. Elise had no doubt that a family court judge would approve their petition for custody. It was clear the little boys belonged with the youngest Haven brother and his soon-to-be bride.

"Nobody got hurt," Ian said as he rushed to

the cook's side as if wanting her protection from Elise. "Midnight isn't even here anymore."

"He's not?" Elise asked at the same moment that Liam asked, "Midnight was here?"

Dusty Chaps, who sat at the table with a baby in his arms, chuckled. Elise recognized him from the old rodeo footage she'd watched, but she didn't recognize the baby he held. It was a little smaller than Lucy and, from the blue knit cap on his head, apparently a boy.

Dusty turned toward Liam and said, "Yeah, didn't you hear, Billy, that I won him in a bet? I think you might have gotten hurt before that happened."

Liam nodded. "I know you won him and that you were going to breed him, but I guess I thought he was in the same barn where you boarded your horse in Nevada."

"Billy?" Elise asked. "Why are you calling Liam that?"

Dusty chuckled again. "Because my ex-father-in-law, Shep Shepard, dubbed Liam Billy the Kid when he first started riding the circuit."

Liam grimaced. "Yes, he did."

A beautiful woman with auburn hair touched his arm. "Sorry about that," she murmured. She was probably in her late forties, maybe early fifties.

Elise had met these people during her investigation of Ian's case, but she was struggling to remember all their names.

"Mom, you are not responsible for what my father did," a dark-haired woman told the older one. She was Dusty's wife, Melanie, and she held a baby, too. This one had a bow headband on, but she didn't have Lucy's bright blue eyes. Hers were turning from brown to hazel.

Melanie's mother sighed. "Well, Shep certainly didn't take responsibility for anything he did." Then she squeezed her daughter's arm. "I'm sorry. I shouldn't speak about your father like that."

"We all know how Shep is," Melanie replied.

"Yes, we do," Liam said.

The younger boys must have tired of the adult conversation and subtext because Ian, with his blond-haired friend/cousin Caleb, ventured closer to her. He and Ian were both five. "Why are you here, Miss Shaw?" Caleb asked. "Midnight got moved to a new barn with another horse."

"He's on the Cassidy Ranch now," Dusty said.

"You have to bring me to see him," Caleb said. "I am sure he's missing his carrots."

Elise remembered how appalled she'd been when she found out that the little boy was feeding the horse, but then she'd personally witnessed during her investigation how gentle the black beast had been with Caleb.

"I'm sure you gave him enough carrots to last

him a lifetime," Sadie said. "And you all need to stop interrogating my guest."

"You invited her here?" Taye asked.

"No, I did," Liam said.

But Sadie had admitted to Elise that he hadn't thought she would come.

"Did Midnight hurt you, too?" Ian asked him.

Liam flinched while Dusty chuckled.

"Yes, he did," Dusty answered for him. "Midnight hurt a lot of riders during his rodeo days. Some of us more than others. That was why everybody needed to stay away from him and why I shouldn't have shipped him to the ranch in the first place, like my big brother Jake kept pointing out to me."

"I could say I told you so," a tall, dark-haired man remarked with a chuckle as he stepped through the French doors that stood open to a big patio. He knocked some dust off his hat before clamping it back on his head. He must have come from the barn.

The names from Ian's case were coming back to Elise. Jake was the oldest of Sadie's Haven grandsons and had been named after her first husband. One of the orphans had been named after him.

That toddler, Little Jake, stood next to Lem Lemmon, holding on to his knees and pointing at the baby girl the older man held in his arms. "Bee bee," Little Jake said. "Bee bee..."

"I'm not here because anyone got hurt," Elise said.

Lucy was staring up at the man who was her great-grandfather, her little hands reaching out as if trying to touch the long white beard that hung from his chin.

That beard was soft; Elise knew because she'd touched it once when she'd sat on his lap in the town square so many Christmas Eves ago. She'd probably been about Ian's age then, and she'd still believed in Santa Claus. And she had really believed Lem Lemmon was Santa.

She might have gone on believing in fairy tales forever if her mother hadn't brought other kids into their home, fosters, and she'd soon lost all her illusions about Santa Claus or even her belief that all parents were good to their children. Because the parents of her foster siblings hadn't been good to them, not like her mom had been. And Elise had vowed then to do something to help them, to save them from any more pain. But there had been so many she hadn't been able to save.

"I'm not here because I believe anyone's in danger," she assured them all and herself. Lucy Lemmon looked happy and healthy. But then Elise wondered, as her gaze met Liam's, if she was the one in danger.

LIVVY WALKED IN with Colton like they'd been told, without knocking, because Sadie hated whenever anyone rang the bell. So nobody noticed them. Not even Feisty.

Everyone was watching the dark-haired woman who stood by Livvy's grandpa. But that dark haired woman wasn't looking at Grandpa Lem; she wasn't even looking at the baby girl he held. She was focused on the man who was supposedly that baby girl's father. And that man, Livvy's brother, seemed focused on her as well.

"Told you," Colton whispered to her. "Sadie strikes again."

Livvy really hoped he was wrong. Liam was the sweetest of her brothers; he deserved to live a happy, uncomplicated life. And there was nothing happy or uncomplicated about Elise Shaw. She was going to hurt him. Livvy had been hurt in love once, or at least what she'd thought was love until she'd found the real thing with Colton Cassidy. But even though what she'd had with her ex hadn't been real, he had hurt her. And she didn't want her youngest brother getting hurt.

But with the way he and Elise Shaw were staring at each other, it might already be too late to save him from pain.

Unlike Colton, Livvy didn't believe Sadie had anything to do with that baby showing up at the Four Corners Ranch, but she'd probably had something to do with Elise Shaw being here at Ranch Haven. With the way Livvy's stepgrandmother was studying Liam and Miss Shaw, Sadie clearly intended to do some meddling in their love lives. And her meddling had never failed to produce a match.

CHAPTER TEN

LIAM SHOULD NOT have doubted that Elise Shaw would show up at Ranch Haven. Despite how much that report to CPS had put her in conflict with the Havens, she had the courage to confront them again. Not to cause trouble but to ease their fears.

She was strong; he'd already known that she had to be in order to do the job that she did. But he'd had no idea how fearless she was. And beautiful—that he'd noticed the first moment he'd seen her. But now...

He couldn't stop staring at her even though everybody else was probably watching him stare.

A man cleared his throat. "Hey, Grandma, what trouble are you up to today?"

Liam glanced over to see who'd spoken and noticed Colton and Livvy standing in the already crowded kitchen. He nearly groaned at the sight of his sister, who was looking at him like he'd lost his mind.

"Me? Causing trouble?" Sadie asked, her tone all

feigned innocence. "Just having a little get-together to meet our newest family member."

Livvy's eyes widened as she turned to look at Elise. "No…" she murmured.

The CPS investigator chuckled softly. "She's not talking about me," she assured the doctor. "She's talking about your niece."

"Geez, Livvy," Liam said. "What are you thinking? That I would marry someone I just met?"

"Hey, don't knock it until you try it," Dusty Chaps remarked, and he stood up to press his lips against his wife's cheek.

Melanie blushed. "Yeah, though it wasn't all smooth sailing."

"But thanks to Grandma's meddling, it worked out perfectly," Dusty said, and then he took a few steps to Sadie's side and kissed her cheek.

"Well, I'm not here to marry anyone," Elise said. "I just came to make sure this little girl is doing well after getting some shots from a mean old doctor yesterday."

Livvy gasped.

"I hate shots!" Ian said, and he sidled a little closer to Elise as if for protection.

Caleb grimaced. "They're the worst."

"Doctors are mean," Liam said.

Livvy glared at him. "I was just doing my job." Then her face flushed a bright pink, and she glanced at Elise, who was smiling.

"Exactly," Elise said, but she turned toward the

boys now. "My job can be bad sometimes. People tell me things, and I have to figure out if they're telling the truth or not. So I have to ask a lot of questions and talk to a lot of people."

Liam's stomach flipped with nerves. Now he knew why she'd shown up at the ranch; it hadn't been because she wanted to see him as much as he'd wanted to see her again. It was because she had a job to do. She was determined to find out the truth. And when she did, she wasn't going to want to see him ever again.

Elise continued, "And I have to be very careful when I decide what to believe because if I'm wrong, kids can get hurt. And I don't want that to happen. I don't want anyone to get hurt."

"Your job sounds really important," Ian said.

She shrugged. "It's not like being a firefighter or a doctor…" And she glanced at Livvy and Colton now with a smile on her face.

And Liam found himself smiling at how well she was dealing with all of them despite their animosity toward her.

"Or a rodeo rider," Caleb chimed in, and he moved away from his friend to come stand beside Liam. "You were a rodeo rider like Dusty Chaps?"

Liam laughed and shook his head. "No. I was never a rodeo rider like Dusty Chaps. He was a champion. I was just trying to break in…" But he had wound up getting broken instead.

"But then Midnight hurt you?" Ian asked. He didn't join Caleb at Liam's side; he stayed next to Elise, so close that he was almost leaning against her. She had gained the little boy's trust with her openness and honesty.

And Liam wished he could be open and honest with her. But then Lucy started crying.

"She wants her daddy," Grandpa said.

"Da…dee…" Little Jake murmured, and the toddler looked from man to man in the room.

Lucy seemed to be looking around, too, and her gaze stopped on Liam. He rushed to his grandfather and took the baby. When she saw him, Lucy stopped crying. He'd taken the trip out to Ranch Haven for Sadie's advice and for help with the baby after the rough night they'd had. But he wondered now if all she really needed was him. He wasn't her daddy, though. And what would happen if Elise or the sheriff figured that out?

He would lose Lucy for certain and whatever chance he might have had with Elise.

HE'D BEEN HURT. Not as Liam Lemmon but as Billy the Kid. During the course of investigating just how dangerous Midnight was, after the bronco had injured Ian, Elise had watched video after video of the horse tossing off rodeo riders.

Liam had been one of them. She remembered watching that horse not just toss Billy the Kid off but fall on him after he had hit the ground. And

that had been Billy the Kid's last appearance on
the rodeo circuit.

How badly had he been hurt?

He didn't limp like Miller, who at seven was
the oldest of the Haven orphans, did. And he was
physically capable of working the Four Corners
Ranch with his brothers, so he must have fully recovered. He'd crossed the room quickly to scoop
up Lucy from his grandfather, and he held her
now, rocking her back and forth in his arms as
he stared down at the little girl.

And Elise couldn't help staring at him again
like she'd been doing when his sister and Colton
Cassidy had walked into the kitchen. She glanced
around to see if anyone had noticed like Livvy
had earlier. Dr. Lemmon met her glance but not
with her usual glare. She even flushed a bit as
if embarrassed over the way she'd been treating
Elise. Or so Elise hoped, not that she'd intended
to embarrass Liam's sister; she'd only wanted to
explain herself and point out how she sometimes
had to upset or provoke people in order to protect the children.

Her job wasn't to protect Liam, though, and apparently it was too late to do that anyway. Her job
was to protect Lucy, and to do that she needed to
find the baby's mother and make sure that Liam
was really her father.

If Liam knew Lucy's mother from his days in
the rodeo, he might not be the only one who had.

So she maneuvered her way around all the people in the kitchen until she managed to get close to Dusty, his wife and his mother-in-law.

Before she could ask or say anything, Dusty said, "I'm sorry, Ms. Shaw. Ian getting hurt was all my fault. Jake was right that I never should have had Midnight sent here. He was too dangerous a horse."

"You would know," Melanie said with a smile. "You got hurt on him, too. That was how we met," she told Elise, "when he came to me for physical therapy."

"Liam got hurt, too," Elise murmured around the sudden lump of emotion in her throat.

Juliet Shepard grimaced. "That was bad. I was there that night, and I wasn't sure if he would live through that."

"I guess it looked worse than it was, or he healed quickly," Dusty said. "Billy the Kid is tough. I was surprised he didn't come back to the circuit after he recovered."

Maybe he hadn't recovered as well as everyone thought he had, including Elise. She needed to talk to him about that; she needed to talk to him about a lot of things. But all those things could have waited until she was back on the clock on Monday.

Instead she'd accepted his invitation, or maybe it had been a challenge, to come out to Ranch Haven. If it was a challenge, she intended to make the most of her win.

"When you all were involved in the rodeo, did you know anyone named Jane Smith?" she asked the trio, who were making faces and cooing at the twin babies Dusty and Melanie held.

Dusty snorted. "Jane Doe was taken?"

"I don't know if it's a real name or an alias like Billy the Kid."

"Not a very catchy or original name if Shep gave it out," Dusty remarked. "Is she a rodeo rider?"

Elise shrugged. "I don't know. She's the mother of that baby girl, though." She pointed at Liam holding his daughter at the end of the long kitchen island.

The former rodeo rider crouched down so Little Jake could see Lucy's face. The baby blinked her big blue eyes at the toddler, and then her mouth sagged open like she was smiling at him. And the toddler laughed with delight.

The laugh made Lucy smile wider while the twin babies started crying. Their parents stepped out through the open French doors onto the patio, rocking them in their arms like Liam had rocked Lucy.

"What a beautiful baby girl," Juliet remarked. "If her mother was a beauty, my ex-husband probably knows her. You might want to reach out and ask him. He's still on the circuit as an announcer."

Elise could imagine why the man was her ex and not her current husband. "So there is a lot of promiscuity in the rodeo?"

Juliet sighed. "I'm giving you a terrible impression. I need to get over my bitterness. I should have known Shep wouldn't change. He is who he is. But he's probably more the exception than the rule. Other riders have families and are true to them, like Dusty."

"What about single riders like Liam...or Billy the Kid?" Elise asked.

Juliet looked away from the baby to the man holding her. "He's a good-looking guy and I recall some groupies hanging around him, but I don't remember him partying much. He seemed very determined to learn as much as he could and work hard to become a champion."

"But then he dropped out," Elise said, and she wondered why. Because he'd gotten hurt? Or could it have been because he'd found out one of those groupies got pregnant?

But if he'd never given them much attention, how would that have happened? While his name was on the birth certificate, he'd insisted that the signature wasn't his. If someone had forged it, it was possible that they'd lied about the real identity of the father just as they might have used an alias for the mother's name.

"Thank you for answering my questions," she told Juliet.

The older woman smiled. "I have a feeling I wasn't much help. It seems like Liam himself would be the best person to answer the questions you have."

"But Miss Shaw has to ask a lot of people questions to find out who's telling the truth and who's lying," Ian said.

Elise nearly jumped, startled that he was sticking so close to her and that he'd paid so much attention to what she'd said. She smiled at the little boy, who had such pretty hazel eyes and such a sweet smile of his own. "You are right," she told him. "You remember so well."

"Now I do," he said, his smile getting even bigger.

But he hadn't always. During her investigation of his case, she'd learned that the accident that had killed his parents had left the little boy with short-term memory loss. He'd kept forgetting what had happened and that his parents were gone. And she felt a twinge of guilt and regret that she'd had to put him through any more turmoil after the tragedy he'd already endured.

"I remember you want to be a firefighter," she said.

He nodded. "And a paramedic like Colton. But I like your job, too. It would be good to keep kids from getting hurt."

Tears stung her eyes at his sweetness. She crouched down like Liam had for Little Jake. And she asked the little boy, "May I give you a hug?"

"I'm going to hug you," he said, and he looped his arms around her neck. "Thank you for making sure that I was protected."

She had to close her eyes to hold in her tears.

It wasn't very often that she got thanked. Cursed out. Threatened. But not hugged and thanked as sweetly as Ian Haven was thanking her. She closed her arms around him and held his little body against her for just a moment before releasing him. She didn't want to upset his family any more than she already had.

But when she opened her eyes, they were all staring at her, and there were tears in their eyes, too. She sucked in a breath and forced a smile. "That doesn't happen enough," she admitted.

"I bet not," Liam said, and he was suddenly standing right next to her, his arm brushing up against hers. He must have moved when she'd closed her eyes, and he no longer held the baby.

She glanced around and saw that Lem held Lucy again.

"Ian is very sweet," she said.

"Uh-oh, I invited you here to get to know you better, and it sounds like I already lost my chance with you," Liam said, and he was grinning.

Her pulse quickened with excitement over his words, but he had to just be teasing her. Or so she hoped because if this attraction was mutual, it would be even harder to fight. "I came here because of Lucy," she reminded him and herself.

"And you haven't even held her yet," he pointed out.

"I don't think anyone will get her away from her great-grandfather but you," she replied.

"You seem to prefer older kids," he said. "Ones not as vulnerable."

She sighed. "All kids are vulnerable." And at the moment, with the way he was looking at her and how close he was standing to her, she was the one who felt vulnerable, especially after being moved to tears in front of his entire family.

"You are amazing, Elise," he said, his voice gruff with emotion. "I have so much respect for what you do and for how hard it must be to do it."

Those infrequent dates she'd had over the years hadn't been as impressed as Liam seemed. They'd told her she should get an easier job, one where she would have more time, presumably for them.

"It is hard," she admitted. Especially now when he was distracting her so much. But she owed it to Lucy to find out the truth about her mom and dad. It still bothered Elise that she didn't know her own dad at all, that he'd never been there for her. Lucy wouldn't remember her mother unless they were able to find her.

Elise hoped the sheriff was having better luck with this investigation than she was. She wasn't getting any answers at Ranch Haven. She was getting more questions and more confused and even more interested in Liam Lemmon. She wanted to believe that her only interest in Liam was to find out the truth about Lucy. But she couldn't lie to herself. She was interested because he was so good-looking and kind.

FOR ONCE LEM wished the ranch wasn't as busy as it always was. He'd struggled to get a moment alone with his grandson since Liam had arrived with the baby, especially when Elise Shaw had been here.

She'd rushed off shortly after Ian had hugged her, though. And some of the others had drifted away to other parts of the house, or out onto the patio, but not before they had all offered to help Liam with Lucy.

"I hope you take everyone up on their offers," Lem said to Liam.

Now that Elise was gone, the young man looked tired, his shoulders a little stooped, with dark circles beneath his blue eyes. "You don't look like you got much sleep last night."

"I didn't," Liam admitted.

"Four Corners Ranch isn't that far away from here," Lem pointed out. "We can get there quickly to help you out there, or you can drop her off here."

"Anytime," Sadie chimed in with a smile. She leaned over his shoulder, peering down at the baby Lem held against his chest. They were both so warm and sweet-smelling—the baby and Sadie.

"I can't believe this little angel kept you awake last night," Sadie said to Liam.

Liam sighed.

Lem wondered if it was the baby who'd kept Liam from sleeping or if thinking about Elise

Shaw had kept him awake. Liam hadn't been able to stop himself from staring at the young woman the entire time she'd been at the ranch. He and Sadie had said that they wouldn't matchmake with his grandsons right now because of the lawsuit contesting Dempsey's will, but this situation had fallen right into their laps.

"I think my sister set me up for that," Liam said.

"What?" Livvy asked as she stepped through the French doors and back into the kitchen from where she'd been sitting on the patio. "I wouldn't set you up with Elise Shaw."

Liam groaned now. "Geez, sis, didn't you listen to anything she said? Even Ian understands she was only doing her job."

And the little boy had given her the sweet hug that had moved her to tears and nearly moved Lem to them as well. All the kids were so loving and open despite the losses some of them had endured. Or maybe because of them. Or because of Sadie who loved them all so fiercely.

"I get that," Livvy said. "And I know it's a hard job that probably consumes her. That's why I wouldn't choose her for you." She shot a glance at Sadie. "Has someone else chosen her?"

Considering how much attention Liam paid the CPS investigator, Lem had a feeling that his grandson had.

Sadie laughed at his granddaughter's question. "I think everyone overestimates my abilities."

"No," Lem said. "There is no overestimating what you're capable of doing."

"But I didn't pick Elise out for Liam," Sadie said. "And I have nothing to do with this little angel showing up at the ranch."

"You really don't know who her mother is?" Livvy asked her brother.

He shook his head. "I told you she must have used an alias on the birth certificate."

"But who were you dating about eleven months ago?" Livvy asked.

He shrugged. "I don't remember..."

Livvy narrowed her eyes with probably the same suspicion that shot through Lem. Liam wouldn't have forgotten who he'd been dating less than a year ago unless he hadn't been dating anyone at all.

Was Lucy even his baby?

Lem tightened his arms slightly around the sleeping baby. He didn't want to lose her. He didn't want to lose Liam either, in that he could lose contact with him like he had for a while with Liam's father. Bob had accused Lem of meddling too much in his life.

Lem had only wanted to help his son, who'd been struggling with his wife's health and with mounting medical bills. But Bob had refused to accept his help or his money and seemed to resent Lem for even offering it. Lem didn't want Liam resenting him for offering too much or for asking too many questions. So he kept himself from prying the truth out of his grandson. But maybe the biggest reason he did that was because he really didn't want to know the truth.

CHAPTER ELEVEN

"So PRINCE CHARMING here got to go to the ball yesterday while us schmucks had to stay on the ranch and work," Blake remarked as he opened the door to his horse's stall.

They were getting ready to head out again while *Prince Charming* was preparing to clean those stalls.

Lucy was strapped into a bouncy chair that Liam held against his chest for now. Once the animals and their riders were out of the barn, he would find a safe place to put her while he cleaned out the stalls. Melanie had loaned him some kind of carrier thing, but it had looked like a shawl to him. He already got so hot mucking out stalls that he couldn't imagine having Lucy strapped to him. They would both get soaked in his perspiration.

"Who are you calling a schmuck?" Frankie asked Blake as she saddled up her horse.

"Me," Brett said. "I missed out on all that good food Grandpa has at Ranch Haven."

Liam didn't know why they were so grumpy. Lucy had only woken up a couple of times last night, and once he'd changed and fed her, she'd gone back to sleep. His sister had made the right call with the change of formula and gas drops. "Tomorrow I'm going to bring Lucy out to the ranch for Juliet Shepard to watch so I can ride out and check the stock and the fences with all of you schmucks."

He hadn't wanted to disrupt the whole weekend at Ranch Haven like his and Elise's visits had disrupted the Haven family the day before. He also wanted Lucy with him for another day in case she had another reaction to her vaccinations or just needed him.

"And I did bring some food back for you," Liam reminded his brother. Taye and Juliet and even the oldest of the Haven orphans, seven-year-old Miller, were amazing cooks.

"Yeah, but I had to share that," Brett grumbled.

"There were more people to share with at the ranch," Liam said. "And you were all invited, too. Grandma Sadie insisted on it."

"Grandma?" Blake asked. "You're calling her grandma?"

Liam sighed. "Not yet, but I think she'd like it if we did."

"But they just got married," Blake said.

"And she's so different from Grandma Mary," Brett added.

"Grandma Cheryl is different from Grandma Mary, too." Cheryl was their maternal grandmother who hadn't been all that maternal. Though his parents had moved to Chicago to be closer to Mom's parents, they hadn't been very involved in their lives. "Sadie is much more invested in us, and she was very good friends with Grandma Mary."

"So much so that she married her widower," Blake said with a chuckle.

"Should I be happy all my family is gone now?" Frankie asked.

"You have a cousin," Liam reminded her.

"No. That woman who is contesting my uncle's will is not the cousin I knew and loved. That woman is gone, too," Frankie said bitterly.

"No, you shouldn't be happy," Liam said. "Our family is very loving and supportive of each other. We're lucky."

Blake snorted. "Wow, they did get to you."

"Remember that Dad warned us not to let Grandpa get too involved in our lives," Brett added.

Liam snorted now. "Dad wouldn't let us get too involved in his and Mom's lives, even when they needed us. No, I think he should have let Grandpa and us help him."

Blake sighed and nodded. "Yeah, you're right."

"All the Havens and Cassidys offered to help with Lucy," Liam added, and he clutched the bouncy chair and the baby closer to his chest. "And this little girl really has no one."

"She has you," Frankie said. "So she's luckier than I am."

"Yeah, I'm not so sure about that," he muttered. He might have made things worse by keeping her since she was getting attached to him. And either her mom would come back for her or someone would figure out he wasn't really her father.

He had a feeling that his grandfather and Sadie already had their suspicions. And Elise Shaw had admitted to not trusting anyone.

A sudden tingling of his skin alerted him to her presence even before he turned around and found her standing just inside the barn.

Had she already figured out that he wasn't Lucy's father?

ELISE HADN'T MISSED what Frankie Dempsey said, but she suspected Liam had. Frankie considered the little girl lucky because Lucy had him.

Did that mean that Frankie wanted Liam for herself? Maybe they were or had once been more than just friends. Frankie smiled at her when she noticed her standing inside the barn, though. If the other woman was interested in Liam, she obviously didn't consider Elise a threat for his affection.

And his brothers looked relieved. "Did you find the mom?" Brett asked.

She shook her head. "No. Not yet."

Then she turned back toward Liam and confirmed that she hadn't imagined the expression on his face when he'd turned and noticed her standing inside the barn. He looked frightened.

Of her?

Maybe he thought she was stalking him since she'd showed up here after going to his grandfather's ranch yesterday.

"Like I said the other day, I need to ask all of you more questions," she said. "Do any of you know a Jane Smith?"

Brett blew out a breath. "I think there are some Smiths in the area that have a small horse boarding operation. I can't remember the first names of the couple, but I know they don't have any kids. Mr. Smith called and asked to buy some hay off us a while ago."

Blake nodded. "Yeah, he was in a bind. We sent someone over with a load of hay to help him out."

"When was this?"

"It happened a few times several months ago," Brett said.

"Did you bring the hay?" she asked Liam.

He shook his head. "No. I know about the horse boarding operation, but I didn't know their last name was Smith." He focused on his brothers. "Are you sure?"

Brett shrugged. "I thought he said Smith."

"It's called Shell's Horse Boarding Ranch,"

Frankie said. "It's been around for decades. The guy who runs it is called Shell."

Brett shrugged again. "Yeah, sorry, I must not have heard him right."

"It might not be the mother's real name any-ways," Elise said. She was trying to find the clinic or midwife to check up on that. "Since Liam doesn't remember a Jane Smith, do any of you remember *any* woman you know being pregnant in the past eleven months?"

Blake chuckled. "Barn cats and cattle are the only pregnant females I've seen. Brett and I have barely left the ranch in years."

Frankie smiled. "When I'm not at the ranch, I'm singing in dive bars, so I haven't seen many pregnant women either."

"Melanie Haven," Brett said. "She was preg-nant at our grandpa's wedding."

"And she has beautiful twin babies," Elise said. "I know them. Anyone else?"

But they all shook their heads.

"We need to get to work," Brett said. "We have to check the livestock. Sorry, Ms. Shaw."

"I might have more questions for you," she said. The sheriff might as well, but she stepped back to let them all pass her. The sheriff would find them if he wanted to talk to them. But maybe the sher-iff already knew who and where Jane Smith was.

Once they'd all left the barn, Liam turned toward her and asked, "Are you working the whole weekend?"

"The sheriff asked me to meet him out here," she said. "He wants to talk to us together."

Liam sucked in a breath, and the color drained from his face. "He…he does? Did he say why? What's it about?"

She pointed toward the bouncy chair and the baby he held. "About Lucy I would assume. Why? What other reason do you think he would want to talk to us together?"

"I…" He shook his head. "I don't know…"

"Are you all right?" she asked with concern. "You look kind of sick."

"I'm guessing he might have found her mother," he said.

"I thought you'd be happy about that," she mused. "And if she's coming here with the sheriff, you will be able to see someone who must've once meant something to you." She felt a twinge of jealousy that she had no reason or right to feel toward Lucy's mother, toward whoever Liam had once dated. He was nothing to her. And he would never be anything.

He uttered a groan. "Oh, geez, this is just such a mess."

She knew he wasn't talking about the barn, but she wrapped her hands around a shovel handle and headed toward one of the stalls his brothers or Frankie had left open. "Then let's start cleaning it up."

With kids, she'd found that if she distracted them with an activity, they were more likely to start talking to her. They usually wound up giving her more information than they would have if they'd just answered her questions.

"What are you doing?" he asked.

"Cleaning up the mess," she said, as she dropped a shovel full of soiled wood shavings into the wheelbarrow next to the open stall.

He set the baby's bouncy chair on a clean patch of concrete in the barn. Lucy was already asleep. Then he walked over to the stall and tried taking the shovel from Elise's hands. He wrapped his fingers around it near hers, their skin touching.

She felt a jolt of awareness and attraction. But she didn't let go.

"Give me the shovel," he said, and he leaned closer to her, his breath touching his face. "This is my mess to clean up, not yours."

Her pulse pounded, but she forced a smile and gestured down the row of open stall doors. "You made all this mess?"

"You know we're not talking about mucking out stalls," he said, and he leaned closer to her.

Her smile slipped away. "No, but we should be doing it. Isn't that why you brought Lucy out to the barn, so you could clean up?"

"Elise…" His gaze slipped to her mouth.

Her heart pounded even harder at the way he said her name, the gruffness of his voice and the look in his eyes…

"What?" she asked, her mouth dry as the attraction she felt overwhelmed her.

"I… I think you're amazing…"

She smiled again. "Because I know how to muck out a stall?"

He smiled, too. "One shovel doesn't mean you know how."

"You won't let go so I can clean more."

"Were you raised on a ranch?" he asked.

She shook her head. "No. A foster home," she said.

"I thought your mom was."

She nodded. "And she wanted to open our home as a safe space for other fosters."

"She doesn't do it anymore?" he asked.

"Oh, she still does."

"Why didn't you want to place Lucy with her?"

She shook her head. "She doesn't take in babies, just older kids."

"Oh…" He continued to hold on to the shovel and stare at her, his gaze going from her eyes to her mouth like he intended to kiss her.

Elise couldn't let him do that. But she couldn't look away either. "Why are you staring?" she asked. "It wasn't a big deal growing up in a foster home. I had my mom."

"But no dad," he said.

She shrugged. "You can't miss what you've never had."

"But you didn't have your mom's full attention either," he said. "You had foster siblings that probably took more of her time and energy."

She shrugged again. "They needed it more than I did." And she'd trained herself to be grateful for what she'd had, which was so much more than those kids had had. "They needed help, and my mom gave it to them."

"So did you," he said. "And you still do with the difficult job you have. You are so incredible and beautiful and—"

She laughed. "Your lies are going to pile up like the mess in these stalls—"

"I'm not lying about you," he said.

She furrowed her forehead. "So you are lying about something else?"

"Elise, will you just let me compliment you without interrupting me?" he asked.

She wanted to press him for the truth, to find out what he considered a mess. But at the moment, with the way he was looking at her, she couldn't help but interrupt him once more. She leaned forward and pressed her lips against his. A jolt of energy, of electricity, shot through her.

He sucked in a breath, clearly as shocked as she was over what she'd done. Then he kissed her back, moving his mouth over hers.

She sucked in a breath and the sweet taste

of cinnamon. His lips were both soft and firm against hers, and he touched his fingertips along her jaw, stroking her skin. She'd never had a kiss like this, both sweet and passionate. And totally inappropriate. She forced herself to step back, to break the contact between them.

"Sorry…" she murmured, flustered. But she was too proud to show that, to admit to how unprofessional she'd been. So she teased, "Sorry for interrupting you again."

"I… I don't remember what I was going to say," he said, his face flushed and his blue eyes bright. He was clearly as flustered as she was.

While she wasn't glad she'd kissed him, she was glad that she hadn't heard whatever additional compliment he'd been intent on giving her. He'd already distracted her enough from what really mattered: the truth. And maybe that was why she'd kissed him—because she had a feeling that after he told her the truth, she wouldn't want to kiss him.

No matter her reason, though, she shouldn't have done it. It was unprofessional. And because of that, she should remove herself from this case and have her supervisor assign it to one of the other investigators.

But she felt a twinge of guilt that she would be adding to their workload. They were all already overworked.

"Hello?" a deep voice called out. "Where is everyone?"

The sheriff. He was the reason she'd come out to the Four Corners Ranch. Not for Liam. Not for that kiss.

Maybe Sheriff Cassidy had found the baby's mother. Maybe instead of handing off the case, Elise would just be able to close it. And then she wouldn't have to see Liam Lemmon ever again.

MARSH HAD LOOKED over the birth certificate and the note left with Lucy Lemmon. But he'd wanted to come out to the place where the baby had been left as well to make sure nobody had missed anything. His trip to the Four Corners Ranch confirmed that there were no signs of any foul play in the barn. Thankfully it hadn't been cleaned since Liam found Lucy there, although Ms. Shaw had had a shovel in her hand when he walked into the barn.

It seemed Lucy's mother had purposely left her baby in the barn for the father listed on the birth certificate to take care of. But was Liam really the father? Was a Jane Smith really the mother?

He understood why Ms. Shaw hadn't closed the case yet. There were still too many questions.

The baby in the bouncy chair was adorable. Mikey, Marsh's soon-to-be stepson, had started asking him and Sarah about a little brother or sister. He didn't care which; he just didn't want to be alone. Apparently Mikey's soon-to-be cousin and current best friend, Hope, was also bugging Marsh's older brother Cash, her new stepdad, and Cash's new wife, Becca, to give her a sibling as well. Marsh suspected the friends might be having a little competition with the winner being whoever got the sibling first. Marsh wanted to marry Sarah as soon as possible, but he hadn't been as convinced about growing their family so quickly. Now...

"She's beautiful," he said of the baby who was awake and kicking her legs out in the bouncy chair. "I can't imagine anyone willingly leaving her." He gestured around the barn. "Though the note and the fact that there's no sign of a struggle make it seem like that was exactly what happened. But just to cover all the bases, I also checked for reports of an abducted or missing baby, and there are none."

Liam Lemmon exhaled a ragged sigh of relief. "That's good. I would hate to think that someone had kidnapped Lucy and then left her here and that her parents are frantic to find her."

"Parents?" Elise was quick to ask.

"Like if the birth certificate wasn't real or something," Liam murmured, but then he clenched his jaw so hard that his cheek twitched.

What was really going on with his new step-cousin?

Marsh nodded. "That is a possibility we're checking out, trying to find out where the baby was born. It's a Wyoming birth certificate, but I can't find the official who signed it."

Liam released another ragged-sounding sigh. Was he relieved that no babies had been reported missing or that Marsh couldn't track down that official?

"What about you?" Marsh asked him. "Any idea who Jane Smith is and where she might be?"

Liam shook his head. "Like I told Ms. Shaw, I don't know any Jane Smiths, but that doesn't sound like a real name."

"We're checking all Jane Smiths in the Wyoming area and not having much luck, so maybe it is a false name," Marsh acknowledged. "So who were you dating eleven to twelve months ago?"

Liam shrugged now. "Nobody serious. Just a few dates that went nowhere."

They must have gone somewhere for little Lucy to have been born nine months later. Marsh wasn't going to crudely point that out in front of Ms. Shaw, though he could imagine with her job she'd heard a lot cruder things.

"Give me their names," Marsh said. "And I'll track them down and see if they are new mamas."

Liam's face flushed, but he nodded. "I'll text you their names and contact information." Almost as if he didn't want to say their names in front of Elise Shaw.

When Marsh first walked into the barn, he had

picked up on some undercurrents between the two of them. And the way they kept sneaking glances at each other...

It reminded him of how he and Sarah had acted before they acknowledged how interested they were in each other. His situation with his father's home health nurse had been complicated but nothing compared to this. Especially because Marsh had a feeling that Liam was holding information back from him and from Ms. Shaw.

Secrets had nearly destroyed Marsh's loving family, had cost him a relationship with his oldest brother for nearly twenty years and with the Haven family he hadn't even known he was part of. They'd recovered because there was so much love there. But not every relationship could handle secrets. And he was afraid that Liam was about to find that out the hard way.

CHAPTER TWELVE

WHILE THE SHERIFF'S visit to the ranch relieved some of Liam's fears, Elise looked more upset after Marsh left them alone in the barn again. Of course she wanted to find Lucy's mother. Liam had figured she would come back, but now he was beginning to wonder if it might be better if she didn't.

"Poor Lucy," Elise remarked. "For her mother to just leave her because she didn't want to be a mother anymore…"

"That is sad," he said. "I wonder why she got so desperate that she would just walk away from her."

Elise sighed. "Maybe she had no family. No one to help her. So she didn't see another way to keep taking care of the baby on her own."

And now he felt guilty for wishing the woman wouldn't return. "Of course she must have been overwhelmed."

"You too," Elise said. "Now she's left you to care for Lucy all on your own."

"I have help," he said. Even though they grumbled about her being around, both of his brothers and Frankie had offered to take Lucy last night when she woke up crying. But he'd insisted they go back to bed. He was the one who'd claimed a baby that wasn't his, so she was his responsibility, not theirs.

"That's good," she said. "A lot of people have no one there for them."

"Like your mother," he said, but then he wondered if Elise felt like she had nobody there for her either, since her mother had given more attention to the foster kids than her. "Or you?"

She shrugged. "I'm fine."

"You're not lonely?" he asked. "Because sometimes I have been, even growing up with two parents and siblings. My brothers were so close in age and to each other, and Livvy was also doing her own thing. I was kind of the odd man out."

"I'm sorry," she said. "I know how that feels. I had friends in school with two parents and siblings that never had to leave like my foster siblings did. I felt like the odd one sometimes." She smiled. "Still do."

"You're not odd," he said. "You're incredible." But still, she was lonely. That was probably why she'd kissed him.

He wanted to kiss her again but not because of loneliness. He wanted to see if the silkiness of her lips and the sweetness of her mouth would affect him the same way, would make him feel as if his legs had been kicked out from under him and his heart was beating so fast and hard that it would explode out of his chest. He'd been scared before she'd kissed him. Scared that the truth about Lucy was about to come out.

That he might lose her.

Now he was worried about losing Elise, too. Not that he had her. But she had kissed him.

"I was hoping the sheriff had found Lucy's mother," she said. "So I could close this case."

"You don't want to be around me anymore?" he asked with a twinge of pain hitting his heart now.

"I shouldn't be around you," she said. "Not in an official capacity."

"I thought you weren't working this weekend."

"I'm not."

"Then you're not here in an official capacity," he pointed out.

"I still crossed the line," she said. "I need to hand this case off to someone else."

"No!" The sharpness of his voice startled the baby, who awoke with a cry. "I'm sorry, Lucy," he murmured as he headed toward her bouncy chair.

Elise beat him to the baby, then unclasped her and lifted her up into her arms.

Liam expected Lucy to keep crying like she had when he'd been in the shower and Brett, Blake and Frankie had tried to comfort her. None of them had been able to, so he'd had to cut his shower so short that he probably still had shampoo in his hair. But the baby settled against Elise with a soft sigh, as if she recognized her, too.

Elise stroked her hand down the baby's back. "I'm sorry," she said. "This little girl should be my only concern right now, and I can't believe that I crossed such a line with you—"

"Elise, please, stop," he said. He hated to see her beating herself up. "I am obviously attracted to you." He hoped that was all it was. But she was so amazing, so strong and generous and determined, that he could see himself falling for her. But he didn't know if she would forgive him for not being completely honest with her about Lucy.

"And I am obviously attracted to you," she admitted. "That's why I need to take myself off this case."

"If that's what you're determined to do, then kiss me again," he challenged her.

She laughed and shook her head. "I don't do things like this..."

"Like what?" he asked. "Kiss? Laugh? Think of yourself for once instead of everyone else?"

She drew in an unsteady breath, then released it in a shaky sigh. "Liam..."

And he wondered if she was starting to fall for him, too. But that wasn't fair to her, not when she didn't know the whole truth about Lucy and about his inability to have any children of his own.

He needed to be honest with her.

About everything...

"KISS ME AGAIN," Liam repeated.

And Elise was tempted. Too tempted. But she shook her head. "This is a bad idea," she said, "for both of us."

"But it felt so good," he said, and he stepped closer to her.

She shook her head again, not in denial that the kiss had been good. It might have been the best one she'd ever had. "This isn't right, Liam," she said. "You already said that everything is a mess, and this...attraction...will just make things messier."

"But if you're dropping the case..."

"Do you want me to?" she wondered aloud. "Or do you want to pretend that the kiss never happened?"

"Can you pretend it never happened?" he asked.

She sighed. "I don't know. But I know we shouldn't do it again whether I'm the one handling your case or not. Lucy's mother could still claim a conflict of interest."

"I don't understand."

"Even if she comes back into Lucy's life, that doesn't mean she'll have the right to take her away from you," she pointed out. "Or even to share custody with you. She abandoned her, maybe when nobody else was even on the ranch. The baby could have been hurt." She tightened her arms around Lucy at that thought. "There were horses in the barn then. What if one of them got out like happened at Ranch Haven when Ian got hurt?"

The baby could have been crushed.

Liam reached out for Lucy then, his hand shaking as he cupped the back of her head. "Oh, my…" His gruff voice trailed off over the horror of that. "I'm sure the mother didn't think anything would happen to her."

"The mother. You really have no idea who she is?"

He shook his head.

And she had to voice the suspicion she'd begun to have. "Are you her father, Liam?"

"That's what the birth certificate says…"

"What do you say?" she asked. "You have no idea who Jane Smith is, and you haven't brought up any other names of women you dated—"

"I'm going to text some contacts to Marsh," he interjected.

"Why not to me?" she asked. "Is it because of the kiss? And if that is the reason…" Then she had no choice; she would have to remove herself from the case and have it reassigned to someone else.

He shrugged. "I don't know. Marsh asked—"

"I asked you earlier," she said.

"You asked me if I knew Jane Smith," he said. "And if I had any idea who Lucy's mother is. I really don't have any idea."

She released a shaky breath. "I wondered if you

had a lot of groupies. Now I guess I have my answer." And she understood those groupies since she'd just kissed him herself and he wasn't even with the rodeo anymore.

He was a rancher.

A cowboy.

A father.

He shook his head. "That's not what I meant."

"Then tell me what you meant," she said. "Tell me the truth, Liam."

He tensed and closed his eyes, as if overwhelmed. Or afraid. Then he murmured, "Elise..."

Before he could say anything more, her cell rang. She passed the baby off to him and picked up her bag from where she'd left it on the floor. With her mom fostering kids, she couldn't ignore even her personal cell in case she needed help. But it was her work cell that was ringing, her boss calling.

She picked up. "Margaret?"

"I'm sorry, Elise, I know you're not on this weekend, but we have a call from the ER in Willow Creek, and everybody else is already over their allowed number of cases."

She was, too, which Margaret had to know, but Elise wasn't the type who made it an issue and refused to take any more cases because of it. "I'm not in town, but I can head there," she said, and she started backing out of the barn, away from Liam. Away from temptation.

But if everyone else was already over their allotted number of cases, who would she pass his off to? Was she stuck working on it despite her conflict of interest?

THE KNOCK AT the door of her and Lem's private suite startled both Sadie and Feisty, who jumped off Lem's lap where she'd been sleeping and rushed to the door. Lem remained asleep. He really needed to get his hearing checked.

Sadie tried to jump up, like Feisty, but she had to push herself up with her arms due to the stiffness in her legs and hips from sitting so long. Her and Lem's easy chairs were comfortable; maybe a little too comfortable, since they'd both fallen asleep this Sunday afternoon instead of watching the football game they'd wanted to watch.

She yawned as she walked over to open the door. Feisty slipped out into the hall and jumped and tugged on the sheriff's jeans. "Is this a raid?" she asked her grandson with a teasing smile.

He chuckled. "I don't know. What are you up to, Grandma, that might get you in trouble?" He leaned down and kissed her cheek. Then he scooped up Feisty, who kissed his chin.

She sighed. "Everybody thinks I've been scheming, and I haven't had a thing to do with the current events."

"Current events being a baby left in the barn at the Four Corners Ranch?"

She nodded. "I would never do something like that."

"No," he agreed. "You wouldn't. But do you intend to match up Lem's grandsons like you did all yours?"

"They're my grandsons, too, now," she said with pride. They would always be Mary's, but Mary was such a dear friend and generous person that Sadie knew she would have wanted the same thing for their family as Sadie and Lem wanted: happiness.

Marsh emitted a soft whistle that had Feisty yipping in excitement. "I knew Liam was in trouble, but I had no idea how much."

"What do you mean?" she asked with concern. "Is he all right? Is the baby all right?"

He nodded, and his white cowboy hat bobbed up and down. "Yes. They are both fine. I just meant he was in trouble now with your meddling."

She held up her hands. "I have not had anything to do with what's going on with Liam. If this is a raid, you can come in and check our suite for babies if you'd like."

He chuckled. "A raid for babies—sounds about right."

"I am surprised that Lem gave Lucy back to Liam when he brought her here yesterday," she admitted.

Marsh's grin slipped away. "I wonder if Liam might have to give her back to someone else."

"The mother? You found her?" she asked.

She heard Lem's chair creak and his groan as he got up, too. She stepped back and opened the door all the way. "Come on in," she told Marsh. Then she turned toward her husband. "The sheriff's here."

"What have you done now, my bride?" Lem asked with a smile, but it didn't quite reach his blue eyes. He was concerned. "And what is this about Liam?" Despite his bad hearing, he must have overheard enough or instinctively knew Marsh was here about his grandson.

"Yes, did you find Lucy's mother?" Sadie asked again.

Marsh shook his head. "He did share contact information for a couple women he dated, but the last time either of them saw him was more than a year ago when he was with the rodeo. Neither of them could be Lucy's mother and not just because of the time span but because they weren't serious with him. He was too busy with the rodeo, and since moving to the Four Corners Ranch, he's been too busy helping his brothers. I don't think Lucy's his." He looked from one to the other of them and narrowed his eyes. "And neither of you are surprised that I said that…"

Sadie shrugged. "I wasn't certain."

"I wasn't either," Lem said. "But I did have my

suspicions. Will he get in trouble over keeping her when she really isn't his?"

"His name is on her birth certificate, so legally he is her father," Marsh said. "He would need to have a paternity test proving she's not his and bring that to a family court judge to get his name removed…and that would only be necessary if her birth certificate is legit."

"You don't think it is," Sadie said.

Marsh shrugged. "Unless she gave birth in the back of a cab and the driver signed as the official, I can't find an *official* official who actually signed that document."

A gasp slipped out and Sadie asked the question that just occurred to her. "You don't think Liam forged it?"

"What are you thinking?" Lem asked as if he knew and was appalled. "That my grandson kidnapped that baby and forged a document so he could keep her?"

"No, of course not," she said. "But he does seem very attached."

"There are no reports of kidnapped babies anywhere around Willow Creek," Marsh said. "She's not been abducted. She's been abandoned, and someone clearly wanted Liam to take responsibility for her."

"So he must have some connection to the mother," Sadie said.

"I'm going to work the case from that angle,"

Marsh said. "That's why I stopped here to talk to Juliet and Dusty about what they know about Liam from his rodeo days."

"But you came by our suite," Sadie pointed out. "I don't think that was just to say hello."

"I just want to see you," he admitted, and he leaned down to kiss her cheek.

She patted his. "And I promise that I am not meddling." *Yet*. "And I think I should be offended that everyone assumes I have been."

"Everyone assumes you have been because you usually have been," Marsh pointed out. "But I don't think you would use a baby, even though that baby is bringing Ms. Shaw and Liam together."

Sadie smiled now with satisfaction. She'd noticed that yesterday. And she'd noticed how remarkable a young woman Elise Shaw was in how she'd dealt with Livvy and Ian and the rest of the family. "Maybe little Lucy is a Lemmon then since she is already helping with the matchmaking," she said.

"But if she's not, and Ms. Shaw finds out that Liam knew the entire time that the baby wasn't his, I don't think he'll be losing just the baby," Marsh warned them.

"What?" Lem asked with alarm. "Will he go to jail?"

"With his name on the birth certificate, I don't

think he would get in legal trouble," Marsh said. "But..."

He would lose any chance of a future with Elise Shaw because the CPS investigator would be furious with him. Like Marsh, Sadie knew all too well how much damage secrets caused. She was lucky she hadn't lost her family over the secrets she'd kept.

CHAPTER THIRTEEN

WOULD HE HAVE told her the truth if she hadn't gotten called away? Liam wasn't sure even now, an hour after Elise had left the ranch. Lucy, fortunately, had fallen back asleep, so he'd been able to finish cleaning out the stalls. He'd also prepped them for the return of the horses and the ranchers who were still out riding the fences.

When they returned, he needed to tell them the truth. They deserved to hear it before anyone else. Except Elise. He should have been honest with her about everything. Not that he had a chance of dating her once he told her the truth. And he wouldn't have a chance of keeping Lucy either.

That was why he hadn't been able to bring himself to do it even though he knew he should, that eventually he would have to. Since it seemed as if Lucy truly had been abandoned, if nobody else wanted her, he wanted her to know that he did. She woke up when he carried her and her bouncy chair back to the house. But she didn't cry because she saw him immediately when she opened her eyes.

"Oh, sweet Lucy..."

Her mouth sagged open with that adorable toothless smile she gave him. Her blue eyes sparkled, too, with happiness. Warmth spread through his chest with a wave of love for the baby girl. From the moment he'd found her, he'd had a connection with her. Like she was meant to be his. And then with his name on the birth certificate as father, it had seemed meant to be.

His cell vibrated in his shirt pocket, and his pulse quickened with the hope that Elise was calling him. She'd only been gone a little over an hour, but he already missed her. He had an instant connection with Elise, too.

He didn't just find the CPS investigator attractive, he admired her so much for what she did, for how strong she was and how caring. And that kiss...

He hadn't expected that, but now he couldn't stop thinking about it. Maybe she couldn't either. Or maybe she was calling to tell him who had been assigned his case since she'd seemed determined to remove herself.

But when he pulled out the cell, it wasn't her number. He noticed he had a couple of text messages from the women whose contact information he'd given to the sheriff. He would text them back apologies in a moment, but right now he answered the call. "Hello."

"Liam, this is Marsh."

He'd figured as much after seeing those texts. "Hey, Marsh, that was quick."

"Yes, your friends were very clear that they hadn't seen you in over a year and that they definitely did not have any children with you."

He winced. "I didn't think you were going to be that blunt with your questions." He was going to have to apologize very profusely for involving them.

"What's the deal, Liam?"

"You asked me for the names of the women I dated last," he reminded the sheriff.

"You haven't dated anyone since them?"

He might have lied if Marsh was just his stepcousin, but he was also the sheriff. "No. I haven't."

"Then Lucy can't be yours."

"That's not what her birth certificate says."

"You're walking a fine line here, Liam."

And he'd already stumbled across it with Elise Shaw. "I know. But there has to be a reason someone put my name on that birth certificate, that they want me to be the father of their baby." Like the note had said: *You take care of her now.*

Marsh's sigh rattled in the cell speaker. "True. So the mother must know you."

"That's why I gave you those names. But I don't

believe either of them would abandon a baby in a barn. They're too nice for that."

"They both said you're a nice guy, too," Marsh said. "So maybe that's why someone put your name on the birth certificate because they know you would step up and take care of her, just like you have."

Liam released a shaky breath. "I hope it's because she thinks I'm a nice guy…" And that he would take good care of Lucy.

"But you don't entirely believe that," Marsh said.

"I don't know what to believe," he said. "I still can't think of anyone I know who would leave her like that."

"No obsessed ex or superfan who might have wanted you to be the father of her baby?"

He laughed. "I have no superfans or obsessed exes."

"That you know of."

"I would think I'd know," Liam pointed out. "I wasn't like Dusty Chaps. I never made it to that level of fame and attention." His interest in joining the rodeo had been about the animals and riding, never about fame. But it had gotten expensive when he hadn't been placing high enough to earn any money.

It was better here at the ranch. But he had no idea how much longer they would be able to stay here if they lost that lawsuit. How would he take care of Lucy if he didn't have a job or a home?

Liam's chest suddenly felt tight. "Are you going to have to tell Miss Shaw what you found out?"

"From those women I contacted?"

"Not just that…"

"That you're not Lucy's fath—"

"My name is on the birth certificate as her father."

"Yes, it is. And I have to find out who certified that thing," Marsh said. "I'll get back to you on that."

"But, Marsh…"

The sheriff disconnected the call without answering Liam's question. Was he going to tell Elise?

It didn't matter whether or not Marsh did, really. Liam knew that he had to tell her…*everything*.

ELISE WAS GLAD the case that had brought her to the Willow Creek Memorial Hospital wouldn't be a difficult one to close. A child had come into the ER with a dog bite, but the dog wasn't in his household, according to his parents. It was at his great-aunt's house, where they'd all been visiting.

"I hope I didn't waste your time," Nurse Sue said as Elise followed her through the ER back toward the waiting room. She was walking out with Elise because her shift had ended a while ago but she'd stayed to make sure Elise saw the child she'd treated earlier.

"I'm going to pop in for a home visit just to make sure it's not their dog," Elise assured her. She'd been lied to before in situations like this, but she didn't think the parents were lying. Still, she would rather be safe than sorry. "I'll follow up."

"You're always thorough," Sue praised her.

"Some might say too thorough," Elise remarked, and she glanced around for Livvy Lemmon as they exited the ER room and passed the intake desk. She hoped that Liam's sister wasn't working today. She knew how the doctor felt about her, that she obviously didn't want Elise getting involved with her younger brother.

Elise felt so exposed and vulnerable after kissing him that she was certain Livvy would immediately know what she'd done, how she'd crossed a line. She had no doubt that the doctor would happily report her unprofessionalism to Elise's supervisor.

"She's not here today," Sue said, and her thin lips curved into a smile. She waved at the intake coordinator as they headed toward the lobby doors.

"Who?"

"You know who. Dr. Lemmon," Sue said. "I am sorry about that…"

Sue was the one who'd reported Ian Haven's injury to CPS.

Elise shrugged. "You were just doing what you thought was right."

Sue uttered a ragged sigh. "I was concerned about the boy, especially after everything he and his brothers went through, but I feel badly that I put them through more. I just… I know their maternal aunt, Genevieve Porter, and I thought they might be safer with her."

"Genevieve Porter…" The name sounded familiar.

"She's married to Dr. Collin Cassidy now. They're in the process of adopting a little girl. Bailey Ann." Sue's face lit up with a bright smile now, and she was really quite beautiful with her silver hair and pale blue eyes. "I watch her for them sometimes."

"Genevieve has a licensed foster home," Elise said. "But she's not currently accepting any more kids." She kept apprised of where the homes were and their availability for children.

"Bailey Ann had a heart transplant earlier this year," Sue said. "She requires a lot of care. I expect that they will open their home up soon, though. Bailey Ann would love to have siblings."

Concern clutched Elise's heart, making her suck in a breath as they stepped out into the parking lot. "Her parents may want to reconsider that. My mom has a foster home, and it was hard for me to see those kids coming and then going back to their biological families."

Sue nodded. "I can understand that."

Something in Sue's tone made Elise ask, "You grew up in a foster home?"

"No. I once…" Sue's throat moved as she swallowed hard. "I once gave up a child."

Seeing how upset the woman was, Elise reached out and touched her arm. "I'm sorry."

"I was young. I wouldn't have been able to care for him. It was for the best." But she didn't sound convinced. And maybe that was why she worried so much about kids being mistreated because she didn't know if her son had been safe all these years.

Elise squeezed her arm. "That must have been a difficult choice for you." One Sue probably dealt with yet every day.

Sue blinked as if fighting tears and nodded. "Thank you, Miss Shaw, for understanding… everything…"

Elise smiled.

"I shouldn't keep you," Sue said. "I'm sure you have a lot of other cases."

"I do," Elise said. But the one that was bugging her most was the one she probably needed to give up. Or close…

Sue turned as if to walk away, toward her vehicle, but Elise held on to her arm. "Can I ask you something?"

Sue stiffened. "About…?"

"I have a case with a baby being left in a barn."

Sue gasped, and then her pale blue eyes widened. "The baby that Livvy's brother brought into the ER?"

She nodded. "Lucy's birth certificate was found with her, but it doesn't look like she was born in a hospital. Do you know any midwives that may have delivered the baby in a private home?"

Sue stiffened again. "I can think of a couple. And there's a clinic I went to…"

"When you had your baby?"

Sue nodded. "My parents didn't want anyone to know, and this place would be very discreet for a price. It's about a two-hour drive from Willow Creek."

A flutter of excitement and fear moved through Elise. She might be close to finding out the truth, but she was also afraid of what that might be. If this clinic specialized in being discreet, there was a reason that Lucy's birth had needed to be kept quiet. Because her mother was too young?

But she couldn't imagine Liam getting involved with an underage girl. Unless she was completely wrong about him. Or he'd been lying about being Lucy's father.

Either way, she'd let her attraction to him affect her judgment and that couldn't continue.

BRETT WAS TIRED and hungry, so while Blake and Frankie walked behind him, he was the first one to step onto the porch after they put the horses away in their freshly cleaned stalls. He could smell something cooking. A roast or stew. And his stomach growled in anticipation.

Despite taking care of the baby, Liam was still pulling his weight around the ranch. Brett knew he would. Liam was a hard worker, always ready to pitch in and get the job done. That was why he'd kept pressuring Liam to come work with them even when he'd been riding with the rodeo.

That and, after losing his mom to cancer, Brett hadn't wanted to lose another member of his family. He'd even tried reaching out to Livvy then, but that jerk ex-fiancé of hers had tried to keep her separated from all of them. He'd done a good job of it until she'd moved back to Willow Creek several months ago. Now she had a great fiancé in Colton Cassidy. She was happy.

While Brett was happy for her, he was a little envious, too. He was so busy with the ranch and with the lawsuit—and missing his boss—that he didn't have time to be happy.

He was just tired.

As he opened the door, a cry rang out, shattering the quiet like it had the last couple of nights. He let out a groan of frustration.

Behind him Frankie sighed and muttered, "She's still here. What is Ms. Shaw doing? Why can't she find the mother?"

"Maybe she doesn't want to be found," Blake said.

"Or maybe she just wants to get some sleep,"

Brett grumbled. While he would like to be happy like his sister, he knew HIS happiness wasn't going to involve babies.

He wanted nothing to do with having a family. The ranch was his baby right now and honoring Frank Dempsey's memory by making it prosper even more than it already had. If they managed to keep it…

CHAPTER FOURTEEN

LIAM FELT A jab of regret seeing the disappointment on the faces of his brothers and Frankie when they walked into the house. Lucy had been quiet and content until they'd come back. At the sound of boots hitting the porch, she tensed up and started crying. Screaming really.

So much so that they couldn't hear each other speak. He pointed toward the pot of stew simmering on the stove and carried Lucy to his bedroom. After he changed her and gave her a bottle, she fell back to sleep.

It must have taken more time than he'd thought because when he walked back out to the kitchen, Brett and Blake's bowls of stew were already empty, and they were getting the last drops of broth with the rolls he'd made.

"I hope you ate some before we got back," Frankie said. "Because I'm not sure they left any in the pot for you."

Dad had taught them all how to cook years ago, probably when Mom had gone through her first round of cancer treatments. They hadn't told them about the first time she'd had cancer. They'd kept secrets.

Liam hadn't wanted to do that. "We need to talk about Lucy," he said.

"She's not yours," Blake said.

Liam sighed. "Does everybody know that already?"

Frankie shook her head. "Not me. I thought you said your name is on her birth certificate as her father. And she has your eyes."

"A lot of people have blue eyes," Brett said. "But why would you keep her if you knew she wasn't yours?" He turned toward Blake. "And how did you know?"

Blake chuckled. "Apparently I'm the only one who inherited our accountant father's mathematical abilities. The baby is two months old, and Liam hasn't dated since he moved to the ranch with us almost a year ago."

"Oh…" Frankie murmured.

"So why would you keep her if she's not yours?" Brett asked him again.

Liam sighed. "Elise said that since my name is on the birth certificate she's legally mine."

"But you know she's not biologically yours," Brett said. "And you could prove that with a paternity test. Did you take one? Are you just waiting for the results or something to prove that?"

Liam shook his head now. "No. I didn't take

one. And I didn't tell Elise that I'm not Lucy's father." That there was no way that he could be.

"Why not?" Brett asked again.

"Maybe he wants an excuse to see Ms. Shaw," Blake said. "She's pretty in that sexy librarian way with her hair all pulled back and those glasses…" He whistled.

Liam tensed with a sudden surge of jealousy.

Blake laughed. "Wow, you should see your face."

"Yes, he likes Ms. Shaw," Frankie agreed.

"Yes, but I don't think she's going to like him back once she realizes he hasn't been honest with her," Brett said. "And I still don't understand why you weren't. If you were interested in her, you had to know that it wasn't going to end well if it started with a lie."

"I didn't think it through," Liam admitted. "And I tried not to lie…"

"You just kept saying that your name is on the birth certificate," Frankie said with a smile and a light tap on her own temple.

"But I don't think Ms. Shaw is going to care about the semantics," Brett said. "And neither do I. I don't understand why you kept her."

Liam sighed then. "I don't understand all that well either. But I just felt so bad her mom left her in the barn like that."

"Like an unwanted cat," Blake said.

Liam flinched. "I didn't want her to be unwanted. Elise said that not a lot of foster homes even take babies. I didn't know where she would wind up."

"Maybe with her real father," Blake said. "Maybe there's another Liam Lemmon out there."

"*Liam*. Not Billy. Not William. Whoever put Liam on the birth certificate knows me," he pointed out. "They want me to be Lucy's father. To take care of her."

"But you don't know who did that," Brett said, then narrowed his dark eyes, "Or do you?"

Liam shook his head. "I don't have any idea."

"Some obsessed ex?" Frankie asked.

He shook his head again. "I don't have obsessed exes. Nobody's ever gone after me but a bronco named Midnight, a few bulls—"

"And my cousin," Frankie said. "She's going after all of us by contesting that will."

"And if she wins, we'll lose our jobs and our home," Liam said. "So I won't be able to take care of Lucy or even myself then."

"What?" Blake asked. "You're acting like we're going to lose. Maci's going to win that lawsuit."

"And even if she doesn't, we'll be fine," Brett said. "We'll always have each other."

Liam shook his head. "You and Blake have each other. I had the rodeo until I got hurt and you all took pity on me."

"We tried getting you to work here before the rodeo," Brett said. "We didn't want you getting hurt in the rodeo."

LISA CHILDS   199

"Still taking care of your little brother?" Liam asked, and he felt even more inept than he usually felt around his accomplished siblings. Maybe that was partially why he wanted to be the one who took care of Lucy, so he could prove that he could take care of someone else and himself.

Brett snorted. "You're bigger than we are now."

"What about Ms. Shaw?" Frankie asked.

"What about her?" Liam asked, even as his pulse quickened at the thought of her.

"Are you going to tell her that Lucy isn't yours?" she asked.

"Or did you already?" Brett asked.

"She wouldn't have left the baby here if he had," Frankie said.

"Is that why you haven't told her?" Blake asked. "You want to keep Lucy?"

His heart ached at the thought of letting her go, especially if she was going back to someone who really didn't want her.

"She's not a cat," Brett said quietly. "You can't just keep her, Liam. Her biological dad might want her even if her mother doesn't. You have to tell Miss Shaw the truth."

He'd already known that without his big brother having to tell him. But telling her was going to cost him more than Lucy…

WHY HAD SHE given Margaret permission to tell Liam Lemmon where she was? Her supervisor had been sheepish when she'd called her. "I am so sorry that I keep bothering you on one of your rare weekends off."

Her mother, overhearing the call, had snorted derisively.

"I'm sure it's important or you wouldn't do that," Elise had replied.

"Well, I don't know if it's important, but Liam Lemmon is desperately trying to find you."

"I didn't notice any missed calls from him." And she would have if he'd called.

"He wants to talk to you in person," Margaret had explained.

Which meant that it was important, or maybe he was just as fascinated with her as she was with him...

But just in case this was about Lucy, Elise gave Margaret permission to give him her mother's address.

The big farmhouse had once been part of a ranch, but when the land had been sold off, the town had grown up around it. It was in the suburbs of Willow Creek now with houses and the new high school built on what had once been the ranch's fields and pastures. The old barn had tumbled down long ago, too, and her mother had turned the stones of its foundation into the patio where they now sat.

Voices drifted out the open windows of the house. Some talking. Some shouting. All the beds were full, and given the square footage of the house, Elise's mother was allowed a lot of beds. And because of her extensive experience as a foster parent, she was given some of the toughest kids to handle.

That was why Elise had stopped over, as she often did when she was in the area, to check on her. But she knew that, like those kids, her mother was tough. She'd had to be, or she wouldn't have survived her childhood.

"You really need to take some time for yourself, Elise," her mother said.

Elise laughed. "Okay, pot. I will as soon as you do."

Her mother waved a hand at the house. "This is what I want to do with my life," she said. "It always has been."

"CPS is what I want to do," Elise said.

Her mother narrowed her eyes and studied her face. "For you or for me?"

Elise sighed. "For me."

Her mother narrowed her eyes even more.

So Elise told her about Ian. How he'd been so sweet and understanding. "I'm doing it for the Ians and the Lucys and the Vivians."

Vivian Shaw smiled. "Cute. What do you do for you, Elise?"

"Mom…" This was a conversation they'd had too many times. "You need to stop nagging me to have a social life."

"You're young. You're beautiful. You should have one."

"Ditto," Elise said. Her mother was only seventeen years older than she was but looked even closer in age.

"I go out on dates," her mother said. "When's the last time you did?"

Elise shrugged. "I don't remember."

Her mother sighed and shook her head as if pitying her.

A little stung by the pity, Elise leaned across the table between them and whispered, "Today I kissed a cowboy."

"Don't lie to your mother," Vivian admonished her, and then she looked over Elise's shoulder and whistled softly. "Oh, you're not lying, and I think I know what cowboy you kissed. And he must be here for more."

She shouldn't have let her mother goad her into making the confession. Heat rushed to her face, and she leaned closer and whispered, "Mom, he's a father on one of the cases. I really screwed up."

She wasn't sure if her mother heard her because she popped out of her chair and turned to Liam. "Hello, I'm Elise's mother. Welcome to my home."

"You're not taking in a baby!" a teenage girl said as she walked onto the patio through the open sliding doors from the kitchen. "I am not taking care of a baby!"

"I need my sleep for school," a teenage boy

said as he followed the girl out. "That's why you cut off the internet at ten, Mama Shaw. So why'd you bring a baby into the house—"

"No," Vivian said softly, but the tone of her voice was like a shout that silenced the teenagers. "You know I have a no-baby rule."

Another teenage girl stood in the open doorway, her belly protruding. "What about mine?"

"Yours isn't born yet," Vivian said.

"She could pop any minute," the boy said.

Vivian sighed. "Let's all go back into the house now and give some privacy to my daughter and her friend." She gestured at them, then turned back to Liam. "I am Vivian Shaw. You must be Liam, and this is…" She leaned closer to the car seat in which the baby was sitting, her blue eyes wide as she took in all the strange voices.

"Lucy," Liam said. "And it's nice to meet you, Mrs. Shaw."

"Miss," she said. "But call me Vivian. Or Mama like the rest of them."

"What's going on?"

"There's a baby here?"

More voices called out from the house.

Vivian sighed. "I will go calm them all down." She slipped into the house and closed the patio doors behind herself. But windows were open, so voices kept drifting out.

"Apparently I shouldn't have brought Lucy

here," he said with a nervous glance toward the house.

Elise stood up. "Why did you?"

"I… I wanted to talk to you," he said.

"You didn't call me."

"I wanted to talk in person." He glanced at the house again. "But I think this might not be the place."

Maybe that was why she had given Margaret permission to send him here, because they wouldn't really be able to talk, not with so many teenagers coming and going. One opened the slider now, but it snapped closed again before she could step outside.

"How many kids does she have?"

"Eight right now," she replied, then remembering the pregnant girl, added, "Er…eight and a half…"

"Wow, was it like this when you grew up?"

"My mom wasn't able to get licensed until I was older. I was nine when she started fostering."

"That must have been an adjustment."

She nodded. "Going from the two of us to a full house? Yes, it was, but I was also old enough to understand why she wanted to do it."

"Because she wanted to protect kids, give them a safe place, like you do," he said.

The way he was looking at Elise had her pulse pounding hard. She wanted to kiss him again like she had in the barn, like she'd foolishly admitted to her mother.

Kissed a cowboy. But Liam was so much more than a cowboy. He was Livvy Lemmon's brother and a rancher with his brothers and a woman named Frankie. And most importantly, or maybe most complicated of all, he was a father...on one of her cases. Elise had crossed a line she shouldn't have crossed.

"I haven't had a chance to reassign your case yet," she said. Because she really didn't want to.

"I wish you wouldn't."

"I need to be objective," she said. "Impartial."

"And you don't think you can be?" he asked.

She sighed. "Liam..."

"You won't do what's best for Lucy?"

"Of course I will," she said and stepped closer to the car seat. Lucy's little mouth gaped open, and her blue eyes sparkled as she stared up at Elise. And something wrapped tightly around Elise's heart. Lucy was adorable, and she deserved the best. And Elise was beginning to believe the best was Liam whether he was the baby's biological father or not.

"Then that's all you need to do, Elise," he said.

"Why are you here, Liam?" she asked, and dread tightened her stomach muscles now. She had a feeling that whatever he wanted to tell her wasn't going to be good.

"Have you talked to the sheriff?" he asked.

She shook her head. "He hasn't called me."

"Oh, I thought maybe that case you got earlier would have involved him."

"Fortunately not," she said. On the way to her mother's she'd stopped by that little boy's house. There had been no dogs, just one very fluffy and bored-looking cat. "Did Sheriff Cassidy find out who Lucy's mother is?"

Liam shook his head. "No. It isn't anyone I know."

She laughed. "That's not how that works, Liam. You must have known her, or you wouldn't be Lucy's father." Her stomach muscles tightened more with nerves that he was confirming the suspicions she'd begun to have. "Are you saying that you're not her father?"

"I..." Before he could say any more, Lucy started crying. He set the car seat on the patio table and unclasped the buckles to take her out. Her cries weren't drowning out whatever he might say, though, because he wasn't saying anything at all.

Then the teenagers managed to get past Mama Shaw through the patio doors. Despite their protests about a baby being in the house, they were fascinated with her. Or maybe the teenage girls were more fascinated with Liam.

He was good-looking. And he was so gentle and sweet with Lucy.

Why would he have kept her if he wasn't her father? And why would someone put his name on the birth certificate if he wasn't? To trap him into a relationship?

But if that was the case, why disappear after leaving the baby?

None of it made sense. But what made the least sense of all was how Elise felt about him. She'd just met him. Yet she was already falling for him.

He stayed for just a little while longer before leaving without an explanation of why he'd had to see her. But she knew... The reason he kept insisting he didn't know the identity of Lucy's mother was because he wasn't really her biological father.

"Wow," Vivian said when they were finally alone again. "I understand why you kissed that cowboy."

Elise closed her eyes. "I wish I did. I've never crossed the line like that before."

"You're human, Elise," her mother said. "All humans make mistakes."

"True," she agreed. "And when we do, we have to make sure that we don't repeat them, that we learn from them." She had to hand off his case to someone else because even though she would make sure she did the right thing for Lucy, she wasn't sure she would be capable of doing the right thing for herself. Especially when she had no idea what that was...

EVER SINCE MARSH left that afternoon, Lem had been on edge. It was probably good that he'd slept through the football game because he doubted he would be able to sleep tonight. But not wanting to disturb Sadie or Feisty, he was sitting out on the front porch instead of in their suite. So he saw the lights of the vehicle that turned into the driveway.

It could have been anyone. With so many people living on the ranch, there were always vehicles coming and going. But he stood up and walked toward the steps. The vehicle stopped and the driver's door opened. It was light enough out that Lem was able to see it was Liam.

Was he alone?

Liam opened the back door of his pickup cab, and after fumbling around, he pulled out a car seat.

And the tightness Lem hadn't even realized was in his chest eased. He hadn't lost Lucy. Yet.

"Are you okay?" Lem asked.

"Yes, is it too late to visit?" Liam asked.

"It's never too late," Sadie said.

Lem hadn't even heard her open the door behind him. Maybe he did need to get his hearing checked.

"And you're always welcome here," Sadie continued. "No matter what time it is."

Liam smiled, and there was a slight sheen in his blue eyes. Then he said, "Thank you, Grandma."

Sadie reached for Lem's hand, squeezing it, and when he turned toward her, he noticed a sheen in her dark eyes. It meant so much to her that their two families fully embraced each other and became one. She'd wanted that even before he'd realized he did.

Bob had gotten so distant from him in his last year of high school. Bob had gotten so distant in his last year of high school. He'd pulled away and then eventually moved away from him. So Lem had been grateful for any contact at all with his son and with his grandkids.

But Sadie had taught him that relationships could be fixed. Hers with her oldest son, Jessup, had been after many years apart. Now Lem's grandson had called her Grandma.

"Come on in then," Sadie said.

"I don't want to wake anyone up," he said.

"The kids are already in bed," she said. "But they can sleep through anything now."

"Too bad that Brett, Blake and Frankie can't," Liam remarked.

"Did they kick you out of the house?" Lem asked. "Because like Grandma said, you're always welcome here—to visit and to stay." He didn't even need to ask her that; he knew it was true. If the Lemmons wanted to move in, Sadie would happily build another wing on the house.

"I just came from seeing Elise Shaw," he said.

"You told her that Lucy's not yours?" Lem asked with concern.

He released a shaky breath. "Of course you two

would have figured it out," he said. "Now maybe you can help me figure out what to do."

After all the years that Lem had tried to help Bob only for his son to reject him, Liam reaching out meant more than he could say. His heart swelled with love and gratitude.

And Sadie squeezed his hand a little more tightly. She knew. He didn't even have to tell her how much this meant to him. How much family meant to him.

Because it meant the same to her: everything.

CHAPTER FIFTEEN

LIAM HAD SPENT the past few days waiting for the fallout from the weekend. For Elise to take Lucy away from him. Or at least to reassign the baby's case and have someone else take Lucy away.

Maybe she was getting a court order for a paternity test so that she would have proof he wasn't Lucy's father despite what the birth certificate said. He'd pretty much admitted to her he wasn't. But he hadn't spelled it out because Elise's mother's house, that foster home full of teenagers, had made him scared for Lucy's future.

That so many kids needed homes and that there were so few places for them was the reason he'd initially stepped up for Lucy—so that Elise wouldn't have to place her in a home in another state or something. He'd wanted to keep her then because he was certain her mother would regret leaving her in a moment of madness and want her back.

But with more days passing and no updates from the sheriff, he realized that might not happen. Elise had said that if the parents couldn't be found, there was a waiting period of several months before anyone could adopt her. Could he keep her during that waiting period?

He had the name of the lawyer his grandparents recommended. Genevieve Porter-Cassidy had recently and quickly become a bit of an expert on adoption law.

Adoption.

That was a lot for him to consider, but as attached as he'd quickly become to Lucy, he wasn't sure how he would be able to let her go. He stared down into the bassinet where she slept peacefully next to his bed where he'd not slept much at all.

Not because she'd been crying but because he'd felt like crying over the mess he'd made of things. He should have been straight with Elise from the very beginning. He should have told her why there was no way he could be Lucy's father.

But then she would have taken the baby away and he wouldn't have had any reason to see either of them again. He couldn't imagine not seeing Lucy. But for the past three days he hadn't seen Elise, and it felt like longer. It felt like much too long.

He didn't dare seek her out, though. He didn't want to give her any more reason than she already had to take Lucy away from him.

Maybe she'd already turned his case over to someone else, but that new CPS investigator hadn't had a chance to contact him yet. No matter the reason for him not hearing from her, he missed her. And he was afraid that just as he'd fallen for Lucy, he'd also fallen for Elise.

LUCY LEMMON'S CASE wasn't a priority one, so Elise excused herself for not following up with Liam again. He was taking very good care of the little girl...even if she wasn't his. So the baby wasn't in any immediate danger. And to remove her from his custody, Elise would have to have a paternity test result proving he wasn't related to her.

Even then some judges didn't care; they went by what was on the birth certificate as that was usually the name of the man who was willing to step up. Like Liam had. But why?

She wanted to talk to him, but he wasn't the Lemmon who'd reached out to her. She was at the ER to meet another one. She expected Livvy to warn her away from her baby brother. But Elise could tell her to save her breath; she hadn't seen him in days.

Except every time she closed her eyes.

And in her dreams.

And every other minute when an image of him popped into her head.

She drew in a breath, bracing herself, as she stepped inside the lobby. Then she walked up to the intake desk where Livvy was either waiting for another patient to come in or waiting for her.

"Ms. Shaw," the doctor greeted her. Then she added, "Thanks for coming. I might have a case for you, but I'm not sure. I don't want to overreact."

"Better to overreact than underreact," Elise said.

Livvy sucked in a breath as if Elise had slapped her.

"I wasn't talking about Ian," Elise assured her. "I know that investigation was unnecessary." But she hadn't known that until she'd concluded it.

"I hope this one is, too," Livvy said. "But a kid came into the ER earlier today with a broken wrist. His teacher says he showed up at school with it. The parents are here now, but they claim they don't know how it happened. And I don't know, but it seemed like the dad was almost daring me to call CPS."

Elise followed Livvy back to the ER bay where a kid sat with his parents, a brace on one of his arms. From his chart, she could see that he was a teenager. "I'm Elise Shaw with Child Protective Services," she introduced herself.

"You called CPS?" the mom asked Livvy, horror filling her eyes. "I told you I don't know what happened." But she glanced at her husband as if she wondered…

Or maybe she knew and was covering for him. That happened way too often.

"Why…why is CPS here?" the kid asked.

"Because you're hurt and we need to know how that happened and make sure that you're not in danger," Elise explained.

The dad chuckled. "The only danger he's in is of getting grounded, but maybe he'd rather go into foster care than have that happen."

The kid's face flushed. "Foster care."

"Yeah, probably won't be as easy to sneak out of those houses," the dad said.

"What are you talking about?" the mom asked. "He didn't sneak out. We have that that doorbell that sends an alert when the door is opened, and it didn't go off."

"Because he didn't go out the front door," the dad said. "Did you?"

The kid's face flushed more and then he sighed. "No. I climbed out my bedroom window."

"But it's on the second floor!" his mom exclaimed.

"I climbed out onto the top of the arbor thing over the deck. But when I was climbing back in that way, I slipped and fell. I caught myself on my wrist…"

"And then had to climb back in with a broken wrist," his dad finished for him.

"I didn't know it was broken," the kid said. "It didn't even hurt then."

"Probably because you snuck out to do something stupid," the dad remarked. "And you weren't capable of feeling any pain."

"I'm sorry," the kid said.

"You will be," the dad promised.

"What will his punishment be?" Elise asked, wondering if it was extreme enough that the kid had a reason to try to avoid it.

"Losing his phone for a week," the dad said.

"Dad, I can't! I have a following. I'm making some money now. And my friends—"

"Two weeks?" the dad asked.

"Dad!" The kid turned toward Elise. "Isn't this cruel and unusual punishment?"

"Keep talking and I'll make it three," the dad continued.

Livvy tried to cover the smile curving her lips. Elise's lips twitched, too, but she shook her head. "Not cruel or unusual at all. I assume they feed you and clothe you and make sure that you have a safe, clean place to live and sleep."

"Yes, of course," the mom replied. "And we can negotiate on that punishment."

"Kids aren't entitled to phones," Elise said. "I would be more concerned about what he's doing when he's sneaking out and how much legal trouble he might get in for that. I know our new sheriff will eagerly enforce all the laws about underage drinking and smoking and curfews. You don't want your son to wind up in juvenile detention, do you?"

"Exactly, Fern," the dad said. "That's why we

have to enforce the rules. It's not going to kill him when he has no phone."

"But if I get hurt or miss the bus…"

"You can use the phone in the principal's office," his dad pointed out. Then he stood up and extended his hand to Elise. "Thank you, Miss Shaw. I think these two needed a wake-up call."

"I think the sheriff might be happy to give them a tour of juvenile detention," she said with a smile.

The kid muttered something under his breath while the mom gasped.

"I'll have Nurse Sue bring in your discharge paperwork," Dr. Lemmon said, and she stepped out of the bay with Elise. Nurse Sue was already waiting for them with papers in her hand. But instead of handing them to the family, she handed them to Elise.

"These are some of the names and that place we talked about," she said.

"Thank you," Elise replied. She knew how difficult it must have been for Sue to admit what she had to her the other day, about having given up a child.

"Hopefully it'll help you find what you're looking for," Sue replied with a quick glance at Livvy.

Obviously Sue hadn't shared her past with the doctor. Elise suspected that not many people knew the nurse's secret, but she'd entrusted it to Elise.

Just as Liam had entrusted her with doing what

was right for Lucy. She wouldn't be able to figure out what was right until she discovered everything she could about the baby who'd been left in a barn.

ONCE NURSE SUE handed those papers to Elise, she'd seemed intent on rushing off with them. So intent that Livvy had to jog to catch up to her in the lobby.

"Hey, wait a moment, please," she implored her.

Elise turned back around and blinked at her. "I'm sorry. I will follow up at the house and with individual interviews to verify that story we heard back there."

"Story? You don't think it was true?" Because Livvy was pretty sure it was, and that the dad was brilliant for acting the way he had.

"I still need to verify it," Elise said. "I'll interview people at the school, too, since they're the ones who sent him to the ER."

"She's thorough," Nurse Sue called out.

Livvy glanced back and saw that the older woman was standing next to the intake desk; she must have followed them out of the ER. Her brow was furrowed and her face pale. Was she worried that Elise would show Livvy those papers she'd handed to her?

Livvy felt a little sick again. What was Nurse Sue up to now? They'd had their differences when Livvy had first started working in the ER. But she'd thought they were good now. That they'd come to respect each other.

Like Livvy respected Elise now.

"Ms. Shaw is really good," Livvy said.

Elise's neck snapped back like she'd slapped her. Either she didn't know how to take a compliment, or she was shocked that Livvy would give her one.

"I'm sorry," Livvy said, offering the long over-due apology. "I realize you were just doing your job over that incident with Ian." And she felt foolish the five-year-old had figured that out and forgiven Elise before Livvy had.

Elise smiled. "He's a sweetheart."

"He's a smart kid, too," Livvy said.

"And perfectly safe," Elise said. Then she lowered her voice and said, "And don't worry about me and your brother…" While she was attracted to him, she couldn't give in to temptation. She couldn't kiss him again. And if she wound up having to take Lucy from him, she doubted that he would want her to anyway.

"I'm not worried about you and my brother," Livvy said.

"You're not?" Elise challenged.

Livvy chuckled. "I'm not worried about you. I am worried about him. I don't understand the whole baby thing. It's not like Liam to date anyone flaky. And whatever women he has dated are still friends of his. Nobody would have his baby and not tell him and then just dump the baby on him like that."

"Would any of them put his name on the birth certificate even though the baby's not his?" Elise asked.

Livvy sucked in a breath as she realized what Ms. Shaw already must have. The baby wasn't his. "I… I don't think any of them would do that. Like I said, they're still his friends. Liam has much better judgment in dating than I do."

"I won't tell the paramedic you said that," Elise offered with a conspiratorial smile.

Livvy laughed. "I'm not talking about Colton. But I can't really take credit for him. Sadie manipulated our paths crossing."

"You thought she manipulated Liam and I meeting," Elise recalled.

Livvy laughed again at how ridiculous and paranoid that sounded. "No. That was Colton's thought more than mine. Sadie isn't going to do anything that might put a baby in danger like leaving her out in a barn."

"So who would?" Elise murmured. And she glanced down at those papers Nurse Sue had handed her.

"You'll figure it out," Livvy said, and she wasn't just offering empty assurances. She was certain. Elise Shaw was thorough.

"But when I do…" Elise murmured, and her dark eyes filled with misery.

She was going to wind up taking Lucy away from Liam. And even though he hadn't had her long, Livvy had seen how attached her brother was to the baby.

Taking her away from him was going to break his heart.

CHAPTER SIXTEEN

LIAM HADN'T BEEN able to bring himself to call Genevieve Porter-Cassidy. He hadn't wanted to talk to a relative stranger when he had a lawyer that he knew and trusted. He intended to call Maci when he wasn't busy with the ranch and Lucy.

Maci Bluff was Frankie's best friend, and she'd been around so much when they were growing up that she'd been like another of Frank Dempsey's daughters, just as Frankie had been more like his daughter than his niece since he'd raised her. Maci was usually around the ranch a lot, too, just not lately.

Maybe Frankie had warned her about the baby, and she didn't want to get manipulated into babysitting, which was what Frankie claimed he'd done with her. He'd gone out that morning to help his brothers recover some cattle that had slipped through a section of broken fence and into some dangerous terrain. As a former rodeo rider, he had the best roping skills of all of them. Frankie had

actually offered to watch Lucy so that, instead
of dropping her at Ranch Haven or waiting for
a sitter to drive from there to the Four Corners,
he'd been able to go out right away to recover as
many head of cattle as possible before they got
lost forever.

But when he walked back into the house, she
pointed at him with her free hand and said, "I
think you broke that section of fence so you could
rope me into watching this sweetie."

"I think the big tree that fell on it in the wind-
storm broke it, but okay," he said with a grin.

He didn't think she was really mad at him
because Lucy was quiet in her arms. The baby
stared up at her while wrapping one of Frankie's
errant curls around her finger. And he suspected it
wasn't just Frankie's curl that Lucy had wrapped
around her finger but the whole woman, just as
the adorable baby had wrapped him around it.

At the sound of his voice, Lucy turned toward
him and cried out. After nearly a week of caring for her, Liam had learned her cries. This one
wasn't because she needed a diaper change or a
bottle. No. She needed him.

And he'd missed her, too. He tossed a towel
over his sweaty shirt and took her from Frankie.
"There's my sweet girl," he murmured, and her
mouth sagged open in the toothless smile that
warmed his heart.

"But she's not your sweet girl," Frankie said softly. "What are you going to do, Liam?"

"I'd like to ask Maci for some advice. Where's she been lately?"

Frankie sighed. "Busy. She feels so bad about Uncle Frank's will. She didn't think this would happen. She was good friends with Trish, too. But because of Trish's mom, Uncle Frank's venomous ex, Maci did her best to make the will ironclad and uncontestable. She didn't want anything like this to happen. But it doesn't matter how busy she is, she'll make time for any of us. We're family to her, too."

Liam's heart warmed even more. Frankie and Maci did feel more like sisters in some ways than Livvy did. He had more in common with them in that they all cared so much about the ranch. But since finding Lucy, the ranch wasn't his primary focus anymore. The Four Corners was still the main concern for his brothers and Frankie, though, and he didn't want to take Maci's attention from the lawsuit.

"Since she's so busy, I don't want to bother her," he said. He would call Genevieve Porter-Cassidy instead. She was actually family now, too, through his grandfather's marriage to Sadie Haven. He was probably related to most of the people of Willow Creek through Sadie.

"You wouldn't be bothering Maci," Frankie assured him. "But what do you want her to help you with? Are you in trouble for keeping Lucy even though you know she isn't yours?"

He shrugged. "I really don't know. I haven't heard from Elise for a few days." And he had a hollow ache in his chest over missing her.

"Elise?" Frankie smiled. "Ms. Shaw? The CPS investigator?"

He felt heat climb up from his neck to his face. "Uh, yeah…"

"You like her," Frankie said in a teasing, sing-song tone that a real sister would have used with him. But Livvy had always been too busy studying to tease him.

He could have denied it, but he'd already been too secretive with his family. And with Elise Shaw.

"Yes, I do."

Frankie's smile slipped away. "How does she feel about you lying about the baby being yours?"

"Like I said, I haven't talked to her in a few days," he replied. "But I keep waiting for her to show up here to take Lucy away from me."

"Oh, Liam," Frankie murmured with sympathy. She stood up and squeezed his arm. "I didn't get it, until today, how you got so attached to her. But she's not even yours, and you took responsibility for her anyway. Are you just that great a guy?"

He snorted, and Lucy made a sound that could have been a giggle. "She thinks you're funny, too."

"She thinks you're a great guy, too," Frankie said. "But what makes you so willing to take responsibility for her?"

He shrugged. "Because nobody else seems to want to..." Her own mother had abandoned her.

"Elise Shaw would find someone else to take care of her until the real parents are found. And if they don't want her, I'm sure she could find someone to adopt her."

"I think I want to be that someone," he admitted.

"That's why you want to talk to Maci," Frankie murmured.

He nodded. "After that bronco, Midnight, fell on me... I was hurt in a way that I can't ever have kids. And then Lucy shows up in the barn, and my name is on her birth certificate. I didn't think that could ever happen."

He'd resigned himself that he wouldn't be like his dad or his grandad; he wouldn't be one of the amazing male role models that he'd had growing up. He'd even worried that he might wind up alone.

"And now I don't want to lose her," he admitted, his voice gruff with emotion.

"Ah, Liam..." Frankie closed her arms around him and Lucy both.

With his arms full of baby, he couldn't hug her back, but he leaned his head against the top of hers, accepting her comfort. Because he had a feeling that even if Maci wasn't busy, she probably wouldn't be able to help him keep Lucy.

Once the truth came out, he would lose her just like he must have already lost his chance with Elise. But then he heard something that drew his attention to the front door he'd left open. And through the glass storm door, he saw her standing on the porch, staring in at him and Frankie and Lucy.

WHOEVER HAD GONE into the house last at the Four Corners Ranch hadn't closed the front door, just the glass storm door. Through the glass Elise could see Frankie with her arms around Liam. Their heads touched with such familiarity and affection.

Embarrassment rushed through Elise, heating her face. She wasn't the only woman who threw herself at him. She cleared her throat, but that wasn't to get their attention. Liam must have already seen her because he moved his head back from Frankie's and stepped out of her arms. She cleared her throat again to choke down the jealousy that had come over her.

She had no right to it. They weren't even dating; they couldn't. And she never should have kissed him because it was unprofessional and because now she couldn't stop thinking about it, about him.

And Lucy…

The sweet baby deserved a home where she was wanted. But first Elise had to find the person who'd given birth to her. She had that lead from Nurse Sue, the clinic where so many unwed mothers went—years ago and apparently in the present as well since it was still open. But nobody at the clinic a couple of hours outside Willow Creek had been willing to answer any of her questions.

Maybe they'd had a problem with CPS taking a newborn away from a mother whose parental rights had already been terminated. Elise had had to do that in the past with a woman who'd gotten pregnant, almost as if trying to replace the child she lost custody of with another. But since the woman was unwilling to give up the drugs or whatever had made a judge rule her unfit as a parent, her subsequent children were removed from her shortly after birth. Some midwives and OBs considered that cruel. Elise just wanted to make sure those babies were safe.

But not everyone understood or appreciated that was part of Elise's job. And the clinic had not been very welcoming or friendly to her.

They'd used HIPAA laws as the reason for withholding information even though she'd explained a baby had been abandoned and she needed to find the infant's mother. Without revealing where she'd received it, Elise had given the information about the clinic to Sheriff Cassidy. Maybe he would have better luck convincing them to answer questions about Lucy Lemmon's birth mother.

And her father.

Lucy's mother might have written down Liam's name because she'd wanted the father to be him. Women really liked him—women like Frankie Dempsey. Frankie followed Liam's gaze toward the door and gestured for Elise to let herself in.

Elise's hand shook a little as she gripped the handle and opened the storm door. Then she stepped over the threshold and said, "I'm sorry to interrupt—"

"No interruption at all," Frankie said. "I was just hugging Liam because I'm grateful he's relieving me from babysitting duty."

"I thought you didn't babysit." Elise remembered what she'd said that first day she'd met the woman.

"Some cattle escaped through a broken fence and Brett and Blake needed the former rodeo rider more than they needed me to get the cattle back," Frankie explained. "I should go out and see if they need my help at all now." She quickly stepped around Elise and slipped out the storm door that had yet to close completely.

Liam cleared his throat, drawing Elise's attention back to him. Maybe because of working so hard to recover the runaway cattle, his face was pale, and he looked a little shaky. He gruffly asked, "Are you here for Lucy?" He held the baby against his chest, against his heart. A heart that clearly belonged to the baby girl.

"I am here about her," she said. "I wanted to update you. I think I found the clinic where she was born, the one with the official that signed her birth certificate."

He sucked in a breath. "They told you about her mother?"

She shook her head. "They wouldn't give me any information. They used HIPAA laws as an excuse."

"But doesn't abandoning a baby take away any right you might have had to privacy?"

"Sheriff Cassidy is going to talk to them," she said. "Hopefully we'll learn more about Lucy's parents soon."

He sucked in another breath, this one even sharper than the first. "You said that my name on the birth certificate legally makes me her father."

"But you didn't sign that, and you don't know who the mother is," she said, and her heart was beating fast as she waited for his full admission.

But he said nothing. He just stared down at Lucy, who stared back at him with her blue eyes wide and her mouth gaped open in that toothless smile of hers.

"Liam?" she prodded him, tears stinging her eyes at the thought of taking the baby away from him.

He shrugged. "I don't know what to tell you…"

"The truth."

"My name is on her birth certificate," he said. "That's the truth."

"But you don't know why it's there."

He sighed. "No. I don't."

She sucked in a breath now, too. She was going to have to do something about this, or maybe she should just have Margaret reassign the case. It wasn't as if she could be objective anymore. Not after that kiss.

"But you know what I do know, Elise?" He crossed the room until he stood in front of her, so close that she could see the sheen in his blue eyes.

He was silent for a moment, as if waiting for her to answer him, but she couldn't talk right now. She could barely think. He was too close, so close that could smell a curious mix of horse and sweat and baby powder. And she could feel the heat of his body and the intensity of his stare.

"Elise, I know that you and I are attracted to each other—"

"Are we?" she interjected. Or was she the only one who was attracted?

"I am to you," he said. "I think you're so beautiful and strong and smart—"

She laughed because she felt like such a fool. "If I was smart, I wouldn't have left Lucy with you without a paternity test."

"But you must not need one when my name is on the birth certificate." he stated. Correctly.

Since she didn't want to confirm that and admit she would need a court order for that paternity test, she continued as if he hadn't spoken, "And if I was smart, I wouldn't have kissed you."

"Elise, that wasn't dumb," he said. "That was bold and exciting and passion—"

She reached out and pressed her fingers over his lips to stop him from saying anything else, from exciting her anymore. But the sensation of his lips against her skin had her tingling, had her pulse pounding.

"Liam…" She couldn't think rationally when he was laying on the compliments and talking about the kiss.

And then he kissed her fingers.

She jerked her hand away from his mouth. "Liam…"

"Kiss me," he implored her. "I can't stop thinking about how your lips felt against mine."

Neither could she. She shook her head. "We shouldn't…no matter how much I might want to."

"It won't change anything with the way you handle this case," he said. "I know that. I'm not trying to charm you into letting me keep Lucy."

But she couldn't help but wonder if that wasn't exactly what he was doing. And she was falling for it because she wanted, badly, to kiss him again.

Then he leaned closer and brushed his mouth across hers, gently, tentatively.

She could have pushed him away, but instead she reached out and clutched his shirt and pulled him closer. For just a moment...

She kissed him back.

Then Lucy cried out, probably in protest of being caught between them even though she had plenty of space because their bodies weren't close. Only their lips.

Elise released his shirt and stepped back, so their mouths broke apart. Then she turned and hurried from the house. It was a mistake coming here.

A horrible mistake. Because every time she saw Liam Lemmon she fell a little bit more for him, for his charm, for his sweetness...and even for Lucy.

But she couldn't keep them, just like all the foster siblings she hadn't been able to keep over the years. They'd gone back to their biological parents. And some of them hadn't survived.

Elise had lost too many people to risk her heart again. Even for Liam—or maybe especially for Liam—because she knew they were both going to get hurt when she had to give Lucy back to her biological family.

INSTEAD OF HEADING to the barn and her horse like she'd said she was going to do, Frankie had waited next to the CPS investigator's state vehicle in case the woman didn't stay long. She wanted to explain what Ms. Shaw had seen.

But when the woman rushed out to her vehicle, her face flushed and a faint sheen of tears in her dark eyes, Frankie wasn't sure she'd done the right thing. Maybe she was only going to embarrass her and make things worse between her and Liam.

Elise Shaw gasped when she noticed Frankie leaning against the driver's side of her vehicle. Then she tensed and drew back as if she expected a fight.

Frankie and her band had sung in some real dive bars, so she had seen a lot of fights. She'd even been in a couple of them. But she didn't want to fight Ms. Shaw, so she held up her hands. "I'm sorry," she said. "I just wanted to talk to you for a minute."

"Without Liam," Elise said. "Why? Do you want to warn me to stay away from him? You don't need to bother. I can't get involved with him."

Frankie wasn't going to point out that it seemed to be too late for that. The CPS investigator was definitely involved with Liam, and she didn't think it was just because of Lucy or she wouldn't have looked so upset when she'd seen them hugging.

Actually Frankie had been the one hugging Liam. He'd had his hands full with Lucy.

"I'm not involved with him either," Frankie said. "I know you saw that hug, and I wanted to make sure that you didn't misunderstand. My uncle saw all the Lemmon boys like his sons. And because my uncle raised me like I was his daughter, that makes them my brothers. That is how I see them. I was just hugging Liam because he's so worried about Lucy. He doesn't want to lose her. He loves her."

Elise released a ragged-sounding breath. "I know."

Clearly she knew what Frankie did, that the baby wasn't really his. But she'd come out to the vehicle alone; she hadn't taken her away yet.

"You didn't have to explain anything to me," Elise told her.

"But I wanted to…" She drew in a breath to brace herself to explain all the chaos in their lives. "There's just so much going on with us, with the ranch. My uncle died recently, and his will is being contested."

"I'm sorry," Elise said.

"Me, too." She hadn't expected her cousin to be so greedy, but knowing who Trish's mom was, maybe she shouldn't have been surprised. "The Lemmon brothers deserve the shares of the ranch that my uncle wanted them to have."

Elise smiled. "To leave them an inheritance, he really must have loved them like sons."

"Yes, he did. And he appreciated how hard

they've all worked on the ranch, making it more prosperous than it's ever been. They're hard workers. They're really good guys." Frankie leaned closer to her. "And trust me, there aren't that many really good guys out in the world." Or maybe she just saw the worst ones in those dive bars where she sang with her band.

Elise sighed again. "I know."

That was probably why she hadn't taken Lucy away yet. Maybe it was also why she'd looked so sad when she'd caught Frankie hugging him.

Frankie didn't know if the CPS agent falling for Liam would make the situation better or worse for him or only more complicated. And Frankie was very glad that she was single.

Life was definitely less complicated that way.

CHAPTER SEVENTEEN

A DAY HAD passed since Elise ran out of the ranch house, but Liam couldn't forget how upset she'd been. He'd screwed up. He shouldn't have kissed her even though his lips tingled from that contact, from the sweetness of her kiss. The sweetness of her.

She was as strong as she was sweet, though. So however upset she'd been in that moment, she would deal with it as stoically as she dealt with all the horrible cases she had to investigate. If she couldn't deal, she would have already passed off his case to someone else.

She hadn't done that yet. And she hadn't taken Lucy away from him either. But he couldn't trust that she wouldn't, especially once the sheriff found Lucy's mother and real biological father. Marsh might have already done that since he'd requested that Liam come to Willow Creek to talk to him at the sheriff's office this afternoon.

Worried about that meeting, Liam had made an appointment with Maci for earlier that afternoon.

Macy had rented an office in Willow Creek instead of working from her home like she used to. Maybe that was why she'd been around the ranch less, since she spent so much of her time farther away from it now.

Unfortunately her office was in the same building as his dad's. His dad had purchased the two-story building after he'd sold their family home. It had once housed a cigar shop, and when Liam pushed open the door and stepped into the reception area in the front, there was still a lingering scent of sweet smoke. He glanced down at Lucy. She slept peacefully in her car seat, but he leaned a little closer to listen to her breathing and make sure that even that faint odor didn't affect her.

While Livvy had given the baby a clean bill of health, Lucy could have other allergies that hadn't presented themselves yet. And Liam didn't want to be the one who exposed her to them.

He hadn't realized it would still smell of cigars because he hadn't visited his dad before this; he didn't know what to say to him. And maybe he still wasn't over the fact that Dad hadn't let them help him with Mom. Maybe he hadn't wanted to burden them and disrupt their lives, or maybe he had just wanted those last moments with her all for himself.

His parents had had a close relationship, so close that it had seemed that they sometimes didn't want to let anyone else in, even their own children. And especially not Grandpa Lem.

But now, after seeing Grandpa and Sadie together, Liam knew that it was possible to be close but still include others in that closeness, that love.

Sadie and Lem brimmed with so much love that it overflowed onto everyone else around them. That was how Liam wanted to love, that was the kind of love he wanted for himself. And he realized now that it didn't matter if he couldn't have biological children. He could still be a loving and supportive father and grandfather someday to the children of his heart.

Like Lucy.

But first he had to find out if he would be able to keep her.

"Knock, knock," he called out to the empty front reception area.

A young man with blond hair rushed down a center hall from somewhere in the back. "Hello," he said with a smile. Then he glanced down at the baby and his smile slipped slightly. "Oh..."

"I'm here to see Maci Bluff," Liam said. "I have an appointment with her."

"Hey, I think I recognize that voice..." a male voice murmured from the back area of the building. There was a reception area in the front, where the cigar shop must have been, and then a center hall that separated offices on either side of it. "Sounds a bit like one of my sons. Not Brett. Not

Blake. I hear from them, so I would recognize their voices instantly. So it must be my youngest…"

Heat rushed to Liam's face. He knew he was the one who talked the least to his father. It wasn't because he didn't love him or because Bob Lemmon hadn't been a good father. Because he had been…

He'd taught all of his children to be independent and self-sufficient and kind as well. He was a good man. And suddenly he was in front of Liam.

"Hey, Dad…" he murmured with a twinge of guilt. His dad was getting older. There was more gray hair than brown on his head. And he looked a little pale, maybe just because he hadn't been in the sun much. Or… "Are you feeling okay?"

Bob Lemmon snorted. "No," he replied.

"Dad, what's wrong?" Liam asked as concern clutched his heart.

"I had to find out about this little girl from one of your brothers," his father said as he leaned close to the car seat. Lucy's lashes fluttered, then her lids opened as she awakened. And his dad sucked in a breath. "She has your eyes."

Liam wasn't sure how that was possible when they weren't biologically related, but they did both have deep blue eyes, like his grandfather Lem.

A little sneeze escaped from Lucy, making her nose wrinkle and her eyes water.

"Oh, shoot," Liam muttered. "I think she is allergic to this place."

"You get used to the smell," the blond-haired man remarked.

"How long does that take?" Maci asked as she stepped out of the back area. She reminded him of Livvy, petite and blond. Though her hair was paler than Livvy's strawberry blond, and her eyes were blue instead of Livvy's green. But she felt as much a sister to him as Frankie did. She wrinkled her nose like Lucy had.

Bob chuckled. "What smell? I don't notice anything."

He'd been known to puff on a cigar himself from time to time. But he'd stopped after his wife died. Maybe Livvy, the doctor, had convinced him to do that. But had it been too late? He did look entirely too pale to Liam.

That twinge of guilt struck again for not reaching out to his father more than he had since moving closer.

The younger man chuckled. "I really don't smell anything either anymore. But then I've been here longer than the two of you. I worked for Katie O'Brien-Morris before she married Jake Haven and moved out to the ranch."

Liam chuckled. "Are there even six degrees of separation from a Haven for anyone in this town?"

"Not for us," Bob said with a bit of a heavy sigh. "Not since my dad married Sadie."

Did that bother him? Liam tried to read his expression, but his dad was focused on Lucy so he couldn't see his face well enough. "Don't you like Sadie?" he asked.

Bob nodded. "I like and respect her, mostly for how she took on my dad over the years, challenging him at every turn and over every decision he made." He grinned. "They're two of a kind."

"Yeah, they are pretty perfect for each other," Liam said.

And his father winced.

"That doesn't take away from how much Grandpa Lem loved Grandma Mary," Liam said. "He adored her, and he took such good care of her when she got sick."

His grandmother had died from Alzheimer's disease.

"Sadie helped him with Mom," Bob said with a smile. "She and your grandmother were good friends."

Liam tentatively asked, "Is it okay if I call her Grandma?"

Bob shrugged. "I don't know how she or your grandpa would feel about that."

"I'm not asking how they would feel about it." He already knew that: ecstatic. "I'm asking how you would feel about it."

His dad shrugged again. And Lucy's next sneeze distracted them both. "Hey, you have an appointment with Maci. And I have some free time. I'll take this little lady out of here."

"This is where you live, too, Dad," Liam said.

His father had an apartment above the office. "Where will you take her?"

"To the park."

It wasn't far from where they were, just a block down and across the street from City Hall. Liam handed over the diaper bag as his dad picked up the car seat. "You sure you remember how to take care of babies?" he teasingly asked. "It's been a while."

"Twenty-seven years to be exact," Bob replied. "But I'm sure it's like riding a bike."

"She is really attached to me," Liam said. "So bring her back if you can't get her to stop crying."

"She's not going to cry," Bob said. "She's going to love hanging out with Papa."

Liam felt a sharp jab in his heart. Obviously neither of his brothers had brought their dad up to date with the news that Lucy wasn't really a Lemmon.

But hopefully, with Maci's help, she could be. Unless Marsh had already found her biological parents and they wanted her back. He dreaded that appointment so much he wanted to put it out of his mind.

INSTEAD OF DRIVING to her next appointment, Elise started across the park that was between the Department of Human Services office in City Hall and the sheriff's office on Main Street. She needed the fresh air and the sunshine to clear her head, to hopefully clear Liam Lemmon right out of it. And it was probably faster to walk than to drive and have to try to find a parking space on Main Street. Or it would have been faster had she not heard a baby crying.

Maybe it was the CPS investigator in her that always made her tense when she heard any child cry, and she had to check and make sure that kid was okay before she continued on her way. But this time she was pretty sure she recognized that cry because she didn't just tense, her pulse quickened, too. And she felt a little flutter of excitement that she might see Liam. That was Lucy's cry.

She followed the sound of incessant crying to one of the duck ponds in the middle of the park. The man holding the baby looked a lot like Liam although there was more gray than dark hair on his head. He also had the same general build, but he wasn't as muscular. Elise wasn't the only one who was aware the man wasn't Liam. Lucy was stiff in his arms as she continued to cry. He kept walking and rocking her and was even singing something under his breath.

"Hello?" Elise called out. He didn't hear her over the crying, so she got closer and spoke louder. "Hello? Do you need help?"

He heard her and Lucy must have, too, because she stopped crying, and she tried to move her head, which was cupped in his hand, toward Elise. The man's eyes widened. "Oh, my goodness, I can hear again."

Elise smiled. "Lucy giving you a hard time?"

"Not as hard a time as my son will give me for not being able to handle babysitting for more than a few minutes," he said. "You know my son Liam and my granddaughter, obviously."

Lucy sputtered and moved in his arms, as if trying to twist toward her. Elise held out her hands, and the man who'd claimed her as his granddaughter willingly passed her off.

"Uh, yes, I know them," she said. But even she was surprised how Lucy settled against her with a soft sigh, like Elise was the one she'd wanted. Something wrapped around her heart, tightly squeezing it.

"I'm Bob Lemmon." The older man introduced himself with a smile.

"I'm Elise Shaw," she responded. And then, in case he thought she was Lucy's mother, she felt compelled to add, "I'm a CPS investigator."

"CPS?"

"Child Protective Services."

His eyes widened. "Oh…"

"I am on Lucy's case," she said.

"My sons told me her mother left her in the barn at the Four Corners Ranch," he said. "And that Liam's name was on the birth certificate."

She was on her way to meet Sheriff Cassidy, who had more information about that now since he'd talked to the staff at the clinic that had refused to talk to her. She wasn't sure if he'd had to get a court order for the information or if they'd just been forthcoming with him because he wasn't CPS.

Who were Lucy's parents? Did the sheriff have that information now? And if he did, would Elise have to take Lucy away from Liam?

"With the way that she was left at the ranch, CPS is required to investigate," Elise explained to Bob Lemmon.

He nodded and said, "So that's why Liam wanted to meet with Maci."

"Maci?"

"Maci Bluff. She's a lawyer who just started renting office space from me."

"So she just got her law license?"

He shook his head. "She was working from home before that. Just does wills, real estate paperwork, stuff like that."

So Liam wasn't meeting with her to have her petition for full and permanent custody of Lucy; he would have met with an adoption lawyer for that. So he must have been meeting with Maci about the lawsuit over the ranch.

Elise's heart ached for him, for what he could lose: his job and his home and Lucy, too.

"Wow," Maci murmured when Liam finished talking.

Liam Lemmon was a good guy like his brothers. That was why Frank Dempsey had put them in his will; he'd loved them. And he would have loved to have had that baby on the ranch. He'd wanted grandchildren so badly.

It was a shame that he would never get to experience them. But Frank had loved his ranch so much that he probably was still there in spirit somehow. Maci had stopped coming around because it was hard to be there without Frank's presence. And it was getting hard for her to be around one of the Lemmon brothers. Not Liam, though.

"What do you think?" Liam asked her.

"I think you need an adoption lawyer," she replied. "I wish I could help, but I'm afraid I would mess it up." Just like she was afraid she'd messed up Frank's will. She wasn't long out of law school—which Frank had helped her pay for—and was scared that she'd missed something, and that the big-city lawyer Trish had hired would find it.

That was why she'd rented an office, wanting to look more professional to him and Trish. Trish probably just remembered her as her friend, the girl that she and Frankie rode horses with and talked about boys with…

She wished she could talk to Trish now about a particular boy. But since Trish was suing him and Frankie was living with him, she didn't dare. Just as she didn't dare take on Liam's case.

"Talk to Genevieve Porter-Cassidy," she said.

Liam sighed. "I know. Grandpa Lem and Sadie recommended her, too."

She smiled. "The less than six degrees."

He chuckled. "Yes. I hope my dad is okay with that."

Maci sighed. "Your dad is a good guy, but he really keeps to himself."

"I think he still misses my mom," Liam admitted. "They were so close."

Was that how all Lemmon men loved? According to the conversation she'd overheard earlier, his grandfather had loved his grandmother like that. Maci wanted a love like that, like her parents had. But she'd been so busy with law school and studying to pass the bar that she hadn't been dating for a while.

And now she couldn't really date the person she wanted or that big-city lawyer might consider it a conflict of interest. With how she felt about Frankie and all the Lemmon brothers, she still had a conflict. But she didn't need that lawyer claiming she'd tricked Frank into writing the Lemmons into his will because of a romantic relationship.

She heard the creak of the outside door opening and then Robert chuckling. "You weren't gone long, Grandpa. And you didn't come back alone."

"This is Elise Shaw from CPS," Mr. Lemmon said.

Liam shot up from the chair in front of Maci's desk.

"Geez," Robert said. "The baby looks fine. How

much did you mess up for CPS to get called on you already?"

"I wasn't called on Bob," Elise said. "I'm just here to talk to Liam. We need to go to the sheriff's office."

All the color drained from Liam's face, and he muttered, "We?"

Maci stood up and whispered, "You need to call Genevieve Porter-Cassidy right now. Or maybe I should call her for you." Maci had heard that before specializing in adoption law, Genevieve had been a criminal lawyer.

She had a bad feeling that might be the kind of lawyer Liam was going to need with the way the CPS investigator intended to drag him down to the sheriff's office.

CHAPTER EIGHTEEN

LIAM STEPPED OUT of Maci's office, shocked at Elise showing up talking about the sheriff. While he had an appointment with Marsh, he hadn't realized she was going to be part of it. Did the sheriff want her there to take Lucy away from him? He was even more shocked when he saw that she was the one holding Lucy, cuddling her against her chest.

"I already have an appointment with the sheriff," he said. He glanced at his watch and muttered a curse. "And I'm going to be late. I didn't think I would be here so long."

"My fault," his dad said. "I wanted to spend some time with my new granddaughter."

He felt a twinge of guilt for not telling his father the truth, but he wasn't about to do that now, in front of Elise. Although it wasn't as if she didn't know the truth…

That Lucy wasn't really his.

Elise's gaze moved from him to the woman who'd walked up next to him.

"This is Maci Bluff," he said, introducing his friend. "And this is Elise Shaw."

"And I'm Robert," the blond-haired man interjected with a big smile at her.

Elise smiled back at the young man, and Liam now felt a jab of jealousy. Then Elise focused on Maci again. "I understand you just opened this office in town. Welcome."

Maci glanced from Elise to him and her smile widened. "Yes, a pending lawsuit made me want someplace better to work from than my kitchen table."

"We are only required to work a couple in-office days, so I work from my kitchen table a lot," Elise said. "But then I live alone, so it isn't a big deal. Now if you had a family or a child..." She glanced from Lucy to Maci. "I could see that not being ideal."

Liam chuckled. "Maci is not Jane Smith." If that was what Elise had been wondering.

"Who's Jane Smith?" Maci asked.

He'd told her about the situation but had just explained that the mother probably used an alias on the birth certificate. "Lucy's mother," he replied. "Which is not Maci, who has no more interest in settling down and having babies than Frankie does."

Instead of laughing with him, Maci frowned as if he'd hurt her. Maybe he was wrong about what

Maci wanted. But he was sure that she wasn't Lucy's mother.

"I definitely have not had any babies, Ms. Shaw," Maci said. "I would have had to actually have a date for that, and I haven't had one of those since before I started law school."

"I'd be happy to take you out," Robert offered with another big grin.

Maci laughed and shook her head. "I think you're great, Robert, but I…" She sighed. "I'm still too busy to date."

Or she was interested in someone else. Liam wondered who that could be. But he didn't have time to pry right now.

"We should get to the sheriff's office," he said. Not that he was in a hurry to learn what Marsh had found out from the clinic where Lucy had been born. He knew that it would change everything, and maybe Elise would take her away from him right there.

Maybe that was why the sheriff, unbeknownst to Liam, had requested them both to be there. So he could supervise the exchange. His stomach clenched with dread at the thought of losing her. Even though he could have asked his dad to keep her awhile longer, he knew he would only be putting off the inevitable. And he wanted to spend every last minute with her that he could.

He reached for Lucy, taking her from Elise's arms. As he did, his hands brushed across her skin. His heart jumped, beating fast and hard over that contact.

And he knew that Lucy wasn't the only one he didn't want to lose. Not that he had Elise. And there was no way that he ever would.

THE OLD CIGAR SHOP was close to the sheriff's office, so Elise and Liam didn't have to walk far. But his steps slowed as they approached it; it was as if he was dragging his cowboy boots along the sidewalk. She didn't think it was because he carried too heavy a load with the car seat and the diaper bag and the baby.

She turned around after passing him and remarked, "You don't want to do this."

He shook his head, and the brim of his cowboy hat slipped a little lower over his forehead, leaving his handsome face in shadow. "No, not really."

"You don't care who Lucy's biological parents are?"

"The mother who left her in the barn is the one who doesn't care," he said.

But he did.

"Why were you meeting with a lawyer?" Was he worried that he was in legal trouble over lying?

"Maci is a friend, too," he said. "I wanted some advice."

"What did she tell you?"

"To call Genevieve Porter-Cassidy."

She smiled with a little rush of relief that he

was just friends with the beautiful blond Ms. Bluff. Heat rushed into Elise's face with a wave of embarrassment; she had no right to be jealous of anyone in Liam's life. And she'd never been the jealous type before. Not even as a kid. She hadn't cared that she'd had to share her home, her room, her toys and her mom with other kids. But for some reason she wanted to be special to Liam, not just one of many women drawn to his good looks and kindness.

She closed her eyes for a moment and forced herself to focus. "We need to get inside."

Liam drew in an audibly deep breath, as if he needed it to brace himself for the meeting. She needed to brace herself as well. Because if the sheriff had found out what Elise suspected, that Liam was not Lucy's father, then she was going to have to take her away from him.

Since Liam was carrying Lucy in the car seat, Elise opened the door and held it for him to pass through. But he didn't pass her; he stopped in the doorway, his body close to hers. And he said, "Whatever you have to do, Elise, I will understand. I know you've got to do your job."

"If I was doing my job correctly, I would have passed this case off to someone else." No matter how busy they were and how many other cases they had, because she couldn't be objective when it came to Liam and Lucy.

"I'm glad that you didn't," he said.

"Hey, you two, come on in," the sheriff said as he held open another door for them, the one that opened to the back. Once through that, he directed them down the hall to his office. When they stepped inside, he closed the door behind them. Then he looked from one to the other of them, his expression very controlled, giving away nothing.

Elise felt uneasy. "What did you find out?"

Maybe it was nothing; maybe that was why his face was blank. But he could have told them that over the phone.

"You're comfortable talking in front of each other with me?" the sheriff asked.

Elise gasped with shock that he must have found out they'd crossed the line. Had Liam told him?

"We're both going to find out whatever you have to tell us," Liam said, his body tense. "So you might as well tell us at the same time."

Elise tensed as well, wondering not just what it was but also how it would change everything. Sure, Liam had said he would understand that she was just doing her job, but doing that job would hurt him.

The sheriff studied her face, as if waiting for her reply. She nodded, and he cleared his throat, then said, "Congratulations."

"What?" Elise asked.

"I was talking to Liam," Marsh said. "Congratulations on your baby girl. She's definitely yours."

Liam laughed, like he had when Elise had told him his name was on the birth certificate. He laughed like it was ridiculous or maybe even impossible for him to be a father.

Marsh reached for a folder on his desk and opened it. "The clinic has been taking precautions recently, and so they get copies of the driver's licenses of the parents before putting their names on birth certificates." He pulled out a photocopy of a blown-up driver's license.

A Nevada license with Liam's face and name on it. Apparently Liam wasn't a nickname for William but his actual legal name. And that driver's license proved that he was Lucy's legal and biological father.

"You said you didn't know who her mother is," Elise said. "You made it sound like you couldn't be her father."

"I…" Liam glanced at the sheriff, and his face flushed a bit. "I don't know the mother. And I lost that driver's license when I first moved to the ranch. When I couldn't find it, I just applied for a Wyoming one."

"So this was an old license?" Marsh asked.

Liam nodded.

So what was he saying? That someone had stolen his license to put his name on the birth certificate?

"What about the mother?" Elise asked. "Do you have a copy of hers?"

The sheriff pulled another slip from his folder and handed it to Elise. An Idaho license for Jane Smith. That was the girl's real name, and she was young. Not a teenager but from her date of birth she'd just recently turned twenty-one.

Liam stepped closer to her and looked at the paper, too. Then he shook his head. "I don't know her."

Elise focused on the license again. "She lives in Boise?"

"Not in that apartment anymore," Marsh said. "I checked. She stayed there last year while she was in college. But she moved out early and didn't renew her lease."

Elise had a pretty good idea why she'd moved out early. Because she was pregnant.

"When were you in Boise last?" she asked Liam.

"Over a year ago," he said. "When I was riding with the rodeo."

Marsh was studying them both with his eyes narrowed. "So you're still saying you've never met this Jane Smith?"

Liam nodded. "I know that you all know what that means…"

"That you're not Lucy's father," she said. But that driver's license accompanying the birth certificate would make it even harder for her to get a judge to grant her petition for a paternity test. And without it, she had no reason to take Lucy from him. Unless…

"Are you going to give her up?" she asked.

"I wouldn't have talked to Maci if that was the case," he said. "And I will make an appointment with Genevieve Porter-Cassidy as soon as possible."

The sheriff nodded. "My sister-in-law is good. But I'm not sure you're going to need to adopt Lucy when legally she's already yours."

"But not biologically," Elise said. She watched his face to see if it was true and noticed how he flinched, like she'd hurt him. "And don't you want to know who used your driver's license to put you down as the father? Who would even have…" Going with who would have had access to his license, she said, "One of your brothers must be her father."

"My brothers wouldn't and couldn't use my license to pass for me. And why would one of them even try to do that?"

Marsh chuckled. "I know my brothers always tried to blame one of our other brothers for whatever they did wrong. Yours didn't do that?"

Liam's face flushed a deep crimson, and he cleared his throat. "When we were kids…it was kind of a joke to blame me…since I was the youngest…"

Marsh nodded.

"But we're not kids anymore," Liam said. "And this isn't a broken TV remote or laptop. This is serious."

"Yes," Elise said. "This is a little human. Lucy

is a person. She shouldn't have been abandoned like she was."

Liam shook his head; he was clearly certain. "One of my brothers wouldn't have done that."

"But who else would have had access to your driver's license?" she asked.

He shrugged. "I must have lost it somewhere. Dropped it at the bank or something." But he sounded confused and upset, and Lucy must have sensed it because she started crying. "I should get her back home."

"Liam, you've admitted you're not her father," Elise said. "I can't let you keep her."

"Why not?" he asked. "You don't have another foster home to send her to—"

"You're not a foster home."

"No, but because of that birth certificate, backed up now with the copy of the driver's license, I am legally her father," he said. "You're the one who told me that. You're going to have to get a court order to get her away from me, Elise. And I'm going to have a lawyer."

"Maybe you should only talk to Ms. Shaw with your lawyer present from now on," the sheriff suggested.

Elise's mouth dropped open.

"You were okay with me talking to both of you in front of the other," the sheriff reminded her.

"I'm leaving now," Liam said, but in a tone that dared either of them to stop him.

The sheriff opened the door for him instead. And when Elise went to follow him out, Marsh Cassidy extended his arm across the open doorway and held her back. "We need to talk, Ms. Shaw."

Elise didn't want to talk to him; she wanted to talk to Liam. But she had a horrible feeling that he was going to take the sheriff's advice and refuse to speak to her unless a lawyer was present.

And that meant no more intimate conversation or kisses.

She'd come to the sheriff's office thinking that Liam was the one who was going to lose Lucy when they left. And now she realized she was the one who'd lost.

Him…

MARSH FELT SORRY for the CPS investigator.

"Why did you do that?" she asked him. "You know that he's not the father. He admits that he's not the father, but you let him take her anyway."

"I think you've known for a while now that he isn't, but you haven't taken her away from him yet," he pointed out. "As the father listed on the birth certificate, he has a legal right to keep her."

"But she's not his," Elise said. "Who is the biological father? And does the birth mother really want to give up her baby? Do you want Liam to get even more attached than he is, and then Jane Smith decides it was all a mistake, hormones, whatever, and she wants her baby back? If Liam has any hope of keeping her, he needs the mother to sign off her parental rights to her."

He sighed. "I'm interested in talking to Jane Smith about endangering the baby by leaving her in the barn. So I'm going to keep looking for her. Now I have the date of birth listed on that driver's license. Unfortunately there is more than one Jane Smith with that birth date."

"Did anyone at the clinic have more information about her?" she asked. "Or about him? Couldn't they tell that license didn't belong to the man who showed it to them?"

Marsh shook his head. "No. They're a pretty busy clinic with a lot of people coming and going. They weren't able to remember much about either of them."

"Why doesn't Liam just say that she's his when he clearly wants to keep her?" Elise asked. "Why admit that he doesn't know the mother?"

"Because Liam Lemmon is an honest man," Marsh said. "And a good man. He will be a great father to that baby."

"But she's not his—"

"That doesn't matter," Marsh said. "My oldest brother is biologically not my father's son. Cash didn't find out until he tried to donate a kidney for my dad, and the doctor said there was no match. My father loves Cash the same way he loves his biological sons, with his whole heart. You don't have to have DNA in common to love someone like family."

"I know that," Elise said, and her voice was a little shaky. "My mother fosters kids, has done since I was nine years old. I loved a lot of my foster siblings. And then I would lose them back to their biological families. That's why we need to find Lucy's biological parents, so that they will sign off their parental rights to her. As hard as it would be for Liam to lose Lucy now, it will be even harder months or years from now."

Marsh sighed. "You're right. I'll try to find the dad, too."

"Someone who would have had access to Liam's license," she said.

He nodded. "He seems pretty sure it's not one of his brothers."

"They really don't look that much like him," she admitted. "And they've been busy with the ranch."

"That clinic is busy," Marsh said. "It's possible that they copied the license without really taking a good look at it."

"Yes."

"Which means the father could be anyone," Marsh said.

Liam had fallen for that baby just like Marsh's dad had fallen for Cash all those years ago. Dad had known that no matter who Cash's biological father was, Cash was *his* son. So he'd willingly put his name down on Cash's birth certificate as the father.

But Elise Shaw was right.

Even though Liam's name was on the birth certificate, the biological parents could come back and take her away from him. And Marsh had a feeling that it wasn't just Liam who would be devastated if that happened but Elise as well.

CHAPTER NINETEEN

LIAM'S HEAD POUNDED and not just because Lucy had cried almost all of the way back to the Four Corners Ranch. He couldn't figure out how or why someone had used his driver's license to verify the identity of Lucy's father. Was it all some sick joke because they knew he couldn't be anyone's biological father now?

But while a lot of people knew about the incident with Midnight, nobody but he and his doctor knew what it had done to him. His brothers didn't even know.

And he'd just told Frankie.

He should have told Elise, too. She knew now that he wasn't Lucy's father. But thanks to the birth certificate, there wasn't much she could do about it. So maybe he shouldn't be mad that someone had stolen his driver's license.

But still…

Like Elise had said, this wasn't a joke; this was about a little human. And like Elise had deserved to know who her father was, Lucy deserved to know the truth someday, too. Even if Liam was able to keep her because of the birth certificate, he still wanted to be able to tell her, when she was old enough and ready to handle it, about her parentage. But first he had to find out what that was.

Who her father was…

Because as much as he wished it was him, it wasn't. He parked the truck close to the porch, jumped out and carefully took the car seat out of the back. Lucy was asleep, but her face was flushed and tearstained from crying. He'd pulled over a few times to make sure that she was dry and not hungry, but she hadn't needed a diaper, and she hadn't wanted a bottle. She hadn't even wanted him.

Maybe she'd grown as attached to Elise as he had.

Or maybe she'd felt his turmoil and frustration and that was why she'd been so upset.

When he walked into the house, he passed the kitchen where his brothers and Frankie were eating a casserole one of his brothers must have made. His stomach flipped despite how good it smelled. Because it smelled good, he knew Frankie hadn't made it. She was not a good cook.

But she was a good friend. She jumped up when she saw him and followed him to his bedroom. She leaned against the frame of the open door and watched as he unclasped Lucy from her car seat and settled her into her pack and play next to his bed. Her voice a whisper, she asked, "Everything all right?"

He grabbed the baby monitor, stepped out of the bedroom and pulled the door shut behind him. Then he looked at her face, which was tight with concern, and remarked, "Maci called you."

She nodded. "Yeah, she said that Ms. Shaw showed up and said you two had to see the sheriff."

"Yup," he said. Then he headed to the kitchen where his brothers had stopped eating. They looked at him, too, with the same concern that was on Frankie's face. Obviously she'd filled them in about the sheriff.

Blake cleared his throat and said, "But you brought Lucy back."

"I'm not giving her up," he said, his heart aching at the thought of having to do that. He'd already called Genevieve for an appointment. When he'd said Lemmon, she'd offered to meet him then, but he wanted to talk to his brothers first.

"Should we be worried that the police are going to show up and arrest you for kidnapping?" Brett asked.

"I can't kidnap a child that's legally mine," Liam said.

"Back to the birth certificate," Blake said. "You admitted that had to be forged. You haven't dated anyone since you quit the rodeo and moved to the ranch."

"Jane Smith is her real name," Liam said. "Apparently she is a twenty-one-year-old college student."

Brett uttered a weary-sounding sigh. "That's young."

Which was probably why she'd been so overwhelmed she'd left her baby in a barn. And it was also why she might change her mind and come back for her.

"Did she tell the sheriff who the real father is?" Frankie asked.

Liam shook his head. "Marsh hasn't tracked her down yet. He only had a copy of her driver's license with an old address on it. The clinic took copies of her license and the father's license."

"So you know who he is now," Brett said.

"Me. It was my license."

"What?" Frankie asked, her dark eyes wide. "You said that after Midnight, you can't..." She trailed off and glanced at his brothers.

"Can't what?" Brett asked.

"I won't ever have biological children after that," he said. "So there's no way that Lucy is biologically mine."

"Why didn't you ever tell us that?" Brett asked, sounding hurt.

"Yeah, why not?" Blake asked, and he sounded hurt, too.

Liam shrugged. "I didn't even want to think about it, much less talk about it. That's why it's really ironic that someone used my license and my name as the father."

"Is that why you're so determined to hang on to her?" Blake asked. "Because you can't have kids of your own?"

He sighed. "I don't know. At first when I found her, I just wanted CPS to pick her up and take her away. But then when Elise was saying how hard it is to find foster homes for infants, I was worried about where she would wind up and if, when her mother came back for her, she would be able to take her back. Then she just started feeling like she belonged here, with me. But now I don't even think I belong here."

"What are you talking about?" Brett asked. "Of course you belong here."

"Elise knows the truth," Liam said. "This is going to get messy. I might even get in legal trouble for lying. I can't get you guys involved in that. I can't give Dempsey's daughter's lawyer an excuse to go after us. I have to give up my share of the inheritance and leave."

Brett jumped up from his chair so abruptly that it fell over onto the hardwood floor. "Don't be a fool! You can't leave! This is your home, too."

The monitor squawked with Lucy's panicked screams. Brett's yelling had obviously frightened her. "I'm sorry," his older brother said. "But this is crazy, Liam. You're not thinking straight."

"I don't want to be the reason we lose that lawsuit," Liam reminded them. "And even if I don't give up my claim on the ranch we could still lose. I can't count on having a job or a home here. And neither can all of you."

"Maci is going to win," Blake insisted, his voice sharp now.

"She'll have a better chance of doing that if I'm not part of the deal and if I'm not even here," he said. "Somebody used my driver's license to make me look like I fathered a child with a college girl. That could go against my character in that lawsuit."

"Someone stole your license," Blake said. "We'll find out who. We'll figure this out."

Liam shook his head. "Not we. I can't keep expecting my big brothers to bail me out. To give me a job. A roof over my head. I have to take care of myself for once, or how will I take care of Lucy?"

He rushed to her now and picked her up to comfort her. "I'm sorry," he murmured as he rocked her in his arms. "I'm so sorry..."

This poor little girl had not had an easy start in life. And Liam had probably just made it worse. If only he'd told the truth from the start...

But it was too late for that. He loved Lucy, and he had to figure out how to keep her.

HOPEFULLY LIAM WOULD ignore the sheriff's advice, or Elise had wasted her time driving out to the Four Corners Ranch. But she had to talk to him…even if he wouldn't talk to her. She had to tell him what she'd told the sheriff. Maybe she could make him understand that the longer he had Lucy, the more it would hurt him to lose her.

When she pulled up next to his truck in the driveway, she noticed that his brothers were heading out to the barn. She stepped out of the vehicle and considered trying to catch up with them to ask if they knew who might have taken Liam's driver's license. But they were moving fast, and their faces were flushed as if they were upset. Had something happened with the cattle again?

Or had Liam already asked them what she wanted to? He'd been adamant that neither of them would have taken his license or been involved with a college student, probably especially since they were even older than he was. They'd also been too busy at the ranch to date, or so they'd claimed. But Elise actually believed them.

Instead of going after the brothers, she turned and headed toward the house. Frankie was coming down the steps from the porch. When she saw her, she shook her head and said, "This isn't a good time."

"Why? What's going on?"

"For the first time since I've known them, the Lemmon brothers fought."

Elise gasped. "Is Liam okay? Is Lucy?" She could hear crying now coming through the storm door behind Frankie.

"They're all fine. It wasn't a physical fight. But…" Frankie shuddered. "They all got pretty upset."

"He asked them about his license," Elise said. "Accused them of taking it?"

Frankie sucked in a breath. "Of course not. As well as being really good, honest men, they've been too busy. Liam isn't the only one who hasn't had time to date. None of them has. Brett and Blake were working their butts off for years to turn the ranch around. That's why it's so unfair that their inheritance is being contested. That's why the brothers fought. Liam doesn't want this… situation…to affect the lawsuit. He's leaving."

"I met Maci Bluff today," Elise said. "She's the one handling the lawsuit?"

Frankie nodded. "And my best friend. She told me about you showing up to bring Liam to the sheriff with you. She said Liam had to make it clear to you that she wasn't Lucy's mom."

Elise sighed. "He just assumed that was what I was thinking." Instead she'd had a moment of jealousy seeing him with the beautiful blonde.

Frankie laughed. "You don't have any reason to be jealous of Maci. Liam is not the Lemmon brother she's interested in."

Elise opened her mouth to deny her interest in Liam, but Frankie gave her a knowing look. "I need to talk to him," Elise said. "He left the sheriff's office in a hurry to get back here."

"I left in a hurry because the sheriff told me not to talk to you without a lawyer," Liam said as he stepped out onto the porch behind Frankie. He held a baby monitor in his hand, but it was quiet now. Lucy must have fallen asleep.

Frankie, still standing on the stairs, turned back toward him. "Do you want me to call Maci?"

"No," he said. "She referred me to Genevieve Porter-Cassidy."

"Want me to call her?" Frankie asked.

He shook his head. "No. I'll talk to Ms. Shaw." His voice was so cold as he said her name that she shivered.

Elise started up the stairs where Frankie hovered on the last step. "Be careful," the dark-haired woman murmured as she passed her.

Elise didn't know if Frankie was warning her to be careful with Liam or of Liam. But she didn't get the chance to ask.

"I'll talk to her alone, Frankie," Liam added, and his voice was nearly as cold to his friend as it had been to her.

While Elise hadn't known him long, she knew this wasn't like him. Frankie confirmed it with a slight gasp of shock, and then she hurried off toward the barn.

"Are you all right?" Elise asked as she joined him on the porch.

"I should be great," he said. "I have even more evidence that I'm legally Lucy's father."

"Thanks to someone stealing your driver's license."

"It wasn't my brothers," he said.

"I know, so why are you leaving?" she asked, and she reached out to touch his arm and comfort him. His muscles tensed beneath her hand, though, so she jerked it back.

"This is my mess," he said. "And I need to clean it up myself. I'm probably making more of a mess right now talking to you."

She felt a pang in her heart. "I've made a mess of this, too," she said. "I should have requested a paternity test right away. I never should have left Lucy with you and…" She shouldn't have kissed him.

"You had her birth certificate with my name as her father," he said. "And now we have the license to back that up. So what makes you think she's not mine?"

"Besides the fact that you admitted to both me and the sheriff that she's not?" she asked. "And that you have no idea who her mother is?"

He lifted his hand to his head and rubbed at his temple. "Yeah, besides that…"

"The first time I told you that Lucy was yours, you laughed, hard," she said. "And you did that today when the sheriff congratulated you on being her dad. Why? What's so funny or ridiculous to you about being mistaken for her father?"

His throat moved as if he was struggling to

swallow. "This is when I shouldn't talk to you… because you're going to use it against me when you go after Lucy."

"Whatever you tell me now will stay between us," she said. "And I will be turning your case over to someone else." Something she should have done right after she'd kissed him. Or probably before she'd given in to that temptation.

"When I got hurt trying to ride Midnight…"

"I saw that," she said. "After Midnight hurt Ian, I watched old footage of the bronco from his rodeo days."

"His rodeo days ended a lot of riders' rodeo days," he said.

"You couldn't ride again after that?"

"I could ride," he said. "I can't have kids. Everything else is okay, but…no biological children for me."

She reached out for him again, grasping just his hand, squeezing it. "I'm so sorry."

He shrugged. "I hadn't even thought about kids or a family then. I was focused on the rodeo. And then that happened, and it seemed like I couldn't think about anything else. I wanted to be the father my dad was to us, the legendary grandfather that Grandpa Lem has been to this whole town. I kept hearing babies everywhere…"

"And then Lucy shows up here with a birth certificate saying she's yours…"

He nodded.

"Is that why you kept her even when you could have told me this then and I would have found a foster home for her?"

"A foster home where?" he asked. "In another state where her mother wouldn't be able to find her?"

"And you wouldn't have been able to see her," she continued for him, knowing that was what would have bothered him most. "That would have been better for you, Liam, because you've gotten so attached—"

"I love her," he said, his voice cracking with emotion.

"But she isn't yours. And the sheriff is going to find her mother who will verify that and maybe want her back."

He flinched as if she'd struck him. "But maybe she won't," he said hopefully.

"Maybe not," Elise agreed. "But the truth is still going to come out that you're not her father. And you're not a licensed foster home either, so she'll have to be removed from the ranch. Or from wherever you go, if you really intend to leave your brothers."

And she hated to think of him doing that. He and his brothers were close and had so much in common with their love of animals and ranching.

"What does it take to get licensed as a foster home?" he asked.

"Your lawyer, if you've hired Genevieve, will

tell you that. She has a licensed foster home. But *I* can tell you that it took years for my mother to get approved," she said. "And fostering is hard. You haven't adopted the kids. You don't have the legal rights the parents do, and all too often they go back to their parents or to other family members who step up to claim them. And judges favor biological family. You don't know how many grandparents or aunts or uncles Lucy has that might want to raise her."

He flinched again and sucked in a breath. Then he focused on her with compassion in his blue eyes. "That must have been hard for you, growing up with kids coming and going in your home."

She nodded. "It was." And she felt that pressure on her chest that was there whenever she remembered some of the really bad outcomes.

"What, Elise?" he asked, and he reached out to grasp her shoulders. "I can tell that you're thinking of something…"

"Awful," she finished for him. "Tragic. There were the kids—Abigail, Taylor, Martin—that went back home and didn't survive. That's why it's smart to not get attached because it hurts so much when you lose them."

"Oh, my God…" He closed his arms around her and held her against his chest that pounded heavy against hers. "I'm sorry. That must have been horrific. But then you put yourself through it all over again with your job."

She wrapped her arms around him, holding on, feeling some of that hollow ache inside her filling with the love she had for him. She'd fallen for him despite her resolve to stay uninvolved, unattached.

He leaned back and touched her face, tipping up her chin, so their eyes met. "Why do you do that, Elise?"

"Because I want to make sure kids are safe in their homes," she said. "Because I don't want to lose another Abigail, Taylor or Martin."

He stroked his thumb along her jaw. "You won't lose Lucy," he said. "I will keep her safe and loved."

"I know," she said, and she covered his hand with hers. He'd comforted her over the past, but he was the one who was really going to need comforting. Maybe her years with CPS had made her cynical, but she couldn't see any way that he wasn't going to get hurt. "But you've been so sure her mom will come back for her. And now, knowing how young she is, I think she will, too. She cared for Lucy for two months, so I don't think she's just going to walk away. I think she's going to want her back, and you will lose her."

He tightened his arms around her, seeking comfort instead of offering it. "I don't want to lose her. I'm going to fight to keep her."

"Good," she said. "But Genevieve will tell you the same thing I have—most judges rule in favor of family, especially in a situation like Lucy's where she's not in any harm with her mother."

"Really?" he asked. "You think it was safe for her mom to leave her alone in a barn? I have a case, Elise. And I would have a better one with your help."

"What are you saying?" she asked. "You want me to bend the rules for you?" She'd already bent so many that when she came clean to her supervisor she might lose her job. But she was going to have to confess all to get Margaret to reassign the case.

"Marry me," he said.

Her heart stopped beating for a moment before resuming at a frantic pace. "That's crazy. We barely know each other." But she knew him well enough to have fallen for him.

"I know that you're strong and smart and beautiful," he said. "You were so brave to show up that day at Ranch Haven, and you explained yourself so well and were so good with the kids, with all of my family, even my sister. And you're so good with Lucy, too."

"That's what you want," she said. "You want a mother for Lucy and to show the judge a two-parent household that her young mother won't be able to give her. You think a judge will side with two parents over one. That's not the way it works. He or she will go with the biological parent over the two that are just in a marriage of convenience."

He snorted. "You think that's all it would be? Elise, I am crazy about you. About your kisses…" He leaned down and kissed her then, moving his mouth over hers.

But before she could even respond, he pulled back and said, "I'm sorry. You must think I'm losing it. And I am all over the place. First I tell my brothers I'm forfeiting my share of the inheritance and moving out and now I'm proposing to you…"

She blinked against the sting of tears. Obviously he couldn't say that he loved her, and he thought now that even proposing to her was crazy. "I understand that you're upset. You don't know what to do…" Because he was terrified of losing Lucy.

"I don't have anything to offer you," he said. "I can't give you my biological children. And I don't even know where I will go if I leave here—"

"Your brothers don't want you to go," Elise said. "I can see that they're upset. Frankie said you fought."

"I don't want to be the reason that they don't win that lawsuit contesting the will," he said.

"You won't be," she said.

"But even if I don't leave and don't forfeit my share, we could still lose. Either way, I won't have a job or a place to live."

None of that would matter to Elise if he loved

her. She would have considered it too soon for him to fall for her if she hadn't just realized how much she'd started falling for him. But his life was in chaos, just like he'd said, with the lawsuit and with Lucy.

He stepped away from her and pressed his hand to head again just beneath the brim of his cowboy hat. "I'm sorry…"

No. Elise was the one who was sorry because she'd been tempted to accept his proposal. But she deserved more than being a means to an end for him to adopt a child that wasn't his. She deserved to be loved.

He already was.

LEM THRUST HIS arms into the sleeves of his sweater and then leaned down to attach a leash to the harness collar he'd already slipped over Feisty's head. Supposedly the kids who usually walked her were too busy with homework to do it tonight after dinner, and the little dog needed her exercise. Lem had a feeling that everybody thought he might need some, too. Since moving to Ranch Haven, he'd been enjoying some of the best meals he'd ever had. Not only was the cook that Sadie had stolen away from the diner in Willow Creek excellent, but Taye was also teaching seven-year-old Miller to cook. And the kid was a natural. Juliet, Dusty's mother-in-law, who was staying to help with the babies, was another excellent cook.

Yeah, he needed the walk, so he headed toward the front door with Feisty, but when he opened it, he found an unexpected guest on his doorstep. And his heart jumped a bit just like Feisty jumped around the visitor's feet. But Lem knew better than to be overly enthusiastic like the pup. This person was already skittish with him. Had been for years.

"Hello, Bob," he greeted his son. "Are you looking for Katie?" Katie was Jake Haven's wife and lived in the house along with all the Haven family.

Bob and Katie were partners in an accounting business, though Katie mostly worked from the ranch, especially since she was heavily pregnant and couldn't easily get around right now.

"Uh, Katie…" Bob murmured.

Lem nodded. "Yeah, you know, Katie."

Bob smiled faintly. "I'm not here about business."

"Lem, why aren't you letting your son in the front door?" Sadie asked from behind him.

He stepped back and gestured for Bob to come inside. Bob, predictably, hesitated for a long moment before stepping across the threshold. He was like a dog that had to sniff your hand before letting you pet him.

"We just finished dinner," Sadie said. "But there are plenty of leftovers that are still warm if you'd like a plate."

Bob smiled but shook his head. "I'm not sure I could eat. I'm too worried about Liam."

"Liam? Is everything all right?" Sadie asked with genuine concern. Lem's wife loved his grandsons like they were her own, just as he loved hers. As he loved her...so very much.

Bob was staring at her, too, with that realization. He blinked as if he couldn't believe his eyes. "Uh, I don't know if he's okay. He was at the office, talking to Maci, and then I stumbled across Miss Shaw when I was in the park with Lucy, and she came back with us and said that they had to see the sheriff."

"You think Elise had him arrested?" Lem asked around the lump of fear in his own throat.

"Liam said that he already had an appointment to see him." Bob sighed. "I don't know what's going on, but I'm worried."

"Have you talked to Liam since this afternoon?" Sadie asked.

He shook his head. "I didn't want to interfere."

Sadie snorted. "You are not like your father at all."

No. He wasn't. He'd made that clear to Lem since he'd gone off to college. He wanted to be his own man and not follow in Lem's footsteps.

"And that's a pity," Sadie continued.

Bob sucked in a breath.

"Your dad is a wonderful man who makes sure the people he loves knows they are loved," Sadie said.

Now Bob narrowed his eyes and glared at her. "My kids know that I love them."

"It's not just your kids who need to know they are loved," Sadie said, and she slid her arms around Lem's shoulders, embracing him, supporting him, loving him as fiercely as she always did.

Lem blinked now, furiously, against the tears rushing to his eyes. "Ah, woman..." he muttered.

"And sometimes to show people that we love them we have to step up," Sadie continued. "We have to interfere. We have to help them as much as we can, so that they know they are never alone."

Bob took a deep breath and then swallowed it down like he was swallowing his pride. "What can I do to help Liam?" he asked. "I couldn't even watch Lucy for him for a few minutes without her crying inconsolably."

"She is very attached to her daddy," Lem said.

"She stopped crying for Miss Shaw," Bob said.

"And Liam isn't biologically her father," Sadie said. "That's why the sheriff is involved. He's trying to find the real biological parents."

"But why was she left in the barn at the ranch? And isn't there a birth certificate that says he is?"

"Ah, for not interfering, you seem to know a lot," Lem said with amusement and relief. He would hate to think that Bob was as standoffish with his own kids as he was with Lem.

"Blake's been coming by the office lately," Bob said.

"He's filling you in then," Sadie said.

Bob chuckled. "Actually he seems to talk more

to Maci Bluff than to me, but then she is a whole lot prettier than I am."

At the risk of getting it bitten off, Lem reached out a hand to clasp his son's shoulder. "Come on into the kitchen. You can have a cup of coffee and a piece of cobbler. Taye's cobbler is legendary."

Bob arched a gray eyebrow. "Like the two of you?"

Lem laughed. "She's the legendary one. I'm just Old Man Lemmon."

Bob stared at him for a moment, and it was as if he was taking note of all the lines in Lem's face, as if he was realizing how old his dad was. "You've had that white hair and beard for so long…"

"Another reason you're probably happy you take after your mother," Lem said. "No red hair that turns to white too soon."

Bob smiled but then he added, "Maybe I should take after you a little bit more. Like Sadie says, maybe it's time I interfere some in my kids' lives. Then Livvy wouldn't have been engaged to that controlling egomaniac neurosurgeon, and I would know what was going on with Liam—like why he would be taking care of a baby that he knows isn't his."

"Because he loves her," Lem said. He loved her already, too. "And she belongs with him. That's why he was the one who found her."

"He found her because he was the first one to

come across her in the barn where her mother
left her," Bob said.

Lem shrugged. "That, too. But sometimes
things happen just how they're meant to." Like
he and Sadie. They'd taken a long time to get together, but they were exactly where they were
meant to be—with each other.

CHAPTER TWENTY

LIAM COULDN'T STAY at the Four Corners, not after telling his brothers he was leaving, that he didn't want their help. He also couldn't get the image out of his head of Elise's face when he proposed. She'd looked horrified or maybe afraid.

He'd messed up everything with her and with Lucy.

So there was only one place he could go. And when he got there, he did as he'd been told so many times—he just walked in. Then he tried not to trip over the little dog as he pressed the door closed with his back and juggled Lucy's car seat and diaper bag and even the portable bassinet.

"Need a hand?" a little boy asked. It was the oldest of Sadie's great-grandsons, the one who had a slight limp. He lifted the dog from the floor into his arms, and it licked his chin.

"He doesn't need help," the boy with the light blond hair said. "He's a rodeo rider, like Uncle Dusty. He can juggle everything."

Liam laughed and was surprised at the sound

coming out of his mouth. He hadn't thought he would have a reason to laugh after today. "I was never a rodeo rider like Uncle Dusty," he said.

"You were Billy the Kid," the boy said with awe.

"I was, but I'm not anymore," Liam said. "And I could use a hand." He passed off the bassinet to Caleb. Their names were coming back to him. The older one was Miller.

Ian was here too, staring behind him at the closed door. "Where's Miss Shaw?" he asked. "Is she with you?"

He shook his head. "No."

Instead of looking relieved, the kid looked disappointed. "Oh, is she out making sure other kids are safe?"

Tears rushed to Liam's eyes, but he blinked them away. "I'm sure she is..."

"That's good then," Ian said. He took the diaper bag from Liam, then grabbed his sleeve with his free hand. "Come into the kitchen. Caleb will eat all the cookies if we don't hurry."

"Caleb is only allowed one cookie before bedtime," Taye Cooper said as they walked into the enormous country kitchen. "And it is nearly bedtime, guys."

A chorus of groans replied.

And Liam chuckled again.

"Speak of the devil..." Grandpa Lem murmured.

"Devil?" Sadie shot back at him.

"As in handsome devil that looks like his grandpa," Grandpa Lem boasted.

Liam grinned and shook his head as he headed over to the long table where his grandparents sat by the fireplace hearth. But they weren't alone. His dad sat with them, a plate of something in front of him that was pretty much only crumbs now. Liam leaned down and kissed Sadie's slightly weathered cheek. The woman probably still rode fences.

His dad's eyes widened with surprise over Liam's instinctive gesture. It was instinct because he already thought of her as family, as his grandmother. Then Bob asked her, "Did you call him?"

"No," Liam said even before she shook her head. "But from the 'speak of the devil,' it sounds like you were all talking about me. Did Brett or Blake call you?"

His dad shook his head.

"Well, they probably will."

"What happened?" Grandpa Lem asked, but he was a bit distracted as he was busily extricating Lucy from her car seat.

Sadie's gaze stopped on the bassinet Caleb had leaned against the island that he was sitting at. The boy reached into a big cookie jar on the stainless-steel countertop. "You need a place to stay."

"Yeah, is it okay?"

"Of course it is," she said, and her dark eyes

looked a little damp. "Ranch Haven is your home now, too."

The crazy thing was that it did feel like home to Liam even though he'd never lived anywhere like it, with so many other people. He'd thought his family was big with two brothers and a sister, but the Haven family just seemed to keep multiplying. He hoped that it would continue to do so, if he could somehow keep Lucy.

Grandpa Lem held her, cooing and making faces at her. And when he leaned closer, her tiny hand reached up to his white beard. When she touched it, something like a giggle escaped from her little rosebud mouth.

He had to be able to keep Lucy. She wasn't the only one he wanted to keep. But it was too late with Elise. Even before she reassigned his case, he'd lost whatever chance he might have had with her.

ELISE PRIDED HERSELF on being tough and independent. But after Liam's proposal and his rescission of it before she'd even had a chance to answer, she wanted her mother. When she'd called and asked her mom if they could meet up, her mother had had to get someone to come by the house and keep an eye on the teenage fosters. A couple of the kids came to physical blows if left with no supervision.

So when Elise went to pick her up, she found her on the back patio with Margaret, Elise's boss.

Tears rushed to her eyes; these were the two women she admired most, and she felt like she'd let them both down.

Her mom jumped up and closed her arms around her. "Oh, no, you've got a rough one."

"What case?" Margaret asked with concern. "I didn't think any of them but the drunk dad was that serious right now."

Elise pulled back. "It's more than a case."

"The drunk dad?" Margaret asked, her brow furrowed with confusion. She was the same age as Elise's mom, but her hair, which she kept short, was nearly all gray. She blamed it on the job.

Elise figured she would find some gray in her own hair soon. "No, not the drunk dad case. Liam Lemmon…and Lucy."

"The baby in the barn," Margaret said. "But hey…you wanted some alone time with your mom. Go ahead and get a drink or something."

"I need to talk to you, too," Elise said. "I should have talked to you before I got in so much over my head." And into her heart—that was where Liam and Lucy were.

"You've been keeping me up-to-date," Margaret said. "You've shown me the progress reports. And the sheriff is tracking down the mom."

"And the dad," Elise said. "Liam isn't Lucy's biological father."

"But his name is on her birth certificate, and it's been verified with his driver's license," Margaret said. "I got the documents you uploaded this afternoon. You're doing a great job on this case."

Elise shook her head. "No…"

"No, what?" her mom asked. "No, you're not doing a good job or no about Liam?"

"He's not her dad," Elise said. She wouldn't share his personal medical information with them, though. She just said, "He's not her biological father. He's even admitted it."

"Well, that does complicate things. We'll need a court order for a paternity test to confirm that and then we'll have to find a foster placement," Margaret said. She glanced at Elise's mom. "You sure you won't take a baby?"

Vivian chuckled and shook her head. "I'm probably going to wind up with one soon enough when Aubrey has her baby. I can't have another one here. And what about Liam? He knows he's not the father, yet he's kept the baby."

"He's attached to her," Elise said. "He's fallen for her." Just like Elise had fallen for him.

"You say that like it's a horrible thing," her mom said with another laugh. "It isn't, Elise. It's okay to get attached. To love someone."

"Not when you know you're going to lose them," she said.

"But will he lose her?" Vivian asked.

"If the biological parents want her back, yes," Elise said. "You know how the judges favor bio family."

Margaret uttered a ragged sigh. "Yes, and sometimes that's a good thing. Sometimes it has a good outcome. You don't see a good outcome with this case?"

Elise shook her head, then she shrugged. "I don't know. I'm too close to it."

Neither of the older women said a thing; they just stared at her, waiting.

A little sob bubbled up and out with her admission. "I think I'm falling for him."

"Oh, Elise!" her mother exclaimed, and she sounded delighted as she threw her arms around her again. "That's wonderful."

Elise pulled back. "No, it's not."

"You said you kissed him," her mom said. "You didn't say if he kissed you back. Doesn't he return your feelings?"

Heat rushed to Elise's face, and she dropped into the chair across from her boss. "I crossed so many lines with this case," she said. "Will I get fired?"

Margaret laughed. "No. I wouldn't reward you like that. I'll write you up if there are any complaints. Is Liam Lemmon going to complain?"

Elise shook her head. "No. He asked me to marry him."

Vivian clapped her hands together. "That's wonderful," she said again.

"It was just because he thinks a judge would look more favorably on a married couple adopting her," Elise said. It wasn't exactly the reason he'd given, but he hadn't said he loved her either.

"What about the bio parents?" Margaret asked. "Will they complain? Will they want her back?"

"I don't know." Elise shrugged shoulders that felt leaden from the burden she carried: the guilt, the regret…the heartbreak.

"You said the sheriff is working on finding them?" Margaret asked.

She nodded.

"Then let's wait until he does and check in with them, see what they want…"

"But they shouldn't just get her back," Elise said. "Not after leaving her in a barn like that. She could have been hurt."

"But she wasn't," Margaret said. "And they could argue that they saw Liam about to walk in. Who knows what they would say in court."

"But hopefully it won't go to court," her mother chimed in. "Hopefully everything will work out how it's meant to."

Elise sighed. Her mother was a lot like Liam in that she maintained positivity. But unlike Liam, her mother should know better. "How can you look at life that way when you know how wrong things can go?" Elise asked.

"Because maybe they won't," her mother replied. "If you're always worried about being hurt or disappointed, you'll never let anyone get close. You'll never love anyone."

That wasn't the situation now. She'd already fallen for Liam.

"And if you keep playing every worst-case scenario through your head, you'll never be able to live the best-case ones," Vivian said.

"I don't even know what we're talking about anymore," Elise admitted. Her head was pounding like Liam's must have been earlier when he'd kept touching his head.

"Your happiness, Elise," her mother replied. "That's what we're talking about. You need to fight for that like you fight for these kids in your cases."

Elise sighed. "I can't make someone love me."

"Maybe he already does."

She wanted to believe that, but he would have told her if he did. Instead he'd retracted his proposal and listed all the reasons why they shouldn't be together. She didn't care about the lawsuit, about whether he had a job or a place to live, though. She just wanted him.

But, if she took her mother's advice, was it a fight she could win?

LIVVY STEPPED OUT of her SUV at the same time that Blake and Brett stepped out of the truck they'd just parked in the driveway at Ranch Haven. "What's going on?" she asked them as her heart pounded fast with fear. "Is Grandpa all right?"

"Dad called you here, too?" Blake asked.

She nodded. "I figured something must have happened." Grandpa Lem had had a scare some months ago. It had been an anxiety attack, not a heart attack. There was always so much going on with their family and with the Havens and Cassidys.

She'd once thought she'd needed to protect Grandpa Lem from that, from Sadie. But she'd never seen him as happy as he was now that they were married, which reminded her to tell Colton that she was ready. They could set a date for their wedding. Hopefully soon because life was too short.

She'd had some tough cases that day in the ER that had reminded her of that. Colton was working the night shift, so she wouldn't be able to tell him. Or see him.

So she was glad she'd gotten summoned here as long as Grandpa was all right. She rushed to the front porch, her brothers following closely behind her. When she opened the door, Brett stopped in surprise.

"You just walk in?"

She snorted. "Yeah, it's Ranch Haven. The only people who ring the bell are trying to sell something. Grandma Sadie will be disappointed if you don't just come on in."

"Grandma Sadie?" Brett asked. "You call her that?"

"Yes."

"Livvy is marrying Sadie's grandson," Blake pointed out.

"Yeah, but Liam calls her that, too, and his truck is here," Brett said.

"So?" Livvy asked.

"He doesn't want us involved in his life right now," Brett said.

"That's why I asked you all to come here," a familiar voice said.

Livvy turned away from her brothers to find her dad standing behind her. She rushed to hug him. "Is Grandpa all right?"

"Yes, of course," her dad replied and patted her back. "I didn't mean to scare you. I just wanted you all here. Sadie's right. We need to reach out to offer help and to take it when we need it. Or maybe just accept that help because other people want to give it."

The sudden urge to cry rushed over Livvy, making her nose tingle and her eyes water. Dad hadn't wanted anyone to help him with Mom, and he'd seemed so alone and cut off since her death. She hugged him again.

But her brothers hung back yet.

"But Liam said he didn't want us doing the big-brother thing anymore," Brett said. "He doesn't want our help."

"What?" Livvy asked. That didn't sound like Liam.

"I'm sorry, Brett and Blake," Liam chimed in

as he joined them in the foyer. "I made such a mess of things…" His voice cracked.

Blake stepped across the threshold. "I know you're under a lot of stress and not getting much sleep, and we haven't been helping much with Lucy."

"Because I wouldn't let you," Liam said. "I made the choice to claim Lucy as mine, and you two already have enough going on with the ranch. That's why I thought I should leave. I don't want to risk you losing the ranch."

Livvy groaned with frustration. "What's going on?" she asked. She hated feeling as left out as she'd always felt with her siblings. But maybe that was her fault. Like her dad had just said, she'd needed to reach out to offer help and to ask for it when she'd needed it. "Tell me why you're fighting."

"Don't you get mad, too," Liam said.

"We're not fighting," Brett said. "I think we're all just exhausted."

"Then come inside," her dad said as he waved them in like he already felt at home there as well. But he'd refused to attend all the parties that happened at Ranch Haven. While he'd attended his dad's wedding, he hadn't been very welcoming to Sadie or even to his own father.

Livvy had never understood that; she loved Grandpa Lem so much. They'd even lived together until he married Sadie. And she missed him. So when she walked into the kitchen, she immediately went to hug him. But he was holding Lucy, so she kissed the top of his head, his soft hair tickling her face. Then she kissed Sadie's cheek. "Grandma, you really are magic, getting all the Lemmons together."

Sadie blinked and gently patted Livvy's cheek. "You sweet girl."

"She really is magic," Lem said, tears filling his blue eyes. And he reached his free hand out for Sadie's. They entwined their fingers, Sadie's long but swollen with arthritis and Lem's shorter, paler ones.

"Okay," Liam said. "Let's use your magic to figure out who Lucy's biological father is." And there was such yearning in his voice, he clearly wished it was him.

So did Livvy.

"Someone who was able to take your driver's license and show it at the clinic," Blake said. "Who would have had access to it besides you, me and Brett?"

Brett grunted. "Frankie. But that is as unlikely as one of us taking it."

Livvy was playing catch-up, so she asked, "Did you get mugged?"

"At the ranch?" he asked.

"Wallet never went missing?" she responded.

"Once…" he murmured, his forehead furrowing as he tried to remember. "It must have fallen out of my pocket. It happened shortly after I moved to the ranch. It wasn't missing long, though, and I found it on a hay bale in the barn."

"Like you found Lucy," Blake said.

"Who was around the ranch then?" Livvy asked.

Liam's blue eyes widened, and he came over to hug her. "Geez, Liv, you really are the smartest one of us."

"What? What did I say?"

"I just figured out who took my license."

"Ah," Blake said and nodded.

"Of course," Brett said.

She sighed. "Well, so much for not feeling left out anymore. You all know who it was but me."

Liam hugged her again. "I wouldn't have figured it out without you, Livvy."

When Liam released her, Blake hugged her. "We never intentionally left you out, sis," he told her.

Then Brett wrapped his arms around her shoulders and leaned his head against hers. "We just couldn't keep up with you. You were so dang smart, sis."

"But even though you ran ahead of us, we were always there behind you," Liam said. "Always admiring and loving and supporting you."

A sob escaped her lips, and she playfully punched his shoulder. "You might have told me that sooner."

"You were just too busy to look back, sis," he said. "But we were always there."

She hugged him again. "You are going to be such a great dad, Liam. Lucy is lucky to have you."

"But she doesn't have me for sure," he said. "Not yet."

Clearly he had a plan now, though, because he looked determined.

"Let me know what I can do to help," she said. "Because I'm not running ahead anymore. I want to walk beside you."

He wrapped his arm around her shoulders. "Just being here helps. This is what I want to give Lucy. A family. *This* family."

"What about Elise Shaw?" she asked, wondering where the CPS investigator figured into her brother's plan.

He drew away from her then. "I screwed that up," he said, his voice gruff with pain and maybe tears. "Now I just have to make sure that I don't lose Lucy, too."

Which meant that he'd already lost Elise.

Once Livvy would have been relieved that her brother wasn't involved with the CPS investigator, but now she was disappointed.

And Liam looked devastated. Elise had been more than the investigator on Lucy's case to him.

He'd clearly fallen for her. So was it really too late?

CHAPTER TWENTY-ONE

LIAM SHOULD HAVE figured out sooner where his license had gone and why someone had taken it.

They all gathered around that long table at Ranch Haven, and Liam shared with the others what he and his brothers had realized. "We had two ranch hands before Frank died," Liam said. "One was a guy in his midtwenties. The other was a twenty-year-old kid. Probably the same age as Lucy's mother when she got pregnant."

"The kid even looks like you," Brett pointed out. "No wonder he was able to pass that license off as his."

"And his name is Levi, so close to yours that he probably had no problem answering to Liam," Blake added.

Surprisingly their father weighed in on the discussion instead of quietly hanging back like he'd done since Mom had died. "I had a friend in high school who used his older brother's license to buy alcohol."

"Jon Fenwick," Grandpa Lem said.

Dad laughed, which was even more surprising than his joining the conversation. "Of course you knew."

"He lost his license several years ago for drunk driving," Lem said.

Bob sighed. "Yeah, I see now that he had a problem. But back then he seemed cool. He spiked the punch bowl with something at prom that was so strong that I still can't remember anything about that night."

"Dad!" Livvy exclaimed. "I had no idea you were such a rebel."

Their father shook his head. "That was the end of my rebellious phase."

Lem snorted. "Yeah, right."

Their dad tensed. "I didn't want to go into politics with you. And I didn't want to marry a small-town girl and stay in Willow Creek."

Grandpa Lem's forehead furrowed. "I don't remember pushing you to go into politics with me. And what small-town girl are we talking about?"

"Sue Lancaster," Bob said. "You kept pushing her at me even when I went away to college and started dating Felicity. You gave her my phone number."

Lem shrugged. "She asked for it. I thought you were friends. You took her to prom."

"You took Nurse Sue to prom?" Livvy asked.

Their dad nodded. "We were just friends, but

taking her to prom, even as friends, gave her the wrong idea."

"She was a beautiful girl," Lem said. "Never figured why you were just friends."

Bob sighed. "Because I didn't want to stay in Willow Creek and she did."

"But you moved back home after college," Liam said. Willow Creek had always felt more like home to him than Chicago. "We were all born here."

"I… I didn't want to deprive Mom of her grandchildren," Bob replied. "But once you all started school, it was time to move."

"To get away from me," Grandpa Lem said.

Bob sighed. "To be someone besides Old Man Lemmon's boy," he said. "To be my own man. And not have every person in town ask me when I was going to run for mayor."

"But you kept the house," Liam said. "We came home for holidays."

"And you moved back after Mom died," Livvy added.

Bob sighed again. "Because Willow Creek is home. And despite how much I pushed you away, I still wanted to be close to you, Dad."

Tears trailed down Grandpa Lem's face and soaked into his white beard. "Oh, Bob…"

Dad smiled. "I just didn't want to be you."

"God forbid there are two of him," Sadie said. She reached out and clasped Grandpa's hand and smiled. "One is just right for me." And she kissed his hand.

They were so in love that Liam's heart contracted with his yearning for that kind of love. For Elise.

He'd been so stupid to propose like he had. To lay out all the reasons for marrying her except the only right one: love. And he did love her. But before he'd let himself admit it, he'd reminded her of all the reasons she shouldn't marry him. His life was a mess, and she deserved more.

Her job was so stressful that she needed a secure home life. He didn't have that now. He wouldn't have that until that stupid court case was settled. And if it went the wrong way, he would have nothing to offer her, just as he'd said.

Livvy leaned close to him, snapping her fingers in front of his face. "You need to call Elise," she said.

He sucked in a breath. Had his sister guessed what he was thinking: that he wanted the love their grandparents had for each other, with Elise? He wanted this life, this family, with her.

"You need to tell her about Levi," Brett chimed in.

He shook his head. "Uh, no, she was going to reassign Lucy's case to someone else. I should just call the sheriff. He's trying to track down the mother, too."

"Oh," Brett said and smacked his forehead. "I ran into Shell the other day at the feedstore."

"Shell?" Liam asked. "The owner of the horse boarding ranch?"

Brett nodded. "Shell is his first name. Short for Herschel. Smith is his last name."

Liam sighed and shook his head. "Does he have a daughter named Jane?"

"Not a daughter. He doesn't have kids."

"A niece, maybe?" Blake suggested. "Frankie always spent a lot of time with her uncle even after she turned eighteen and he was no longer her guardian."

"I didn't have a chance to ask him," Brett said. "He didn't even tell me his last name. I just saw it when he signed his name on the invoice. But the place was so busy that there was no opportunity to talk to him."

"I'll tell Marsh about that, too." Jane Smith was probably a lot closer to home than Boise, which meant that Lucy's parents were close.

Would they want her back?

Would he lose her just like Elise had warned him he might? He reached out and took her from his grandpa then, just to hold her close and cuddle her. He wanted to hold on to her forever. But he had a feeling that wouldn't be possible.

THE LAST THING Elise needed was a new case, but she was next up in the rotation even though Margaret had refused to take Lucy's case away from her. Bleary-eyed from not sleeping the night before even after talking to her mom and Margaret, Elise stumbled through the lobby doors of the ER.

Livvy Lemmon was waiting at the intake desk. And not just for the next patient. She was waiting for her since she'd personally requested her to come by the ER. Dark circles rimmed Livvy's eyes like they did Elise's.

"Late night in the ER, Doc?" Elise asked her.

"Late night with my brothers and my dad and grandparents out at Ranch Haven," she said.

A flutter passed through Elise's heart. "Brothers? They were all in the same room?"

Livvy nodded. "They made up."

She released a shaky breath. "That's good. I know they're close."

Tears pooled in Livvy's green eyes. And Elise reached out to grasp her shoulder. "What's wrong? Are they okay?" she asked.

"They're great," Livvy said. "The best brothers I had no idea I had."

"What do you mean?"

"They were always close to each other," Livvy said. "But not to me."

"I'm sorry."

"It was my fault," Livvy said. "I never made the effort. I just thought we had nothing in common."

Elise offered her a tentative smile. "Well…you really don't. They're ranchers and you're a doctor."

"But we're family," Livvy said. "And that's all that matters. Family, Elise."

Elise narrowed her eyes and studied the doctor's beautiful face. "You didn't call me here about a kid, did you?"

"Yes, I did," Livvy said. "I called you about Lucy."

A pang of concern struck Elise's heart. "What about her? Is she all right?"

"She will be if Liam will be able to keep her," Livvy said.

"He's not her biological father."

"I know," Livvy said. "But he is still her dad. He loves that baby so much. And that's what she deserves. Love. We all do, Elise."

If only Liam loved her…

"Well, if her parents can be found and sign off their rights to her, it's possible he could adopt her," Elise said. But if he didn't have a job or a house, it wasn't going to happen. She didn't dare point that out now, though.

"He found her parents," Livvy said.

Elise's stomach dropped. "*He* did? Liam? He found them?"

"Well, he figured out who they are, and he told Marsh," Livvy said.

Elise pulled her cell from her purse, but there were no missed calls from the sheriff's office. "Who are they?" she asked.

"A kid who used to work at the Four Corners as

a ranch hand, and a girl who has some connection to the horse boarding ranch nearby," Livvy said.

Elise closed her eyes. She should have followed up on that lead herself. "I didn't know there were ranch hands."

"They fired them after the wedding."

"What wedding?" Elise asked. "I don't understand."

"When my brothers were at Lem and Sadie's wedding, the ranch hands were supposed to be helping Frank Dempsey. They were both goofing off instead and Frank had an accident. Got thrown off his horse and hit his head."

"That's how he died?" she asked.

Livvy shook her head. "Not right away. He lay out there awhile before Frankie found him."

Sympathy clutched Elise's heart. "Poor Frankie. He raised her. She adored her uncle."

Livvy's eyes got bright with her own tears of sympathy. "Then he was in the hospital for weeks but never regained consciousness. It was sad for everybody. My brothers loved him a lot."

"And he loved them," Elise said. "Or at least that's what Frankie's told me. That they were like his sons."

"That's why he included them in his will," Livvy said. "Too bad Frank's daughter doesn't realize how hard they worked for him, how much they cared about him…" She trailed off and sighed. "That will work itself out. But for now…"

"Why did you request that I come to the ER?" Elise asked.

"Because I think my brother loves you," Livvy said.

Elise shook her head. If he'd loved her, he would have told her so when he'd proposed. No. He didn't love her. But she wasn't going to argue with his sister. Again.

"And I think you would be great for each other and for Lucy," Livvy continued.

"And you all complain about Sadie's meddling and matchmaking," Nurse Sue said. She must have slipped out the doors from the ER sometime while they were speaking, and she now stood behind Livvy.

Livvy smiled. "I don't complain. Not anymore."

"I need to leave," Elise said. She had to talk to the sheriff, find out if he'd found Lucy's parents. And if he had, what they wanted to do.

Officially give Lucy up or take her back?

Either way might not work out in Liam's favor. And if Elise had to take the baby away from him, he would never forgive her let alone love her like his sister claimed. Too bad that this time she had gotten attached, to him and to Lucy, and she was already hurting…

TUESDAY MORNING MARSH STARED ACROSS his desk at the young adults sitting in his office. It had taken a few days but he'd had a deputy track down Levi at the rodeo, and Jane Smith had been found at her uncle's house, but just for a visit. Marsh had had his deputies escort them here because he wanted to talk to them together. Their heads were down. They wouldn't look at him or at each other.

"Jane, why did you leave your baby in a barn?" he asked.

The girl's face flushed nearly as bright a red as her hair.

"You left her in what barn?" the boy asked, and he pushed back his cowboy hat and turned his blue-eyed gaze on her. With his black hair and those blue eyes, he really did look a lot like Liam.

"Your barn," she said. "At the Four Corners."

His face flushed now. "I don't work there anymore. You just left her there? Was anybody even around?"

"Liam found her," Marsh replied.

"So you did find her," Jane said, her voice full of accusation.

"He's not Liam," Marsh said.

The girl jumped up. "You lied to me about your name? I don't suppose you're a rodeo rider either who won so much that you were able to buy that ranch?"

Levi's face flushed. "Well, you were so snooty visiting your uncle from the big city, acting like we were all hicks."

"You are a hick," Jane said. "That's why I can't wait to get out of here."

"You're not going anywhere until you tell me about your daughter," Marsh said.

And he hoped they wanted to give her up because Lucy would be a lot better off with Liam Lemmon than either of these two. He glanced at his cell and saw an incoming text from Elise Shaw. She'd been texting him the past few days for updates on whether or not he'd found Lucy's parents yet. And he'd let her know this morning that they would be in his office shortly.

She was a better person to handle this situation than he was. So he would happily step aside and let her take over. He just hoped that she was legally able to do what was best for Lucy.

CHAPTER TWENTY-TWO

GENEVIEVE PORTER-CASSIDY'S OFFICE WAS too small for Liam to pace. But he couldn't sit still in one of the chairs in front of her desk, so he tapped his foot on the floor. "What do you think? Do I have chance at adopting her?"

He'd left Lucy at the ranch with Frankie. But maybe he should have brought her with him; maybe she would have helped make his case for him. But Genevieve wouldn't be the only one he needed to convince.

"Any family court judge is going to want to make certain that you can take care of her," she said.

"I've been doing that for nearly two weeks now," he said. "She's healthy. She's happy. She's thriving really." She hadn't even cried when he'd left her with Frankie. She was getting used to the other people in their family. Like Elise.

But Elise wasn't truly family. His proposal hadn't even tempted her; he'd seen that. Maybe it was too soon like she'd said. But while it might be too soon for her to have fallen for him, he loved her. She was so amazing, so strong and resilient, that he hadn't had a chance of not falling for her.

"I meant financially as well as physically," she said. "You told me about how the will is being contested. If you and your brothers lose…"

"We will lose our jobs as well as our home," he said. "But I can find another job. And I could live at Ranch Haven. Grandma Sadie will do everything within her power to help me."

"And Grandma Sadie's power is considerable," she agreed with a smile.

Genevieve reminded him a bit of Maci, with blond hair and blue eyes, but Maci was shorter and younger. And not nearly as cynical he realized when Genevieve's smile slipped away and she added, "But Sadie won't be able to convince a family court judge to take a chance on you when there are so many other families wanting to adopt babies."

"So even if her parents don't want her back, I could lose her?"

"If her parents do want her back, most judges would side with them," Genevieve said.

He sighed. "That's what Elise said."

"Elise Shaw?"

His heart fluttered at the sound of her name. "Yes, she has Lucy's case." Unless she'd passed it off like she'd said she would.

"Elise is good," Genevieve said. "Everyone

speaks so highly of her. She's been around awhile in a job that people usually can't stick with. It's a rough one."

"I realize that."

"And she and I don't always get the outcomes we want," Genevieve said. "While I'm sure we can both see how much you love Lucy, it might not be enough."

"When isn't love enough?" he asked. Maybe if he'd told Elise that he loved her, she would have accepted his proposal. Or maybe she would have just thought he was crazy and desperate.

"When a judge says you need something more," Genevieve said. "But we'll make a case. We'll be ready."

"Can we fight the parents if they want to keep her? The mom left her alone in that barn. Lucy could have been hurt," he said, cringing at the thought of what could have happened to her. Something bad could happen so fast, like when Ian Haven was hurt in that barn with Midnight... and when Liam got hurt.

"That will be up to CPS to get their parental rights terminated," Genevieve said. "And to the sheriff's office if they want to press charges for child endangerment."

Liam hated this feeling of helplessness. "So there's nothing I can do right now?"

She shook her head. "We can't file to adopt a child until she's up for adoption, until her parents have no more rights to her," she said. "But once we know she's available, we'll petition the court."

"But I have her now," he said. "Isn't possession nine-tenths of the law or something like that?"

She smiled. "With property, sometimes, but not people, Liam. I'm sorry I can't do more."

"And I can't do anything..." he muttered.

"But love her while you have her," Genevieve said. "My husband and I adopted a child who's had a heart transplant. Chances are she will need another one someday, and she has a lot of health issues. I've had people ask me why we would want to adopt her, and by people I mean my heartless mother and stepfather."

Sympathy rushed through him; he really was lucky to have the loving family that he did. "You love her. That's why you adopted her," Liam said.

Tears filled her eyes as she nodded. "Yes, and every day with her, every moment, is a gift that I will treasure."

So that was what he would do, go back to the ranch and treasure every moment he had left with Lucy.

WHEN ELISE DROVE up to the house at the Four Corners Ranch, she didn't see Liam's truck. Livvy had told her days ago that he'd made up with his brothers, so he should have been here. Unless he'd taken Lucy somewhere.

Maybe after he'd realized who her parents were,

he'd been so concerned about losing her that he'd taken off with her. Or maybe that was just where Elise's cynical mind went because of all the parents who'd pulled that on her in the past. When they'd realized they were about to lose their children, they'd gone on the run with them. A lot of them had never been found.

But Elise needed to find Liam. She didn't want him to do something stupid, something dangerous, that would get him in trouble with the law and ruin whatever chances he might have to adopt.

She opened her door and headed toward the porch. And as she approached it, she heard a familiar cry. Lucy was here. He hadn't taken her with him wherever he was.

But she didn't want to do what she had to do before he had a chance to say goodbye. Her throat filled with sobs that wanted to come out. But she couldn't cry like Lucy was. Instead she climbed the porch steps and knocked on the glass of the storm door.

Frankie came out of the kitchen, Lucy clasped against her chest. "I thought she and I were good," she said to Elise as she pulled open the door. "But Liam was just gone a little while before she became inconsolable. I've changed her, tried feeding her, but I think she wants him."

Elise could identify with that want all too well. She reached out and Frankie happily passed off

the baby to her. "Hey there, sweet girl," she murmured. "Are you giving your auntie Frankie a
rough time?"

The tension drained from Lucy's body, and she
opened the eyes she'd squeezed shut. She blinked
the tears from them and focused on Elise's face.
And the crying stopped.

"Wow, she's attached to you, too, now," Frankie
said.

A pang struck Elise's heart so hard that it took
her breath away for a moment. Elise was attached
to Lucy, too. She'd fallen for the baby and for
Liam. But she had to do her job as well. "Where
is Liam?" she asked.

"He's in Willow Creek meeting with that other
lawyer, Genevieve Porter-Cassidy."

"Good," Elise said.

"No, it wasn't," a deep voice remarked.

He must have left his truck at the barn because
she hadn't heard him drive up. Or maybe he'd
driven up while Lucy was crying, and she hadn't
been able to hear the engine over her.

"It wasn't good?" Frankie asked with concern.

Liam shook his head. "No. If the lawsuit was
settled and I had a permanent job and residence,
it would be different."

"Damn Trish," Frankie said. "I don't understand what's going on with her."

"Greed," Elise suggested, and her bitterness
for a woman she'd never met surprised her. But

she was hurting Liam, and anyone who hurt him deserved to be resented. Too bad she was going to have to hurt him now herself.

"I thought you were taking yourself off the case," Liam said.

"My boss wouldn't let me," she admitted. "She thinks I will do what's right for Lucy no matter what my personal feelings are."

"And what are your personal feelings, Elise?" he asked, and he stepped closer.

Love. She had so much love for him and this baby. And she wanted to tell him, but she didn't think her love would be much consolation if he still lost Lucy. And she didn't know for sure how all this would turn out.

Five years on the job had taught her just how unpredictable life could be. Because she had certainly never expected to fall in love so quickly and so deeply.

"Uh, I think I will run down to the barn and see if Brett and Blake need some help," Frankie said. She rushed out of the house, leaving them alone with the quiet baby.

"My personal feelings don't matter right now," she said.

He stepped even closer and touched her face, and until he wiped away a tear with his fingertips, she hadn't even realized she was crying.

"I don't want to do this," she said.

"I know…"

"But the sheriff found her parents, and they want to see her."

He nodded. "I know he found them."

"You figured out who they are," she said.

He nodded again. "Lucy deserves better," he said.

"She does. She deserves you."

"But even if they sign off their rights to her, I probably won't be able to adopt her," he said, and now tears slid down his handsome face.

Holding Lucy with one arm, she raised her other hand to his face and wiped away his tears. Then he lowered his head and kissed her, and their tears blended together. When he pulled away, his face was as wet as hers.

"I don't want to do this," she said, her heart aching with her love for him. "I wish it was anyone else."

"I'm glad that it's you," he said. "Tell them, Elise, how much I love her. How special she is."

She nodded. "But I can't make any promises."

"I know."

She sucked in a breath. "A lot of times, when the parents see their baby again, they change their minds. They want to keep her."

He nodded. "I can't imagine being able to give her up." Yet that was exactly what he was doing right now.

Because he wasn't fighting Elise like so many other parents or guardians had in the past. In fact he helped get all of Lucy's stuff together and even loaded it into her car as she buckled in Lucy's car seat.

"You don't have to do this," she said, and she couldn't stop the tears from flowing again.

"I know, but they're young. They probably don't have any money. They'll need all these things. And I won't anymore. I won't have any children."

His loneliness and despair filled her, and she reached out for him, wrapping her arms around him. She wanted to profess her love then, to tell him that he would have her if he wanted her, no matter what. But now was not the time. He was so vulnerable and heartbroken.

And her heart broke as well.

He clutched her against him. "Elise…"

But no more words came out, just a sound like a wounded animal might make. She didn't want to pull away. She didn't want to leave him. "They're waiting at the sheriff's office," she whispered. "I have to go."

He dropped his arms and moved toward the open door to the backseat. He had a small pink stuffed animal in his hand. A poodle. "This is her favorite," he said. "Grandpa Lem bought it for her." And he put it in the car seat next to the sleeping baby. But he didn't touch her. He just stared at her with so much love and so much pain before he turned and walked away.

And all that pain and regret filled Elise, and for the first time ever she considered quitting her job. She considered calling him back and asking him to run away with her and Lucy. But she knew how that would all end.

Badly.

FOR NEARLY TWO weeks Brett had walked into the house wishing for quiet, hoping that the mess with the baby would be sorted out, and their lives would go back to normal. But when he walked in with Blake and Frankie and heard the silence, his heart broke. And that was even before he saw his baby brother sitting alone at the kitchen table, his face in his hands, his shoulders shaking while he wept. He rushed to him, pulled him up from the chair and into his arms, and held him tight.

But he didn't lie. He didn't promise that everything would be all right. He had no way of knowing that. Not anymore.

Frank had promised that he would be all right if they left him alone at the ranch to attend their grandfather's wedding. He'd said he could handle things for a few days with the ranch hands and Frankie and that they deserved some time off.

But when they'd come back, he was barely hanging on. The strongest man Brett had ever known, and he hadn't been able to recover.

What would happen to Liam? How would he survive losing the baby he loved so much?

CHAPTER TWENTY-THREE

LIAM FELT AS if someone had reached inside him and ripped his heart from his chest. Could he live like this? Could he go on?

And it wasn't just Lucy he was missing but Elise, too. He was even missing how his brothers used to treat him. The teasing, the goofing around. Right now they were treating him with kid gloves, staring at him like they thought he was going to fall apart.

But he was already hurting more than he could probably survive. So he focused on the ranch the rest of that afternoon. And he was out early the next morning, riding the fences, checking for missing cattle. A few head were still out there somewhere.

He turned his horse toward the crevices and ravines near the foothills of the mountains. And he heard a cry. His heart flipped with his first thought that it was Lucy. But it wasn't. It was a cow, caught in some underbrush. How long had the poor thing been there?

It was fortunate that no predator had taken advantage of her vulnerability. He got off his horse, a tan buckskin named Honey. She'd been his mount in the rodeo, for the roping contests. She was good. She'd made him better than he was. Between the two of them, they got the cow out and back into a pasture.

Dirty and tired from his sleepless night, Liam headed back toward the barn. After being out in bright sun all morning, the barn seemed especially dark. He couldn't see anything as he led Honey inside toward her stall. She knew where it was, though, and she led the way. Someone had already cleaned it. Either one of his brothers or Frankie. They were all clearly worried about him.

So was he.

He didn't know what he was going to do without Lucy. Then he heard her. It wasn't a cry, more like a gurgle, but it was her. And he turned toward the pile of hay bales where he'd found her almost two weeks ago. Her car seat was sitting there, and she pushed against it and the straps holding her into it, as if wriggling to get out. To get to him.

He pressed his hand over his eyes. He had to be imagining things. But he pulled his hand away, and she was still there. She wasn't alone, though, like she'd been the first time he'd found her. Elise stood beside her, unclasping her from the car seat. Then she held the baby out to him. "Here, she misses you."

"I don't understand," he said, but his arms automatically closed around the little girl. She settled against his chest with a soft sigh. And the ache inside his chest eased a little. "Her parents wanted to see her, and then you didn't bring her back."

He'd thought he'd lost them both forever. And even though they were back now, after his meeting with Genevieve he didn't believe he could keep either of them. Maybe it would have been better had he not seen them again.

"I don't understand, Elise. Are you here just so that I can say goodbye?" he asked.

TAKING LUCY AWAY and leaving him yesterday had been one of the hardest things Elise had ever had to do. Unfortunately there had been harder things because sometimes her job was life and death and death won.

And maybe she'd let all those negative experiences take away her positivity and her hope for the future. She wasn't as able to look on the bright side or to trust people to do the right thing. But Lucy's biological parents had done it yesterday.

Her mind went back to that meeting yesterday in the sheriff's office. Neither parent had reached for Lucy like Liam had. And the baby hadn't looked at either of them like she recognized them. "Don't you want to hold her?" she'd asked them. "Isn't that why you wanted to see her?"

The young man, who looked eerily like Liam, shook his head. "I'm not good with babies. I've never held one before."

"What about you?" she asked the mom. "Weren't you taking care of her the past two months?"

The young woman shook her head. "No. My dad's housekeeper was, but she quit. And Dad said that I had to grow up and figure this out on my own."

And instead she'd left Lucy in a barn at the Four Corners Ranch.

"You don't want her?" Elise had asked, her heart aching for Lucy. This was why Liam had kept her, because he hadn't wanted her to feel unwanted.

They'd both shaken their heads.

"What about your family?"

The girl had let out a bitter laugh. "Not anyone in my family."

The guy had shaken his head. "My parents would kill me if they knew. I just wanted to see her before I sign whatever I gotta sign."

"Me, too," Jane had said and smiled. "She's really pretty."

"Yes," Levi had agreed.

And for a moment Elise had thought they were going to change their minds and that her worst fears would have been realized. But then...

"The reason her parents wanted to see her was to say goodbye," Elise explained to Liam. But she hadn't been certain that they would be able to, so she hadn't wanted to give him false hope. She wished now that she hadn't been so cynical.

"But you said that a lot of people change their minds then," he reminded her. "That when they see their baby again they can't let her go. But here she is…"

Elise reached out then to touch Lucy's slightly flushed cheek. She wasn't sick; she'd just been upset. "That was not the case for Levi and Jane. They could barely stand to be in the room together, kept blaming each other for her very existence. And when I brought her in to see them, she was quiet for a little while and they were commenting on how pretty she is." She smiled over what had happened next. "But then she let them know what she thought of them. She projectile vomited on Levi and Jane. It was like a scene from *The Exorcist*."

He laughed. "No…"

"Oh, yes, and they couldn't wait to sign away their parental rights," she said. "Jane dropped her off in the barn because her dad's housekeeper, who was taking care of Lucy, quit, and Jane is leaving soon for a study-abroad program. Honestly, I don't think she'll ever come back to the States. And Levi is getting tossed out of his parents' house if he can't find a job and keep it. Neither of them wants the responsibility of raising a baby."

"And their parents don't want Lucy either?" he asked.

She shook her head. "No, Jane just has her dad, who is very busy with his job and younger women according to her. That's why she visits her aunt and uncle so often, but they're too old and uninterested in kids, too. She never even told them about the baby or Levi. And Levi's parents told him that if he got a girl pregnant, they didn't want to know and they wanted nothing to do with it."

"It? She's not a cat to be left in a barn," he said.

And she smiled because that was what she'd told them. "I told them that you already love her, and that you would take the very best care of her."

He sucked in a breath. "But Genevieve told me that a judge would never approve a guy in my situation. I have too much unsettled in my life."

"A judge wouldn't," she agreed. "But Genevieve, Maci and I came up with a plan for a private adoption."

Now his breath escaped in a shaky sigh. "What are you saying?"

"Levi idolizes you," she said.

He snorted. "What?"

"While he stole your license so he could buy alcohol, he also did it because he wants to be you. He's trying to join the rodeo right now."

Liam snorted again. "He wasn't that great a rider."

Elise shrugged. "He wants to be just like you.

And he said that you're the nicest of the Lemmon brothers."

He grinned. "Well, I am."

"This is true," she said. "Also the cutest."

He grimaced. "I hope he didn't say that."

"No, I did."

He grinned now. "And Jane, what did she say?"

"She never met you so she can't weigh in on your cuteness, but she could see that Lucy looked healthy. And I told her that she was crying because she misses you, that she's very attached to you. So she agreed to the private adoption, too."

She expected his grin to widen, but instead it slipped away, and his face got pale. "Liam, what's wrong?" Had her negativity and distrustfulness rubbed off on him?

He shook his head. "I asked you to do what was best for Lucy," he said, and tears filled his blue eyes. "Am I what's best for her? We might lose that lawsuit. We might lose our jobs and our house…"

"If that happens, you'll still be able to take care of her. You have a big, loving family."

"Yes, I do."

"You'll find another job and a place to live," she said.

"What about you?" he asked.

She sighed. "I can't lose my job even when I get personally involved in my cases and act unprofessionally," she said.

"So you just used me to try to get fired?" he asked, his blue eyes sparkling with amusement.

She sighed again. "Yup, and Margaret refused to take me off the case, much less fire me."

"I need to meet this Margaret," he said.

"Yes, you do," Elise said. "She's pretty great. She's also my mom's best friend."

"So she has a conflict of interest with you working for her," he said.

"It's Willow Creek, pretty much everyone in town has a conflict of interest with being related to or personally involved with someone else."

"Definitely less than six degrees of separation," he agreed. "But I meant what about you, Elise? What about that proposal I gave you? Do you care that I can't pass along my DNA to children, that I might not have a job or a house?"

Her pulse quickened. "I told you that you don't have to go before a judge. This is a private adoption. They've signed the papers. All you have to do is sign, and she'll be yours."

"What about you?" he asked again.

"You don't have to marry me," she said.

"I *want* to marry you, Elise," he said. "I love you. So much that my heart is about to explode. I can't believe how incredibly smart and beautiful and kind you are. And I don't want to let you go. But I feel like I'm being selfish with you and Lucy, like you both deserve so much more than I can give you."

"All we deserve is to be loved," she said. "That's all I want. That's all Lucy wants."

"I love you."

"Then yes," she said as tears pooled in her eyes. "Yes, I will marry you."

With his free arm, he pulled her close and lowered his head to hers, kissing her. Lucy let out a little squeal of excitement or maybe approval. Elise blinked against the tears stinging her eyes.

"Are you okay?" Liam asked.

She nodded. "Just happy..." Happier than she'd ever thought she could be.

"Good, I was worried you might be changing your mind."

"Never. I love you, Liam, and I love Lucy. I can't wait to expand our family whenever we decide."

"You really don't care that I can't give you my baby?" he asked.

She touched Lucy's cheek. "You already have," she said. "You're sharing her with me. There are so many kids that need homes that I always intended to adopt. And I have a feeling that our next baby will find us just like Lucy did." Something brushed against her bare ankle, something furry. Thinking it was a rat, she let out a squeak. Then she looked down and saw an orange cat winding around her ankles.

"Of course it would be a cat," Liam said and then he laughed.

And Lucy let out her little squeal of joy again.

SADIE'S HEART SWELLED with love as she stared around her kitchen table. It was full, and more people sat around other tables out on the patio. Kids ran in and out and up and down the stairs.

Lem brushed a tear from his cheek as he followed her gaze around the table. And she reached out to squeeze his hand. "I can't tell you how much this means to me," he said. And he turned to smile at her. "Our family, all together—you did this."

She followed his gaze to where Elise and Liam cuddled Lucy between them. "She did that," Sadie said. "Elise Shaw is an incredible young woman." And Sadie knew a lot of incredible young women; they were all family now. Soon Elise would be as well. "The private adoption idea was brilliant."

"Yes, it was," Livvy agreed.

Elise glanced over at everybody studying them. And she shook her head. "I didn't come up with it on my own. Genevieve and Maci helped."

That way it was more legally binding since everybody had had their own legal representation. Elise had assured Liam and his family that she wasn't worried about the biological parents changing their minds. Both had left town the minute they'd signed the papers, and she doubted they would come back.

Lucy wouldn't miss them. Not like she would have missed Liam and Elise. They were her parents now. Lucy was a legally a Lemmon.

So the family was expanding. But Sadie had a feeling it was going to expand even more. After all, there were a couple more Lemmon boys.

And Frankie and Maci were strong, beautiful young women...

Lem laughed.

"What?" Sadie asked. Had she missed something funny? Maybe she needed to get her hearing checked now that he had his new aids.

"You're scheming again already," he said.

She didn't bother denying it; he knew her too well.

"Thank goodness," he said. "We're going to have to step in and help."

"Yes, but Maci is holding her own with that fancy lawyer so far," Sadie said.

"I wasn't talking about the lawsuit," Lem said.

And she followed his gaze to his son. Bob had visited a few times now. They were making progress with him. "What about Bob?" she asked.

Lem sighed. "Things are definitely better than they've ever been with him. But he's so sad. So lost."

"He lost his wife," she reminded Lem. "And I think for a while he lost his children, too."

Liam approached his father now and passed the baby over to him. Bob looked awkward at first but then he got her settled comfortably in his arms and stared down at her with awe and love.

"He has his children back now, and a grandbaby," Sadie said. "He'll be all right." Especially if he found his second chance at love like Lem and Sadie had. She had to be out there.

But right now Sadie was focused on Bob's sons. They couldn't lose their shares in that ranch they'd worked so hard on, but she would be very happy if they lost their hearts.

* * * * *

Harlequin® Reader Service

Enjoyed your book?

Try the perfect subscription for Romance readers and get more great books like this delivered right to your door.

See why over 10+ million readers have tried Harlequin Reader Service.

Start with a Free Welcome Collection with free books and a gift—valued over $20.

Choose any series in print or ebook. See website for details and order today:

TryReaderService.com/subscriptions